BLUE SKY

By

Trish Finnegan

Burning Chair Limited, Trading as Burning Chair Publishing
61 Bridge Street, Kington HR5 3DJ
www.burningchairpublishing.com

By Trish Finnegan
Edited by Simon Finnie and Peter Oxley
Book cover design by Burning Chair Publishing

First published by Burning Chair Publishing, 2022
Copyright © Trish Finnegan, 2022
All rights reserved.
Trish Finnegan has asserted her right under the Copyright, Designs and Patents Act 1988 to be identified as author of this work.

This is a work of fiction. All names, characters, businesses, places, events, locales, and incidents are either the products of the author's imagination or used in a fictitious manner. Any resemblance to actual persons, living or dead, or actual events is purely coincidental.

This book may not be reproduced in whole or in part, in any form or by any means, electronic or mechanical, including photocopying, recording, or by any information storage and retrieval system now known or hereafter invented, without written permission from the publisher.

ISBN: 978-1-912946-28-0

Also by Trish Finnegan

Blue Bird

Dedicated to my mother who has always loved what I write (even the rubbish). She cannot see well enough to read anymore, but she enjoys listening to me talking about it. Or maybe she's just a really good actress. Love you Mum.

Prologue

The river, often fast flowing and powerful, was slow and low in the first lightening of the sky. This was not the industrial part of the river where myriad coloured lights would bounce from the waves. Here, the wind gently rustled the leaves, and the three mile wide, sweeping bend of the river offered attractive views. At this time of the morning, nothing disturbed the tranquillity apart from the panting of the fleeing youth.

The youth had been surprised when his boss' mate had invited him to the airfield club. He'd always thought it was for posh folk, not lads like him more used to backstreet pubs and sessions in a mate's home. He'd wondered if he had been selected for a job, a big one that would pay well, and he'd snatched at the opportunity. He'd grown tired of selling drugs to kids on street corners and was disillusioned with the life he'd thought would be so glamorous when he had been one of those kids. One last, well-paying job would mean he could afford to move away, start again in a new area, somewhere he couldn't be found. He'd find a proper job and maybe meet a girl who would forgive his past.

At the club he'd enjoyed a few pints before his boss's friend, now his new friend, had suggested that he might enjoy a sample of the latest import. The youth had been trying to get clean in preparation for his new life. It was hard and sometimes he slipped but, little by little, he was winning the battle. Perhaps one little sample wouldn't hurt though. He'd get back on plan tomorrow and work towards that bright future he'd envisioned for himself.

When he woke up, he realised that he was outside. Stars

twinkled above him and he could hear the river. He sat up and rubbed his head. When had they left the club? A noise close by made him turn his head. His companion was preparing a syringe. How long had he been out of it? Was it too soon to be shooting up again?

His new friend held up the full syringe. 'I told you it was good stuff. Why don't you have a bit more?'

The youth didn't want any more, he wanted to think about his future. Then he noticed that his new friend was stone cold sober and he began to feel a little uneasy. How had he shaken off the effects so quickly? Why had they bought the gear into the woods? Why had they come to the woods at all?

'No, that's okay, mate. I think I'll get off now.' The youth stood up but pitched forwards as his companion grabbed his ankles. 'What the fuck are you doing?'

His new friend didn't answer him. The youth felt a sharp prick in his ankle.

'What the fuck was that? What was it!?' Without waiting for an answer, the youth hauled himself to his feet and ran blindly into the wood but his legs felt disconnected, as if something was creeping along his legs, dulling their response as it went.

He slipped on wet leaves and mud as he fled. Stones and ferns ripped at his hands as he tried to pull himself up but he felt no pain. He looked behind him. He couldn't see anything but he could hear twigs snapping and leaves moving as someone brushed past. His new friend-turned-enemy was stalking him like a lion stalks its prey. With a jolt, the youth realised that was exactly what he was: he was prey! Somehow, the boss must have got wind of his plan to leave and set him up. The boss wouldn't deal with things himself; he was meticulous about keeping himself tidy, but he happily passed on the dirty work to his underlings. The boss's friend was hunting him down!

The youth hauled himself upright and tried to run again. Not towards the river; he would stand a better chance if he went the other way. He had seen a small housing estate close to the airfield: if he could make it there, he could get help.

'Help! Help me!' he yelled, but he could feel it was useless; nobody would hear him.

The youth ran until he burst into a clearing and tumbled over a fallen tree. He felt something give in his wrist and cried out from the pain. He heard a noise and held his breath to listen. His pursuer was coming through the trees. He didn't sound as if he was rushing, but he didn't sound far behind. The youth wondered if he was running in a circle and his hunter—for that was what he was—his hunter was waiting for him to exhaust himself, or for whatever he had injected to take effect.

The youth didn't have time to see to his wrist; he understood that if he was caught, a broken wrist would be the least of his problems. He stood on jelly legs and nursed his sore arm with his good arm as he lurched back into the trees. His best chance would be in thick, tangled wood that would hide him.

Then the familiar feelings ran through his body and he began to relax. His new friend and he worked for the same boss and the youth had felt that they had connected when they were in the club. Perhaps his friend was as unhappy as he was. They could escape together. This wasn't so bad. They could watch the sunrise over the river; it would be glorious but even if his new friend didn't want to leave, the youth thought he would go alone. Stuff the next job, he'd leave today. Who knew where he'd end up? Not London. Scotland perhaps, or Cornwall. Yes, Cornwall. He'd been on holiday there once and he smiled as he remembered the white sand and blue water.

A sudden pain in his chest brought him back to reality. He realised he was still in danger. The pain grew worse and the youth dropped to his knees. He couldn't run any more so he had to hide. He rolled underneath a bush and curled up. Maybe if he lay still he wouldn't be discovered. The youth closed his eyes, and gradually the pain eased as consciousness left him.

*

The man shone a torch down at the youth's body at his feet. He looked asleep, like a mucky child who had crashed out after a hard day's play. He had lasted longer than the man had expected. He considered leaving the youth where he lay, but he was quite well hidden and might be there for some time. Families came to walk in the woods, and it would be horrific if a small child happened upon a partly decomposed body.

'Well, I can't have kiddies coming across you, so we'd better get cracking.'

He took the youth under the arms and dragged the body so it was easily visible from the path by a passing early-morning jogger. Better that than a child seeing a dead person. Satisfied he had done all he could, and any threat this youth posed had been eliminated, he turned and jogged away. He needed to report back to the boss.

Chapter One

'*Wednesday September 14th, 1977.*' As I did every day, I wrote the date in my pocketbook ready for the start of my shift at Wyre Hall police station, a two-storey box of a building named after a long-demolished mansion house. I underlined my words just as Steve Patton, who sat next to me, nudged me. A thick, black line of ink snaked across the page.

'Dammit, Steve, look at my book. You know how strict they are about it.' There was no point trying to erase it: the pocket notebook was classed as an official document and erasures were not permitted; neither were gaps, alterations, or anything else that might look like I was trying to hide or manipulate evidence should I ever need to produce my book in court. I'd just have to write around it.

'Sorry, Samantha,' said Steve, not sounding sorry at all.

I looked at him and stared. 'Why have you put sunglasses on? This is England, land of rain and clouds, not the California Pacific Highway. Also, it's seven in the morning so you look a complete berk.'

Steve grinned. 'I look cool, don't deny it. Remember you once told me that I had to be an aviator to look good in mirror lenses.'

'Yeah, yonks ago,' I said wondering where the conversation was going.

'Well, I am now an aviator.'

'No you're not. You're a police constable, the same as me,' I argued.

'Well, yes I am, but I'm also an aviator.' He folded his arms and waited for me to react.

I took the bait. 'Go on, explain.'

'I was talking to Desmond Monaghan, that bobby who belongs to a flying club.'

'I know him.' I rotated my hand to indicate he should get on with his story; parade was due to start.

'Desi was telling me he's got part-ownership of a Piper. A small plane,' Steve explained when he saw my quizzical expression. 'Long story short, it's stored at Hornthorpe Dell. He told me they do lessons there. I went and I had a lesson.' He sighed. 'Sam, it's brilliant. It's not like going on your holidays in a big jet, it was a little Piper, like Desi's plane, and you can feel every bump.'

That did not sound like fun to me. I didn't really enjoy flying and, when I did fly, I liked to be in a big plane with lots of engines that could cut through the air with minimal turbulence.

'You're going again?' I asked.

Steve nodded. 'Tony, my instructor, says I've got a natural aptitude for flying. It's expensive, but I can just afford it if I keep my motorbike and stay living with my parents for another year.' He leant forward and addressed Ken Ashcroft, the policeman sat on my left. 'You should try it, Ken. You'd love it.'

'It does sound interesting but I'm saving up for a deposit on a house. I'm getting married next year, remember,' Ken replied.

'Take out one of those hundred-and-five percent mortgages they've brought out,' Steve suggested.

'We don't want to drown in debt, Steve. We could still only borrow so much, and even that wouldn't be enough to get a house on that new estate Gaynor's got her eye on.'

Typical Ken: practical and sensible. He was due to finish his probation in November, but they weren't tying the knot until Gaynor had finished her probation in just over a year. They were favouring a Christmas wedding, which I thought sounded fantastic, especially if it snowed.

'I thought you'd be in your own place and driving an MGB

BLUE SKY

GT now you've got through your probation, Steve,' I said.

'I always said that, but now I want to get my pilot's licence, and even though my pay has increased a bit, I couldn't afford if I moved out of my parents' place.'

Trevor, the Mike Three driver came in. He stopped when he saw Steve in his sunglasses.

'Not again,' he groaned. He took his seat at the big table at the front, the one that all the drivers sat at. We foot patrols sat on wooden chairs arranged in short rows behind them, which gave plenty of opportunity for the type of mischief you'd normally expect in a classroom.

Steve leaned forward. 'Hey, Ken mate. I see Rovers didn't exactly cover themselves in glory at the weekend.'

'Wazzer. Give it time,' Ken replied with a big grin.

'How much time do they need? The season is almost over,' Steve replied.

'Ugh, if you two are going to talk football, one of you swap places with me,' I said.

Before we could move, the door opened, and conversations around the room ceased as Inspector Gary Tyrrell entered, followed by Sergeants Alan Bowman and Shaun Lloyd. It was dull in the parade room, not least because of the filth that covered the high windows. Shaun flicked on the light, which cast a sick-yellow, fly-spotted glare over everything. Someone should have a word with the cleaners.

'That's better.

Inspector Gary Tyrrell headed B Block: our block. He was referred to as Sir, or Boss, by most people. Outside work, I called him darling, or Big Bird because he was almost a full foot taller than me. We'd been together for several months now. We tried to be discreet because the brass upstairs didn't really approve of relationships between ranks from the same block, or even the same station. Discipline problems, they said. They especially disliked relationships between probationers and higher ups, even unmarried ones, in case the probationer felt coerced. I still had four months of my probation to do, so they were highly likely to move one of us away if they found out.

Other recruits had arrived at Wyre Hall after me, including a couple more women, but they had gone onto other blocks. I reckoned it was B Block's turn for the next sprog, whatever the gender. I couldn't think of anyone from my intake who was still the sprog on their block, so it was about time we got someone with less service than me.

Gary, Alan, and Shaun sat down, and we all followed suit. As usual, Alan started parade by giving out duties. He believed that it was good for a police officer to get to know an area well and for the people in the area to get to know them. I could see what he was trying to do, but people in some areas of my patch didn't want to get to know the police. They had an innate dislike of the police and, to be honest, sometimes the feeling was mutual. However, there were a lot of decent people there, too. Whatever their feelings, these were becoming my people and I would do my best for all of them.

I had a lot of respect for Sergeant Alan Bowman. He had enough service to leave, but he was still here: station sergeant, father figure, judge of our paperwork. He said he'd retire in the new year, but we were laying bets that he'd remain with us until they prised him out with a crowbar.

Shaun was our patrol sergeant. I liked him too. He was a newly promoted sergeant and Wyre Hall was his first posting at that rank. He'd been with us for around six months, admirably filling the gap left by the late and unlamented Sergeant Brian Lewington. Shaun did what Brian had been supposed to do—supervise incidents and deal with the outside stuff—without any illegal extracurricular activities.

Once everyone knew what they were doing, Inspector Tyrrell went through the parade book, talking about observations, suspicious incidents and so on. Nothing was relevant to my beat, so I spent my time admiring his high cheekbones and blue eyes.

'Finally, that body found in the woods by the airfield has

been identified as Kevin Lynch. Nineteen years old. Cause of death was a heroin overdose,' Gary said.

'That's no loss to society,' Frank Moreton, the Mike One driver said. 'That little scrote has been dealing for months. Better he killed himself than drag another poor kid into addiction.'

'It's still sad though,' Ken said.

Frank *hmphed* his disagreement.

Parade ended and we all went to the tiny, glass-surrounded control room to collect our radios and do our test calls.

'Are you covering Kensington Road?' Ray Fairbrother, our radio operator, asked me. He drew deeply on his cigarette and puffed out smoke like a dragon.

'Yes. Do you have a job for me?' I replied.

'Suspicious male hanging around.' Ray handed me a sheet. 'Caller is a Muriel Jackson from number ten, and she sounded genuine. He's wearing jeans and a striped zip-up cardigan.'

'I'll give you a lift out,' Phil Torrens said. Phil was the Mike Two driver. The park end of my beat was in his area. He had been my tutor constable when I first arrived at Wyre Hall. He was still my first port of call if I came across something I wasn't sure of.

'Thanks, Phil.'

Steve wandered through the control room, still wearing his glasses. 'I thought the boss told you not to wear them outside yonks ago,' Derek Kidd, our other control room operator, said.

'Eyeguard glass.' Steve tapped the side of his glasses.

'Do your test calls and get out,' Alan shouted over the chatter.

Steve and Ken walked out to their beats together, while Phil and I went to Kensington Road, in a pleasant area of post-war semi-detached houses known as the "palace streets" because all the roads were named after royal residences. A lot of areas in the town were given nicknames over the years, as the town planners of the time named the roads after a particular theme.

'Nothing suspicious here,' Phil said when we arrived. 'You go and speak to the caller and I'll take a slow drive around and see what I can see.' Phil pulled over and let me out, then slowly drove down the road.

I found number ten and knocked on the door, pretending not to notice the ubiquitous curtain twitches from neighbours.

A woman in her fifties peered out of the front bay window at me, waved and disappeared. A couple of seconds later, she opened the door.

'Come in, come in.' She glanced nervously along the road and shut the door behind us. 'Please, come in to the sitting room. I've just made breakfast. Would you like a cup of tea and some toast or a biscuit?'

'A biscuit would be nice, thank you,' I said.

I sat on a brown leather sofa and felt as if I had stepped back into the 1950s. A heavy mirror hung by thick chain from a picture rail. The fireplace was surrounded by a beige, marble-effect, tiled hearth and mantelpiece. An embroidered screen covered the opening. Two china dogs sat either end of the mantelpiece and between them a large clock loudly ticked away the seconds. A dark wood display cabinet occupied one alcove beside the fire, and a television cabinet sat in the other alcove. An armchair in the same material as the sofa filled the bay window. Pride of place was a black-and-white wedding photograph in a glass frame, supported on each side by dark wood shoulders. Photographs in silver and brass frames covered the flat surfaces. No children, I noticed: just pets and photos of a younger Mrs Jackson and her husband. I could have been in my nan's house.

The large clock bonged out 8am. Mrs Jackson came in with a tray of tea and biscuits and put it on the coffee table. I was pleased to see chocolate bourbons there.

'Thank you for coming,' she said as she poured tea and handed me a cup. 'I hope you don't mind if my husband doesn't join us. He's in the dining room finishing his breakfast. He's diabetic so he needs to eat at regular times, but I can get him if you need to see him.'

'Did he see the man?' I asked.

'No, he didn't,' Mrs Jackson replied.

'Then please don't disturb him,' I said. 'Tell me about the man outside.'

'He was ever so odd. I opened the curtains and he just stood there looking at the house.' She held out the plate of biscuits and I took a bourbon.

'Thank you. Was he looking at your house in particular?'

'I think so,' she sat in the armchair and sipped at her tea. 'I'm glad I've got nets up.'

'Did he wave, or try to interact with you in any way?' I asked.

'No, he just stood there, watching.' Mrs Jackson took a digestive and bit it in two.

'My colleague is driving around to see if he can see anything. Meantime, I want to take a full description from you.' I got out the suspicious incident form and began to fill it in. Mrs Jackson gave me a fairly good description, which I radioed to Ray to give to Phil.

After we filled in the form. I finished my tea and stood up. 'Thank you, Mrs Jackson. If you see him hanging around again, don't be afraid to ring us.'

'Thank you, dear.' Mrs Jackson saw me to the door.

I decided to speak to a couple of the neighbours to see if I could get any more information, so I went to the house next door and tapped on the door.

A younger woman opened the door and gasped.

'Don't be alarmed,' I said. 'Your neighbour has reported a suspicious man staring at houses in the road a little while ago and I wondered if you had seen anything?'

'No, nothing,' the woman said. A baby wailed from inside the house. 'I've been busy with the little one.'

'Okay, thanks. I'll let you get on.' I went across the road to the house opposite and spoke to a man who hadn't seen anything either.

I radioed in the result to Ray and scribbled the update on the form, then put it in my handbag. I would submit it when

I got back. I would also check with Irene, our collator, to see if anything similar had been reported in the area recently. Sergeant Irene Kildea knew everything that was going on in the town and anyone of note. She kept files on any little thing that often came together to make big things. All most helpful in an investigation.

Phil drew up beside me.

'Any joy?' I asked.

'Nothing.' Phil said. 'Area searched, no trace. Hop in, I'll let you ride with me for a while. Save your feet.'

I got into the passenger seat. In a single shift we could walk fifteen to twenty miles, so I was grateful for a ride.

Phil drove us around the surrounding streets, past the allotments and the playground and on to the park. I couldn't see anyone fitting the description of the suspicious man.

'Was she overreacting?' Phil asked.

'She didn't seem the hysterical sort, and she was quite firm on what she had seen. I'll check in the collator's office if there have been similar calls,' I said.

'Sometimes, that's all you can do,' Phil said.

It was frustrating when a complaint could not be verified. I had no reason to disbelieve Mrs Jackson, but I would have to write this up as ASNT. NOD: Area Searched, No Trace, No Offences Detected. It wasn't good to get too many of those against an address; eventually patrols would begin to wonder if a caller was being genuine.

Phil parked up by the park railings and I took advantage of the peace and quiet to write up my pocketbook

A tapping on the window drew my attention. I looked up from my pocketbook and saw a lady, at least seventy-five years old, peering in at me.

I wound down the window. 'Can I help you?'

'I wonder if you would call to my house. It's not far. Windsor Close, number 4. I think my friend, Joan, has given me a cannabis plant.'

Well, that was unexpected.

'What makes you think it's a cannabis plant?' I asked.

'She's grown some plants in her greenhouse and she gave me one. She told me it was a hibiscus, but I saw a programme on television last night and I think it looks more like a cannabis plant. I was taking my morning walk through the park and saw you here so I thought if anyone knows a cannabis plant, it's a police officer.' She stepped back and smiled awaiting our response.

I still wasn't convinced the plant would be cannabis, and there was the possibility she was just a lonely lady who wanted a chat. However, I said, 'We'd be happy to take a look. Climb in and we'll drive you home.'

'It's only around the corner. I'll walk home and put the kettle on. I'll see you there. My name is Winifred Platt by the way.'

Phil waited for her to go out of earshot then guffawed. 'No way that'll be a cannabis plant.'

'I heard the local Derby and Joan club are fundraising,' I joked. I called up control, told them where we were going and asked Ray to start a job sheet. I would need an incident number when I came to write this up.

We drove around the corner to a neat bay-fronted terraced house in a nice cul-de-sac. We got out of the Panda and walked up the short drive. Winifred Platt had left the front door ajar. I could see into a hallway that was crammed with plants.

'Someone has green fingers,' Phil commented. 'It looks like a jungle.

'Hello?' I called.

Winifred Platt came into the hall. 'Please come in, the kettle has just boiled. Tea or coffee?'

'Tea please,' Phil said.

'And me,' I added. 'May we call you Winifred?'

'Of course. The plant is in the living room, on the table. Go in, I'll bring the tea in a minute.'

Phil and I went into the living room, which was as full of greenery as the hall. One plant had been isolated on a low coffee table.

'Hellfire,' Phil muttered.

'What do you think?' Winifred brought a tea tray in, set it on the table next to the plant and began pouring the tea.

'I'm sorry to tell you, Winifred, but this is indeed a cannabis plant,' Phil said.

Winifred almost dropped the teapot. 'I knew it!'

'We'll need to take the plant, and we'll need to speak to your friend, but don't worry, I'm sure there's a reasonable explanation.' Phil accepted the cup Winifred held out to him.

Winifred passed me a cup of tea before speaking again. 'Joan must have a dozen plants like this.'

'We'll need to establish where she got the plants from, but I'm sure she will have no idea what the plants are.' Phil sipped from his cup.

We stood around the table, drinking tea, and staring at the offending plant.

'Right,' Phil placed his empty cup on the tray. 'Let's get this back to the station.'

I put my cup next to Phil's. 'Can you give me Joan's name and address please.'

'Joan Fletcher, 14 Westbourne Road.'

I jotted it down. Phil picked up the plant and carried it out to the car. I hurried ahead and opened the door for him. He placed the plant on the back seat, and we got in the front and drove back to Wyre Hall to collect the van in case we needed to transport a lot of plants.

I put my head around the door of the collator's office. Irene was typing something. Her fingers flew across the keyboard and the white, short-sleeved, police-issue blouse she wore enhanced the tan she still had from her Spanish honeymoon several weeks ago. She had to be using a sunlamp to keep it going.

'Breaking news, Irene,' I said.

She looked up from her typing. 'What's happened?'

'Phil and I have just busted a drugs cartel based by the park and run by pensioners,' I said maintaining a straight face.

Irene leant back in her seat, ran one hand over her dark, cropped hair and grinned. 'Okay, what's the story?'

I laughed out loud. 'A pensioner asked us to look at a plant her friend gave her, and it's cannabis. We're just going around now to collect the others.'

Irene grinned. 'The Godmother.'

I glanced at the typewriter and saw what she had been typing. 'Is that the overdose? It's a suspicious death now?'

Irene pushed the typewriter to one side. 'You didn't see that.'

I sat beside her. 'I did, but I know not to repeat it. So, what gave it away?'

Irene sighed. 'They've upgraded it because the pathologist found a puncture mark on one leg that that goes in at an angle the deceased would not have been able to do himself. Eamon and Mike are following it up.'

'He was found in woodland. Couldn't it have been caused by a scratch from a bush or something?' I asked.

'Scratches around his leg almost caused the pathologist to miss it,' Irene said. 'It was lucky he took time to remove a thorn from a wound and spotted it. He thought it was a bit odd for Lynch to have injected there, because he only had marks on the crook of his elbow.'

'Sometimes they do inject in other places,' I said.

'If they want to hide their addiction, or they're so far gone their veins have collapsed,' Irene said.

'Sam!' Phil called down the corridor.

'Got to go. I won't say anything.' I trotted after Phil and we drove to Westbourne Road.

We parked outside Joan Fletcher's large Victorian house and Phil knocked on the heavy door.

'Hello,' said the short, elderly woman who opened the door. 'Winifred phoned to say you'd be calling to take some plants away.'

'That's right, Mrs Fletcher,' Phil said.

'Plain old Joan is fine. I was surprised when Winifred told me the plant was cannabis. Come in.' Joan led us through the house to a greenhouse in the walled garden at the rear. Phil and I gawped at the cannabis plants lining the glass walls.

'Where did you get them?' Phil asked.

'I grew them from bird seed.'

'Bird seed?' I echoed. I was hearing a lot I hadn't been expecting today.

'Winifred and I are members of the horticultural club. We're quite a competitive lot. I wanted to find something a little exotic to display, so I came up with the idea of planting bird seed to see what came up. I got several shoots that I transferred to pots and these plants grew up. I thought they looked like a variety of hibiscus.'

I wasn't interested in horticulture and didn't know what hibiscus looked like, so I couldn't comment. I wandered up and down the greenhouse examining the plants.

'They're in good shape, aren't they? My grandson, Jason, likes helping me,' Joan said. 'I was looking forward to showing them at the club AGM.' She cackled. 'I'd love to have seen their faces if I had. Imagine: me growing cannabis!'

Phil pulled his gloves on. 'Let's shift this lot, Sam.'

I put my gloves on and, together, Phil and I moved the cannabis plants into the van, then Phil made out a receipt for the property and handed it to Joan.

'I'm afraid you won't get the plants back, they'll have to go for destruction,' Phil said.

'Don't worry, I've never knowingly done anything illegal in my life and I don't want to start now. I'll display my *Plumbago Auriculata* instead.'

'Sounds lovely,' I said. I didn't know what *Plumbago Auriculata* looked like either.

*

Back at the station once more, we got the plants into the property store and I settled myself in the report writing room to complete the paperwork.

'What are you up to?'

I straightened up and rubbed my aching back, smiling at Gary who was leaning on the door jamb.

'Writing up about the cannabis plants Phil and I seized. I'm recommending no further action other than destruction of the plants, because neither lady realised what they really were. They weren't even obtained illegally because they were grown from bird seed.'

'I'll endorse that then,' Gary said. He pulled a chair out and sat opposite me.

'What? Have I done something wrong, or have I not done something I should have?' I asked.

'I want to talk to you about a new posting,' he said.

My heart flipped. Did this mean the brass upstairs knew about us and wanted to separate us? There might be a rank difference but there wasn't that much of an age gap. I was twenty-two and Gary was only thirty years old.

'You or me?' I asked.

'Me,' he replied.

'You can't cope with life on the spike so you're going back into CID,' I teased.

He laughed. 'Spoken like a true plod.'

I put my pen down. 'Go on.'

'Do you remember a while ago I told you about a posting to Hong Kong?'

I remembered. He'd seen it in a police publication, something to do with anticorruption, but I hadn't paid much attention. He'd applied but because of his young age, despite being of the required rank, he hadn't expected to hear any more.

He chewed his lip for a moment. 'I've been invited

for interview.'

'When?'

'I have to contact them to confirm I'm still interested, and they'll give me a date,' Gary said.

'That's good isn't it?' I asked.

'It's good that I've been invited…'

'But?' I definitely heard a big but.

'Things have changed since I applied. I didn't know how we were going to work out, and there's my mother…'

'Gary, your mother is fifty-four, not ninety-five. We have people working here who are older than she is.'

'But she's by herself,' Gary argued.

'Your mum is a feisty lady who only needs you to reach things off tall shelves and to remove lids from jars. I think she'd be cross if she thought you let opportunities pass you by because of her. She has your sister and her family to keep her company while you're away. Also, the posting won't last forever,' I said.

'And us?'

I folded my arms. 'I think we can survive a few months apart. Think of the benefits of going over there. Experience: life experience as well as professional experience. Also, I remember you said it was more money.'

'So, it's my money you're after,' he joked.

'Of course. Why else would I be associating with a handsome, kind, very tall senior officer.'

Gary stood up and plonked a kiss on the top of my head. 'You're right; this is too good an opportunity to miss.' He blew another kiss at me and left.

I slumped on the desk. I might have been encouraging, but I would miss him. However, like his mum, I didn't want him not to do things because of me. We could survive this.

Blue Sky

*

I wasn't in the mood for Steve's chatter at refs, our meal break. I just kept thinking about Gary being so far away if he got through the selection process.

'Hey, Sam.' Steve nudged me.

'What?' I snapped.

'Would you like to come with us?'

'With you where,' I asked.

'Have you listened to a single word I said?' Steve complained. 'Desi said when I've had a couple more lessons, I could go with him on a flight to the Isle of Man one weekend and bring someone with me if I wanted. He's licenced to take passengers and he might even let me take the controls for a while.'

I couldn't think of anything I wanted less, but I had time to think of an excuse before we went. 'Sure, let me know when you're thinking of going.'

Steve turned back to Ken to discuss future uses of his pilot's licence and his chances of being selected, if the rumours were true and the force went ahead and bought an aircraft.

Phil came in and, as was his habit, he put his bag on the table then went to set up a game of snooker. I spotted a Baker and Wilkie's textbook peeking out of the bag. There were a number of books in the series, which contained everything a police officer needed to know. This could only mean one thing.

'Hey, Phil, are you revising?' I called.

Phil came back to the table and pulled the book and a box of sandwiches from the bag and laid them on the table. 'I thought I might try for the promotion exams.'

'About time! You'll make a great boss,' I said.

Phil grinned. 'Glad you think so.'

'Wyre Hall won't be the same without you,' Steve said.

Oh yes, the downside of promotion: Phil would move to another division. If Gary and Phil went, things would be very different here.

'Do you think the force will buy a plane?' Steve asked Phil. 'I'm taking flying lessons and I wouldn't mind being the pilot.'

Phil thought for a moment. 'I think it would be better if they got a helicopter, because planes don't hover.'

'Phil's right,' Ken said. 'A helicopter would give someone a steady bird's eye view of something. That would be hard to do in a circling plane. Will you be able to fly a helicopter, Steve?'

'No.'

I had to agree: a helicopter sounded much better. But as yet we had neither, so it was pointless discussing it.

Alan came into the refs room and turned the radio over to Radio 2.

'Do we have to listen to old fogey music, Sarge,' Steve complained.

'It's better than the caterwauling that those long-haired louts call music,' Alan said.

I didn't mind a spot of Perry Como or even Glenn Miller or Gershwin, so I left Steve and Alan to debate the merits of their chosen music. Alan would win; he was the sergeant after all.

Chapter Two

The following day, Steve pulled me to one side as we queued to collect our radios.

'I want to talk to you about something. Let's walk out together.'

No doubt it was connected to flying. It seemed to be all he could talk about these days. I began to think of excuses in case he asked me again to go to the Isle of Man with him.

'I've got the town centre beat, so I'll walk with you too.' Ken joined us.

'The three musketeers,' Steve said. 'One for all and all for one.'

Like the three musketeers, we strode out to face the night. Okay: they strolled, I strode and occasionally trotted to keep up.

'I want to sound you out over something,' Steve said.

'Go on, you've got us interested now,' Ken said.

Steve took a deep breath. 'I'm thinking of making a career change. I researched it and I meet the requirements to enter the RAF as an officer and begin pilot training.'

I was speechless. 'You've finished your probation. You can specialise now and take your promotion exams. There are so many directions you can go in. Isn't that as good as a career change?'

'Not if I can't fly,' Steve said.

'Isn't there an age limit,' Ken asked.

'And a height limit so you don't cut off your knees when you eject?' I added.

'Yes, but I'm still young enough for that not to be a problem, and I'm just within the upper height level,' Steve replied.

'Have you told anyone apart from us yet?' I asked.

'Not yet. Don't tell the boss, Sam. I know it's cheeky of me to ask you to keep secrets from him, but I need to be certain before I burn any bridges.'

'What does your dad say?' Ken asked. 'I heard there's some rivalry between the services.'

That was a good point. Steve's dad had been in the Royal Marines, his older brother was still a marine, and they had expected Steve to follow suit. The life hadn't appealed to Steve, who had grown up on military bases, so he had joined the police. Only now he was thinking of becoming a pilot.

'It's all military,' I said. 'Surely they'll be proud, especially as you'd be an officer.'

'Yeah, probably. So, what do you think?' Steve asked.

Ken and I exchanged glances. Neither of us wanted to flatten Steve's enthusiasm, but we were a bit shell-shocked.

'Well, you have to balance what you have now against what you'll gain if you move,' Ken said.

'I think you have to do what makes you happy,' I said.

'I'm happy here, but I think I would be happier flying,' Steve said.

'This is my stop,' Ken said. 'Have a think, mate, and we'll speak later.'

'Don't spend too much time in Smith's Yard. I heard Shaun is on to it and might do a spot check. You don't want to be on a fizzer,' Steve said.

'Thanks.' Ken turned away and began his patrol. Steve and I walked on to our own beats.

'What's Smith's Yard?' I asked. I didn't normally work the town beat, so it wasn't somewhere I'd come across.

'It's a yard opposite the market. I think it was a coaching station. There's a cellar in the far corner that's usually open and you can hide in there when the weather's bad,' Steve said.

'Who owns it?' I asked.

'Don't know. Maybe nobody. The stairs that would normally lead to a house have been bricked off.'

'Maybe it was a place the stable lads slept in the olden days and they wanted to keep them away from the master's house,' I said.

'Could be. Anyway, you'll have to come to visit me if I'm accepted.' It sounded as if Steve had already made his decision about leaving.

'It looks like B block is completely changing,' I said. I liked our block, and I was comfortable with things as they were.

'I'm the only one thinking of going as far as I know,' Steve said.

'Remember Phil's taking the promotion exams,' I said.

'But he'll have the promotion board interviews to get through if he passes. I know of at least one person who has passed the exams through to inspector but can't get through the boards.'

'Phil will pass, and he'll do well in the interviews,' I said. 'He'll leave and now you're thinking of leaving.'

'He won't go at once.' Steve put an arm around my shoulders. 'Hey, you're not going to cry are you? You know, nobody has cried about me before, apart from my mum and that was because I was in hospital after I knocked myself out falling off a climbing frame.'

I shook his arm off. 'Of course not. I'm just not looking forward to being left behind on the block.' I needed to lighten the atmosphere. 'You fell off a climbing frame and got knocked out? That explains so much.'

Steve elbowed me and we laughed.

'Seriously, is there anything else happening?' he asked. 'People move around all the time in this job.'

'Gary has applied for a posting to Hong Kong,' I blurted out. 'Nobody must know, so if you tell anyone I told you, I'll tell them about you leaving for the air force.'

'You're going to Hong Kong?' Steve exclaimed.

'Not me. Gary, if he's accepted,' I said. 'It's a temporary

posting, but it'll be hard to be here without him. And now you and Phil will be leaving too.'

'We'll still all be friends,' Steve said. 'We just won't be working together.'

'Yeah. Nothing stays the same, does it. The world turns, we all adjust and life goes on.' I remembered my uncle saying that to me when I was staying with him and my aunt in Canada after I left school. I smiled, then I had a thought. 'Hang on, if you're accepted, the safety of the whole country might lie in your hands.'

'The country doesn't seem to mind me looking after this bit of it, so I expect it'll be okay if I see to the rest of it,' he said.

'It's a bit scary, and I don't just mean the flying,' I said.

Steve shrugged.

'4912 from control.' Ray's voice came over the radio.

'4912 go ahead,' I replied.

'Mrs Jackson of 10 Kensington Road reports a suspicious male. Long hair, wearing a dark leather jacket and jeans.'

'Roger, but I'm still on my way out from the station. Will you tell her I'll be at least ten to fifteen minutes, please.'

'Roger that. Mike Two from control, what's your location?'

I listened to the beeping over the air, indicating that Phil, the Mike Two driver, was replying.

'Roger, Mike Two,' Ray said. '4912.'

'Go ahead,' I replied.

'Stand down. Mike Two is closer and he'll attend.'

'Roger.' I responded.

'You know, it would be much easier if they had it on Talkthrough, then we could all just talk directly to each other,' Steve said.

'They do that in some divisions, but the superintendent here says all the chatter is confusing. He likes one voice on the radio,' I said.

We walked on for five minutes.

'This is where I leave you,' Steve said. 'See you at scoff.'

'See you later,' I replied.

I would be patrolling alone now, barring running into Phil as he patrolled, until our meal break, or "scoff" as most police referred to it. Or "refs", which probably was short for refreshments. Between words like that and the various acronyms that were used as nouns and verbs, I now spoke fluent jargon, which spilled into my everyday speech. Sometimes I had to consciously alter the way I spoke, to avoid confusion outside work.

I walked past the park. It was a well-used area during the day but at night we usually only found drunks and druggies. Heroin was becoming a bit of a problem, so recently it had been more druggies. I spotted a man jogging through the park, his long hair blowing from his shoulders as he moved. He was dressed in a leather jacket, flared jeans, and a striped shirt. Not usual exercise gear, and close enough to the description of the suspicious male to warrant a stop check.

I headed to the main park gate. As I walked I radioed control to let them know where I was. I had been warned on a couple of occasions about rushing in without telling anyone and I didn't want to annoy Gary.

'4912 to control.'

'Go ahead, Sam,' Ray replied.

'Do you have any further description from Phil yet?' I asked.

'Not yet, Sam,' Ray replied.

'Roger. I can see a long-haired man in a leather jacket, striped shirt and jeans running through the park. I'm headed for the main gate and I'll stop him there.' I trotted towards the gate, keeping an eye on the man.

'Mike Two from control.'

I stopped paying attention to the radio and concentrated on my quarry. The man slowed as he reached the gate.

I timed it perfectly. I got there just as he turned out onto the road.

'Good evening,' I said. He jumped. 'You seem breathless.'

His cheeks were red even in the poor evening light, but at least he didn't stink of sweat: he wore too much aftershave for that.

'So? I've been running.'

'We have had a report of a suspicious male in the area, so you won't mind answering a few questions will you.' I made sure it didn't sound like a request.

'And if I do mind?' He faced me full-on and squared his shoulders. He intended to intimidate me, which never went down well. I carried on regardless.

'I'll ask them anyway. Why were you running?'

'Who says I was?'

'You did, and I saw you in the park,' I said. 'What's your name?'

'Donald Mallard.' He jutted his chin.

'Good one. It makes a change from the usual Michael Rodent I hear. Now, what's your real name?' I asked.

He smirked. 'Elmer Fudd.'

I heard the sound of a clapped-out Panda engine crunching through the gears, about fifteen seconds before Phil drove the car around the corner and screeched to a halt.

'All right, Sam?' He strode towards us.

Phil wasn't as tall as Gary, but I reckoned he was about six feet and he looked like he could benchpress a small elephant. Elmer, at least two inches shorter than Phil and several pounds lighter, lost the attitude.

'Fine thanks, Phil. Elmer Fudd and I were just having a chat, weren't we, Elmer.'

'Description of our man is white, average build, long hair, wearing a striped shirt and leather jacket.' Phil bobbed his head towards Elmer. 'I think you have an exact match.'

'What's your real name,' I asked Elmer.

'None of your business.' Elmer glanced at Phil.

'Were there any offences?' I asked Phil.

'No, unfortunately. But a nice lady has been badly frightened, which I think is despicable.' Phil directed the latter half of his sentence to Elmer.

'If no offences have been committed, you have no reason to detain me any longer.' Elmer made to walk off, but Phil grabbed his arm. For a moment, I thought Elmer was going to thump Phil, but he backed down and turned towards us. 'This is police harassment.'

'A lady has been frightened by a man fitting your description, and my colleague thought you were suspicious enough to stop you and that's good enough for me. Turn out your pockets.' Phil released Elmer's arm and stood with his hands on his hips.

Elmer emptied his pockets of a lighter, a packet of cigarettes and a wallet. Phil patted him down then took the wallet and checked inside.

'Oh, so that's what this is about. You won't find more than a fiver in there,' Elmer sneered.

Phil curled a lip at him then pulled out a driving licence. 'Vincent Boyle. The address here is in Portsmouth. That's a long way away. What are you doing up here, Vincent?'

'I came to find work,' Vincent snarled.

'Where are you living?' Phil asked.

'I'm staying at the YMCA for a while.'

'And why were you hanging around Kensington Road?' Phil asked.

'I wasn't hanging around; I was just walking past. It's not my fault some daft old bat has jumped to the wrong conclusion.'

Phil nodded and handed back the wallet. 'Right, thank you for your cooperation. You'll find nothing has been taken. Good evening to you, Mr Boyle.'

Muttering under his breath. Vincent Boyle pocketed his wallet and left.

When Boyle was out of earshot I said to Phil, 'You realise that you hijacked my stop check?'

'I had the details of the incident,' Phil said.

'But it was my stop check,' I countered. 'We've talked about this, Phil; you don't have to ride in like Sir Galahad. I'm a big girl and I can work alone, even on nights. If I need help, I'll call for it.'

Phil knew he'd been rumbled. 'Yeah, well, I wouldn't like to think of Jo or one of our girls doing stop checks out alone at night.'

'Your wife isn't in the job and it'll be about eight years before either of your daughters is old enough to join up.' I patted his arm. 'Thank you for caring but please stop thinking you have to look after me any more than you would one of the lads.'

Phil nodded. 'Okay, let's update this incident with the control room then I'll let you ride with me for a bit.'

Professional pride satisfied, I wasn't going to turn down a ride.

*

The rest of nights passed without major incident. I paid some extra attention to Kensington Road, but there were no further calls. I visited the collator's office, but couldn't find anything on Boyle. I left a note for Irene asking her if she would make enquiries with the Hampshire Constabulary and speak to the collator that covered Portsmouth in case they knew something about our suspicious male.

I couldn't find much on 10 Kensington Road apart from a couple of calls about the suspicious male that had been made during our weekend off. Each incident had been marked *"ASNT, NOD: Area Searched No Trace, No Offences Disclosed"*. Phil made some enquiries and found that Boyle was indeed staying at the YMCA. Everything appeared to be in order so that was the end of that, until lates.

Chapter Three

Just before 6pm, Ray transmitted, 'Any patrol please to number ten Kensington Road, report of a disturbance.'

I was on foot near the park, so I shouted up my number and ran for the address. I got there at the same time as Ken, who was coming from the opposite direction.

Several neighbours were in the front garden of number ten, gathered around Muriel Jackson who was kneeling beside a prone man who was holding his stomach and retching onto the grass.

'I told Leonard not to go out, but the silly fool wouldn't listen. He shouldn't be sick; it upsets his blood sugar.' Mrs Jackson rubbed Mr Jackson's back.

'4912 to control,' I radioed.

'Go ahead,' Ray responded.

'Stand down patrols; the offender has made off, all quiet here now. Ken and I are dealing.' Ray cancelled the patrols and I knelt beside the man. 'I'll get you an ambulance, Mr Jackson,' I said.

'I don't want an ambulance. I'll be fine.' Mr Jackson wiped his mouth and stood up.

'I advise you to have a check-up all the same because of your diabetes,' I said.

'I told you: no,' he insisted.

'Do you want us to contact family for you?' I asked.

'We have no family,' Muriel Jackson said. 'Just each other.'

'I saw everything,' the Jackson's young next-door neighbour said. 'I was getting the baby out of his pram and Leonard came out of the house and I saw a man with long hair punch him in the stomach. I shouted at him and Muriel came out and he ran away.'

'What did he look like?' I asked.

'Long hair, jeans, chunky boots, black leather jacket,' the young mum answered.

'When was this,' I asked.

'About ten minutes ago. He went that way.' The neighbour pointed to a footpath a short distance away that lead to the allotments behind Sandringham Boulevard.

Ken ran to the path and I began to follow. I needed to get statements, but I knew where everyone was so I could go back and do that later.

Mr Jackson grabbed my hand. 'It was nothing, really. We won't make any complaint. I just don't want him to come back here.'

'Okay, we'll talk about it later,' I said. 'We'll check the area first.' I heard shouting coming from around the pathway. 'Stay here,' I ordered; not that anyone was in a rush to follow me.

I ran towards the allotments and saw Ken grappling with Vincent Boyle. As I ran towards them, Boyle gripped Ken's jacket, pushed him backwards across a hedge and rained punches onto his face. Wishing I hadn't cancelled the back up, I called a scramble to the location and hurled myself at Boyle. Scramble was the most urgent of all calls; nobody ignored a scramble.

I grabbed the arm Boyle was using to punch Ken and pulled it backwards. Ken was able to escape and grabbed Boyle's other arm. However, that didn't stop him from kicking out at us. One well-aimed kick got me in the knee. My leg gave way and I fell to the floor. Boyle tried to kick me again, but Ken pulled him away in time, earning another punch to the side of his face. Perhaps Phil's instincts hadn't been so far from the mark when I had stop-checked Boyle on nights. My gender had saved me from a couple of beatings in the past because there was still something of a taboo about hitting women, but not everyone thought like that. Boyle evidently had no qualms about it: proved when I had to dodge another kick from him.

I swung my handbag at Boyle and it connected with his head with a satisfying clunk, thanks to the can of pop I always carried in there. Boyle stopped trying to kick me and staggered back a couple of paces, which gave me a moment's grace to bring him to the ground and sit on his back. Ken lay across his thrashing legs. I was a bit concerned by the way Ken kept bringing his hand up to his eyes. Something to check out later.

A second later, Phil screeched up the path and, without bothering to turn off the engine, leapt from the car and handcuffed Boyle. Phil frisked Boyle and, together, we wrestled Boyle into the back of Phil's Panda and slammed the door. Boyle screamed and kicked at the headrests and windows.

'Are you all right, Sam?' Phil asked wiping the sweat from his brow.

'Fine, thanks. But I think something's wrong with Ken's eyes,' I replied.

'Hellfire,' Phil said. One of Ken's eyes was swollen and scarlet. It looked horrific.

'I can't see properly.' Ken rubbed at his eye.

'Don't rub it, you'll make it worse. You need to go to hospital,' Phil said.

I radioed in cancelling the scramble, which didn't stop Gary arriving with Steve a moment later.

'You've missed the fun,' Ken said to Steve.

'Looks like you've got a right charmer in there,' Steve nodded towards Phil's Panda.

'It's our suspicious man,' I said. 'He's assaulted Leonard Jackson at number ten, and there's witnesses.'

'Are you all right, Sam?' Gary dipped his chin towards my grazed legs, visible through the gaping holes in my tights. Great: more scabby knees.

'I'm fine, thanks. But look at Ken's eye.'

Gary went over to Ken and recoiled. 'Bloody hell! It looks like a plum tomato. I want you to go to the general to get that checked out and make sure there's no permanent damage.'

'But the prisoner?' Ken asked.

'Sam can deal with him,' Gary said. 'Steve, you sit in the back with the prisoner so Sam can ride shotgun with Phil. Ken, you're coming with me.'

We obediently got into our designated cars, and Phil took us and the prisoner to the bridewell while Gary took Ken to the hospital.

*

In the charge office, Phil stood close to Boyle as I recited the details of the arrest to the bridewell sergeant.

'What's your name,' the bridewell sergeant asked.

Boyle had evidently served in the military. National Service probably. He stood to attention and spoke in a deferential tone. 'Vincent Boyle, sir.'

'I'm a sergeant; you don't have to call me sir.'

'Yes, Sergeant.'

'And you can stand easy.'

'Yes, Sergeant.'

Boyle relaxed his stance.

The bridewell sergeant glanced at Phil who was still looming over Boyle, ready to jump on him if he misbehaved, but Boyle answered all questions courteously and went to his cell as meekly as a kitten. To anyone who had not been at the allotments, it would have been hard to believe that this apparently nice man could have been so vicious.

I went to my locker to get a new pair of tights from the stock I kept there. I seemed to go through them at a fast rate. The adrenaline was leaving my body and, as normal when I was coming down from an adrenaline rush, I was feeling a bit shaky and nauseous, which made me narky. Who thought it practical for a female police officer to go out and deal with incidents in a skirt and tights, and with nothing to defend herself but a soft leather handbag? Didn't they realise how hard it was to climb walls and wrestle with prisoners without showing off your knickers? It was all so undignified. If they wanted us to do the same job as the men, we should be allowed the same things as the men: things like trousers and deep pockets so we didn't have to lug a bag around. Batons would be good, too.

I went to the control room and begged some of their stash of antiseptic that they used to sanitise the equipment from time to time. Then I went to the ladies' toilet, bathed my knee, dislodged the little stones from my skin, then changed my tights, repinned my hair and touched up my lip gloss.

Feeling refreshed and looking more presentable, I returned to the Bridewell. Irene's new husband, DC Eamon Kildea was in the charge office when I went in.

'Hello, Sam m'darlin',' he said in his lovely, honey-smooth Irish voice.

'Hi, Eamon,' I replied. 'Still enjoying married life?'

'I highly recommend it. I can't think why I didn't do it sooner,' he said. 'But then, if I had, I wouldn't have met Irene.'

'Good point,' I acknowledged. 'Are you here to interview Boyle?'

'I am, m'darlin'. I could do with knowing more about Ken's injuries though.'

'I can tell you that Boyle repeatedly punched Ken in the face and caused injury to his eye. He looks like an extra from a Hammer film; that's why the boss took him to the hospital. Even when we managed to restrain Boyle, he kicked at us and my leg gave way. I've just had to bathe my knees and change my ruined tights.' The smell of antiseptic was still strong.

Eamon nodded. 'Let's leave it a few minutes and see if we can learn a bit more.'

*

Gary came back without Ken about fifteen minutes later.

'Have you sent him home?' I asked.

'They're transferring him over to the eye hospital in the city. The damage to his eye might be serious: the doctor said his optical nerve might be affected,' Gary said.'

'Section 20 sounds right then,' Eamon said.

'Isn't Section 20 too lenient? Section 18 GBH seems more fitting to me,' I said.

Eamon considered my words, which I appreciated because not everyone listened to me. However, he said, 'For Section 18 we have to prove intent to cause serious harm.'

'He repeatedly punched down on Ken. I saw it. Boyle had to have known Ken would be badly injured,' I said.

'Ah, but the devil is in the detail, Sam. We can prove he would have known he'd cause some injury to Ken, that's Section 20, but not that he intended to cause serious injury,' Eamon said. 'Better to get a conviction of Section 20, than have him go to trial and be found not guilty of Section 18 because we can't gather enough proof of intent.'

The old proving-versus-knowing problem again. I hated it, but Eamon was right.

'I need to let the brass know, and his family,' Gary said. 'Sam, can you tell Ray and Derek to take Ken off the rota?'

'Will do,' I said.

'I'll let DI Webb know,' Eamon said.

'Thanks.' Gary went to his office and I went to the control room.

'The boss asked me to tell you that Ken's been taken to the eye hospital and to take him off the rota,' I told them.

Ray marked the call sign sheet with a brief note of what had happened.

'Is the optical nerve damaged?' Derek asked.

'Possibly: his vision is impaired,' I replied.

Derek's lower chin wobbled as he shook his head. 'He could go blind. He'd have to leave the job, then.'

'You're a proper misery arse,' Ray said.

Blue Sky

Derek was right, though; if the damage turned out to be permanent, Ken would go. Gary, Steve and, eventually, Phil were going. Sergeant Bowman said he'd retire in the new year. These were the people I cared most about at Wyre Hall. Only Ray and I would be staying. Don't get me wrong, the other lads were okay, but I didn't work with them often, so I didn't have the same level of friendship with them.

I returned to the bridewell and met DS Mike Finlay there.

'Want to practice your interview skills?' he asked me. 'You can ask some questions and we'll jump in if we think of anything,'

I leapt at the chance. Mike, Eamon and I went into the interview room, where Boyle was being guarded by one of the bridewell officers.

'Hello, Mr Boyle,' I began.

'I'm not talking to that little bitch,' Boyle said to the men.'

We sat down and the bridewell officer left.

DS Finlay leant towards Boyle. He played on the force rugby team with Phil and had an imposing appearance. 'Constable Barrie has more balls that you will ever have. If she asks you a question, you'll fucking well answer it. Understood?'

Vincent Boyle immediately calmed down. It wasn't hard to spot the pattern. Small people, especially women, he tried to intimidate and probably succeeded most of the time; big people, and he behaved.

Mike cautioned him and turned to me to begin questioning.

'Okay, Vincent,' I said. 'What were you doing in Kensington Road?'

'Walking,' he replied.

'Just walking?' I asked.

'Just walking.'

'You walk there a lot. Why?'

'It's on the way to the park,' he replied.

'Why do we get calls saying you're staring at number ten?' I asked.

'I don't stare. I go past.'

'It's not on the route from the YMCA to the park, so why Kensington Road?' I asked.

'I didn't know we had prohibited areas around here,' Boyle said.

'Why Kensington Road?' Eamon's lovely voice had an edge to it that Boyle caught.

'It's a pleasant walk.'

'So you haven't been staring at number ten,' I asked.

'I'm sure I already said that.' Boyle folded his arms.

'Wind it in,' Mike warned.

Boyle gave an exaggerated sigh. 'No, I haven't been staring at houses.'

'Why did Mr Jackson come out to you?' I asked.

'I don't know. He raced out shouting and raised his fist. I thought he was going to thump me, so I thumped him. It was self-defence.'

'Okay,' said Mike. 'Let's move onto the assault on Constable Ashcroft.'

'That was self-defence too,' Boyle said.

I was outraged. 'No, it wasn't! I was there. You might have blinded him!'

'Then he should have kept his hands to himself, shouldn't he?' Boyle shouted back. 'After that lunatic at the house attacked me, I went to the allotments to think. Then that bastard came running at me, shouting that I was under arrest for assault. He grabbed me. and we got into a bit of a struggle. Then you showed up.'

'And saw you battering him! And you kicked me!' I was too angry to think logically anymore, which Eamon noticed.

'Sam, m'darlin', we'll take over here. Go and get the kettle on and have one yourself.'

'Milk, two sugars,' Boyle called after me.

'I wasn't including you, gobshite,' Eamon snapped.

I shut the door and went to make tea in the alcove behind the charge office. I'd blown the chance Mike had given me. I'd allowed myself to get angry because my friend had been injured. So unprofessional.

*

I gave the bridewell sergeant a mug of tea, because it was important to stay on his right side. I was just adding milk to my tea when Eamon and Mike came out of the interview room. I quickly made two more drinks.

'Ah, lovely.' Eamon said when I handed him the tea and took a large mouthful.

I handed Mike his mug. 'I'm sorry I got angry in there, Sarge. I know it's not professional,' I said.

'Don't worry,' Mike said. 'I was only letting you flex your muscles. You'll be properly trained in conducting interviews before you come into the CID.'

The bridewell officer brought out Boyle from the interview room and took him to his cell. He glowered at me as he walked past; I glowered back.

'We need to speak to Mr Jackson,' Eamon said.

'Can you deal with that please, Eamon? I have to be off soon, I'm meeting Jill.'

'No problem, Mike. I'll take Sam with me seeing as she has had dealings with the family.'

Mike waved an acknowledgement as he disappeared down the corridor, eager to meet his girlfriend.

Boyle was charged with Assault on a police officer for me and Section 20 GBH on Ken. Of course, he denied it. Also, he was charged with common assault on Mr Jackson. Leonard Jackson had refused help so we couldn't be sure if a higher charge would be appropriate. We could withdraw or amend the charges when we knew more about Ken's injuries and had spoken to Mr Jackson, but there was no doubt in my mind that Boyle had intended to hurt Ken and me.

I was pleased that he was refused police bail. He'd remain in our cells until he attended remand court in a day or two. Then it was up to the magistrates to set the date for his trial and decide on bail. I looked forward to his trial; Ken's doctor would have to supply evidence and you can't argue with a surgeon.

Chapter Four

Eamon and I went to Kensington Road and knocked at number ten. Mrs Jackson let us in and settled us in the dated front room before going to make us a cup of tea.

'It looks like my mammy's house,' Eamon whispered to me while she was gone. 'But I'm not allowed in the parlour there, except for special occasions.'

Mrs Jackson came in with a tray of tea, closely followed by Mr Jackson. We all shook hands and Mr Jackson settled himself into an armchair while Mrs Jackson busied herself with the tea.

'Mr Jackson, was the man who assaulted you the same man Mrs Jackson has been seeing in the road?' I asked.

'Yes, he was there again, and I called out to Leonard,' Mrs Jackson answered before Mr Jackson had a chance to speak.

'Could you tell us exactly what happened from the start?' Eamon asked.

Mrs Jackson sat on the edge of the sofa. 'Should I start?'

'You may as well, Muriel,' Mr Jackson said. 'I only saw him after you shouted.'

'All right then,' she said. 'I was dusting the window ledges and saw him outside again, staring. I shouted to Leonard and he swore and ran out; he never normally swears in front of me. I called after him not to go near the man, but he went out shouting for him to get lost. Then I saw the man punch him and Leonard fell over. I rushed out and my neighbour, Lisa, was on her path holding the baby saying that she had seen everything and was going to ring the police.'

Eamon turned to Mr Jackson. 'Would you tell us what

happened from your perspective, please.'

Mr Jackson drew a long breath. 'When Muriel shouted, I was upstairs. I came down at once and saw the man. I remember saying, "bloody bastard".' He smiled at Mrs Jackson. 'Sorry my dear. Then I went out to confront him for upsetting Muriel. He saw me coming towards him and raised a fist at me. I shouted at him to get lost and not come back but he didn't leave. I decided he needed stronger encouragement and went up to him to tell him to eff off, I didn't want to shout a word like that in the street. However, he punched me in the stomach before I could say anything.'

'Your neighbour rang the police, and we arrived a few minutes later?' I asked to confirm.

Mr Jackson nodded.

'Do you have any idea who he is?' I asked.

'Not a clue,' Mrs Jackson said.

'I need to take a statement from you both about what happened,' I said.

'I still don't want to make a complaint about the assault,' Mr Jackson said.

'Why not, Leonard?' Mrs Jackson cried. 'He should be arrested.'

'Actually, the offender has already been arrested. He assaulted Constable Barrie and another officer, who's in hospital,' Eamon said.

'That young man who came with you?' without waiting for me to reply, Muriel jabbed a finger towards her husband. 'See, he's a violent criminal. You have to complain about him hitting you.'

'I don't want the faff of going to court,' Mr Jackson said. 'One more charge won't make a difference.'

'You can't let him get away with it,' Mrs Jackson insisted.

Mr Jackson sighed. 'All right, if you think it best, my dear.'

I got a couple of statement sheets from my handbag and using the tea tray to rest on, I began to write.

Blue Sky

*

A couple of days later, when we came in for refs, we heard that Ken had had to have an operation on his eye. I didn't understand the details, just that pressure was building up, something had detached and needed reattaching and they wanted to deal with a clot that had developed.

'I tell you, that lad is on his way out of the job,' Derek intoned.

'Let's hope for the best,' I said and handed him the "Get Well Soon" card I had bought in for the block to sign, along with a jar to collect donations for a gift.

'I hope I get to meet Boyle in a dark alley.' Trevor took the card from Derek and scribbled a lewd message.

'Not the wisest thing you've ever said,' Ray advised.

Maybe not, but I agreed with Trevor's sentiment. However, we had to trust the system to bring Boyle to justice, even though we were all dismayed that the court had granted him bail on condition he stayed away from Kensington Road and the Jacksons. However, on the bright side, if he breached those conditions, we could arrest him again and it would be unlikely he would be granted bail again.

With that happy thought, I went upstairs to the refs room.

Steve was already in the refs room, looking pleased with himself.

'I've applied for the RAF,' he whispered.

'I don't want to pour on cold water, but you seem to be moving fast on this,' I said.

'It is what I want. I could wait but, as Ken pointed out, there is an age limit so I don't want to leave it too long. I'll continue to have lessons while I wait to hear,' Steve said.

'What about your current job?' I asked.

'The process will take a while so, when I'm given my starting date, I'll resign. No point in taking promotion exams or trying to specialise now; I'll just bumble along until I know the outcome of my application.'

So that was that. Steve was going to leave. I'd only have Ray left.

'Hey, want to come with me to visit Ken at the weekend?' Steve asked.

'Great. I'll drive us over.' I had never seen such an injury to an eye, so I would be reassured if I could see Ken in person. Also, it would be a good chance to take the block card to him, and a present I was yet to buy.

*

On Friday, I stared at Steve as he came towards my car dressed as a pirate, complete with a gold coloured, plastic hoop clipped to his ear. Under his arm he carried an inflatable parrot, the type of thing that could be found in one of the seaside souvenir shops at Lyseby. In his hand, he had a plastic bag.

He opened the back door, laid the plastic bird on the rear seat and climbed into the passenger side.

'You're a pirate?' I asked.

'Arrr,' Steve replied.

'You can't go into a hospital dressed as a pirate.'

'Why not?'

'You look silly,' I said.

'When have I ever cared about that?' he said. 'This is to cheer Ken up.'

I sighed. 'Okay then, if you're sure.' I started my car and drove to the General Hospital.

Steve collected a few strange looks as we made our way to the ward. If Steve caught anyone's eye, he shook the parrot at them and made pirate noises. Luckily, everyone laughed. They probably assumed he was entertainment for the children's ward.

'See, people like it,' he said.

We peered into the ward and spotted Ken sitting on his bed about halfway down the ward. He had a huge dressing across one eye but otherwise looked well.

Steve passed me the plastic carrier bag, threw back the door and strode in, I could only follow in his wake.

'Arrr, where be me old shipmate?'

Everyone, including the nurses, turned and gaped. I thought Ken's good eye was about to pop out as he stared at Pirate Steve.

'There he be.' Steve walked over to Ken's bed with a strange limp, which I think was his interpretation of walking with a wooden leg like Long John Silver. 'Why are ye still abed ye scurvy landlubber, ye should be swabbing the deck.'

Steve held out his hand to me and I passed him the bag. Steve brought out a pirate captain's hat. 'I bought ye hat wi' me, Cap'n.' Steve gently put the hat on Ken's head, taking care not to dislodge the eye dressing. 'An' ye'll be needin' a proper patch for that eye.' He got out a black, plastic eye patch, like his own and placed it on Ken's lap. 'And ye weapon. Arrr.' Steve passed a child's plastic cutlass to Ken.

Ken stared at the patch and the cutlass, then laughed long and hard. The spell was broken and everyone else laughed too.

'Be careful you don't burst a blood vessel in that eye,' I warned.

Ken brought his laughter under control. 'Oh my God, I needed that laugh.' He dissolved into giggles again making everyone around him, including me, laugh again.

Finally, Ken calmed down. Panting, he held his side. 'Don't make me laugh again, I think I've pulled a muscle.' He removed his hat, carefully put the plastic eyepatch over the dressing and replaced his hat. He pointed the cutlass at Steve. 'Behave Master Patton, or I'll have 'ee walk the plank.'

'Aye Aye, Cap'n,' Steve replied. He turned the inflatable parrot towards himself. 'What's that Polly? Ye want to stay with the cap'n?' He put the parrot on the bed. 'She wants to stay here with 'ee.'

Ken picked up the parrot and said, 'Pieces of eight, pieces of eight,' in a squawky parrot voice.

'I got you Roses.' I placed the box of chocolates on Ken's

beside. It was the largest box I could buy, but it seemed paltry after Steve's efforts. 'And this is from everyone on the block.' I handed over the card. I hadn't been able to decide on a suitable present so I'd got a gift voucher, which I'd put in the envelope. I reasoned that Ken and Gaynor could put it towards something for their wedding.

Slipping back into his normal persona, Steve said, 'How are you, mate?'

'A lot better now,' Ken replied. 'The doctor said that the operation went well so they're optimistic of a good outcome. I might be back at work by Christmas.'

'You need to make sure you don't come back too soon. Make sure your eye's right first,' I said.

'Aren't you missing me?' Ken asked.

'Who are you again?' I joked.

Ken chuckled.

'Did you hear that the scrote that attacked you has elected for trial?' Steve asked. 'Bloody cheek of him. And he's been given bail.'

'Conditional bail,' I clarified.

'Even so, it's bloody galling,' Steve said.

'I had heard,' Ken pointed at his eye. 'I think I hold the trump card.'

The lads started talking football so I sat back, enjoying listening to my two friends chatting normally. I felt much better and slightly less hostile towards Boyle.

*

Afterwards, I dropped Steve off at his home and went on to Gary's flat. He lived in The Crags, a modern block situated on the outskirts of Lyseby that had wonderful views out to sea. He'd given me a key and I spent most of my time there.

Gary had finally got the date and instructions for his interview, and sod's law meant that it fell on the first Monday of nights.

Blue Sky

Gary would have to travel down to London on the Sunday and travel back for nights on the Monday. However, that was almost a month away. This evening, I snoozed next to Gary on his big, comfy sofa while he watched a film.

'I've had a thought,' Gary said, jerking me awake.

I lifted my head. 'Oh?'

'Why don't you come to London with me? Let's go down on the Saturday and make a weekend of it. We can do the full tourist thing then travel back home after my interview on the Monday, and still have time to get some sleep before nights.'

'I love that idea,' I said, instantly fully awake. 'Can we ride in a black cab and go to the Tower of London, and see the Natural History Museum and Madame Tussauds, and go up the Post Office Tower and see the Houses of Parliament and Buckingham Palace?'

Gary laughed and put up his hand to stop me babbling. 'We'll only be there for a weekend.'

'I love you.' I kissed him. I felt a familiar tingle in my stomach. A normal person would have acted on it and led their beloved to the bedroom. Not me; that little gremlin in the back of my mind flashed me a picture of a reeking, stringy-haired man advancing on me in the back of a van, and I couldn't, I just couldn't. I shivered. I had to get over this block. Gary had been patient with me up to now, but how long could it last?

'Cold?' Gary asked.

'A bit,' I lied. Gary switched on the electric fire and I snuggled back in. One day, I would make love to my boyfriend like I wanted to. One day: just not this day.

Chapter Five

I called in on Karen Fitzroy on my rest day, when I knew she'd be awake ready for her night shift. Usually I saw her when I was on duty, but as we had become more friendly, I had taken to calling around off-duty from time to time. If anyone at work were to ask about our relationship, I'd say she was an informant. However, I liked her; I enjoyed her company.

She lived in a rundown area known as the "ship streets": each narrow road named after a type of sailing vessel. Police generally were not well liked around there, but very few people looked past the uniform to the person. It was unlikely that I would be recognised off-duty with my hair loose and wearing my new jeans.

From habit, I glanced around to see if any of Karen's neighbours were watching as I knocked on the door. I had a tin of biscuits under my arm. I ate so many biscuits in Karen's tiny living room, I felt I should repay her.

The door opened and Karen squealed when I handed her the biscuit tin, her default sound of delight.

'You do spoil me. I haven't had posh biscuits since… since the last box you bought me,' she said.

I wouldn't have called the biscuits posh, but they made her happy so that was good enough for me.

Karen disappeared into her miniscule kitchen to make a pot of tea. She brought in two mugs of tea and placed one on the slightly scuffed coffee table beside me.

'Is this the table you retrieved from a skip?' I asked.

'Yes. I gave it a good clean and it's come up okay, hasn't it?'

she replied.

'Not bad at all,' I agreed.

'I want to show you something.' Karen rummaged in the sewing box she kept beside her chair and brought out a bundle of material. She shook it out and an exquisite christening gown unrolled. 'What do you think?'

'It's gorgeous.' I ran my fingers along the smooth silk. 'You really do have a rare talent, Karen.'

Karen beamed. 'My friend's expecting a baby. This is my present to her.'

I sighed. 'Karen, I've said it before and I'm saying it again: why the hell do you go selling yourself on the ships when you can sew like that?'

Karen rolled her eyes. 'It's how I earn a living. My mum was on the game and I followed her before I left school. It's all I know.'

'Your friend got out of the game,' I said.

Karen sighed. 'You never give up, do you? She was lucky. She found a decent man with a good job on the buses. That won't happen for me. Even if I found a man who wasn't put off by what I do, who would want a wife who can't have kids?' For a moment, Karen looked wistful and stroked a hand down the beautiful gown. I felt sorry for her; she had been beaten almost to death as a teenager, an attack that took her spleen and her fertility.

Karen shook herself and packed the gown away. 'Anyway, it's not like I walk the streets like a common prostitute looking for johns. I cater for the officers these days.'

I refused to give her the validation she was seeking. 'You're still selling yourself.'

Karen scowled at me. Perhaps I should stop putting my own values on her life and just let her get on with things. I held my hands up in surrender. Karen smiled.

'Have you heard from Bernadette Pritchard at all?' she asked.

'I had a letter from her, as it happens.' I picked up my mug and took a sip. 'She's taking her O-levels in a few months. She's applied to a college in Manchester and she's going to train as a hairdresser.' I had been instrumental in removing Bernadette from her dreadful mother. She had settled with a caring foster family and was thriving.

'That's all Bernie ever wanted.' Karen drank from her mug. 'I'm a bit worried about her sister. Have you seen Ruthie recently?'

'Last month. She was brought in to the bridewell for the usual,' I said.

'Common Prostitute Loitering?' Karen asked. I nodded. 'She's not well,' Karen said. 'She's lost loads of weight and I've seen corpses with more colour in them than she has.'

'Is she still on heroin?' I asked

'Smacked up to the eyeballs,' Karen said. 'Ruthie's alone and not coping. I've heard the other girls talking about her becoming reckless. She goes off with anyone, no thought of danger; she'll even let them ride bareback.'

That wasn't good. Only the most inexperienced or desperate girls allowed customers to leave condoms off. Ruthie was far from inexperienced, so this alone was a testament to how far she had fallen under heroin's spell.

'And she's been begging by the shops, completely off her head,' Karen continued.

'Perhaps I can ask for a referral to drugs services or social services,' I said.

'She's an adult now, so social services probably won't be interested. The drugs services sound like a good idea though.'

'I'll do that, then.' I would also contact social services, maybe there was something they could do to help her.

'Changing the subject: have you told anyone you're dating your boss yet?' Karen tilted her head.

'We're still keeping it quiet.'

'Doesn't it get confusing having to call him "sir" at work? Do you ever slip and call him "darling" or something?'

'I haven't so far, but I have called him Big Bird; luckily when nobody was around.'

'Is that because he has a big pecker?'

'Karen!'

She threw her head back and gave her dirty Sid James laugh. 'So, have you done the deed yet?'

'Karen!' I could discuss anything with Karen, even stuff I wouldn't discuss with my mum, but there were limits.

Karen's eyes narrowed. 'You haven't, have you? Have you even seen each other naked? What are you waiting for? You're not a teenager, and it's the 1970s not the 1870s.'

I squirmed. 'Gary said he didn't mind waiting until I was ready. After what happened.'

Karen folded her arms. 'That doesn't mean he'll wait forever, Sam. I know you had a bad experience; you were kidnapped and another girl died, and you were only fifteen. It must have been awful and I know it's left you with some issues, namely sex, but you have to get over this block or you'll die a virgin.'

'Since when was sex compulsory? And anyway, we have seen each other naked, and we do sometimes share a bed and… touch.' I sounded defensive even to me.

'Touch?!' Karen shook her head. 'You're missing out. Sex with the right person is fantastic, and Gary is the right person for you. Don't forget, I understand what you went through better than most. I was almost killed by a customer; but I recovered, came to terms with infertility, and moved on, eventually. Sex is an important part of a relationship for most people, and you shouldn't be afraid.'

'I'm not afraid!' I paused. 'Okay, maybe a bit nervous. We get so far then I think of being in that van and I just can't…'

Karen smiled sympathetically. 'Then Gary must work a bit harder to keep you distracted from thoughts like that. I'll tell him next time I see him.'

'Don't you dare!' I cried. Then I remembered what Karen and I had originally been talking about. 'Karen, I'm sure the childrenswear factory would take you on. You could sign on the dole while you're waiting. Most of the other girls do, even though they're working the streets.'

Karen snorted. 'Sam, I have never signed on. I can make more in two nights on the ships than I could working a whole week in a factory.' She crunched on a biscuit for a moment. 'Tell you what, I'll do a deal with you. You don't nag me about my work choice, and I won't go on about your non-existent sex life.'

I shrugged. 'Okay, it's your choice.'

'Hallelujah!'

I took a swig of tea. 'Actually, I want to place an order with you, and I expect to pay you for it.'

Karen raised an eyebrow. 'Nagging hasn't worked so you're resorting to bribery?'

I laughed. 'No, this is a genuine order. I want a present for my mum.'

Karen thought for a moment. 'I have some silk left over from the christening gown so I could make a nice scarf. Maybe I could embroider it. Do you want to choose a design, or should I just use my imagination?'

'You choose, you have a much better imagination than me.'

'What's your mum's favourite flower?'

'Roses or freesia,' I replied.

She closed her eyes. 'Red roses at each end and green ivy running along the borders.'

I approved. 'That would be lovely against the white material.'

Karen beamed. 'I can have it ready for your next weekend off.'

'No rush, Karen. Actually, Gary and I are going down to London on our next weekend off. I'll collect it at some point the following week.'

'There's your chance to pop your cherry. Get some stockings and saucy undies and seduce him. You've got two nights, no distractions, no work, no rushing back home. You can take as long as you want. Perfect.' Karen sat back evidently satisfied by her plan.

I thought for a moment. Karen was right: it would be a good opportunity to face down my fears in a relaxed and comfortable environment. I just had to keep a lid on my anxiety.

'I'll think about it,' I said.

Karen jumped up. 'Don't think about it. Seduce him.' She slinked across the room in four steps. 'Walk towards him like that and he won't be able to resist.'

'I don't have lovely long legs like yours,' I complained.

'Doesn't matter. I'll let you see some of my books, if you like. I keep a decent selection for clients. I even have a couple of films that might give you some ideas.' Karen started to move as if going to get them. I had seen some of Karen's books and films as part of my work. They came from abroad and there were some things in there that I would definitely never ever try.

'That won't be necessary, thank you, Karen. The theory is sound, it's the practice that's lacking. I'd better get over the first obstacle before I start trying anything fancy.'

'You're probably right,' Karen agreed.

'Shall we start talking about when you'll start earning your living by sewing?' I asked.

'No, we shall not,' Karen said. 'I was only trying to give you some ideas to kick start your love life.' She nodded at my empty cup. 'Do you want another brew?'

'Yes, please,' I said.

Karen went back into her kitchen and I had a think. By the time she returned, I had decided I would follow Karen's advice when Gary and I went away, minus the books. He was so patient with me but even I knew this couldn't carry on indefinitely. I decided that, in London, we would make love properly, like normal couples did.

*

'Evening, Biggles,' I said to Steve on the first parade of nights.

'Did you have another lesson?'

'I've had two lessons. One on Saturday and one this morning.' Steve said. 'I'll have to wait until payday until I have another.' He sat down. 'Next long weekend, Desi is going on that trip to the Isle of Man. Do you still want to come?'

'I'm sorry, I can't. Gary and I will be in London.' I was pleased I hadn't had to fib to get out of the flight.

'A dirty weekend?' Steve winked.

'Behave. He's got an interview there, so we thought it was a good excuse for a little holiday and to see the sights,' I said.

'A dirty weekend then,' Steve grinned.

I grinned back. I had no intention of explaining how things were between Gary and me to Steve; it was easier to let him believe what he wanted.

Chapter Six

It was a grey, drizzly, Saturday afternoon when the train pulled in at Euston station. Christmas decorations were already popping up. We got a black cab to our hotel, which was close to the building where Gary's interview would be held. One tick on my to-do list. The hotel was a bit expensive, as it was located close to the river, but we didn't want to risk Gary being late on Monday morning, so it was worth it.

A large Christmas tree filled a corner of the foyer, and colourful baubles hung from the ceiling. Holly surrounded the reception desk, making it a little difficult to get too close.

'It's nice, isn't it,' I said.

'It's still November,' Gary muttered.

'Bah, humbug,' I whispered back.

Gary booked us in, and an ever-smiling receptionist pointed us towards the chrome-fronted lifts.

We got to our room, which was painted in hotel neutrals with orange and scarlet soft furnishings and curtains. No Christmas decorations here.

Gary looked around. 'I've slept in worse.'

'Don't let your enthusiasm overwhelm you.' I bounced on the bed, which, thankfully, didn't creak. I didn't want anything to get in the way of my plans. 'Why are you so grumpy?'

'I'm not grumpy. I'm tired from the journey and, to be honest, I'm nervous about Monday. Do you want to have a walk then we can get ready for dinner?'

'That's a good idea, if you feel up to it. We could just rest if you're tired.'

'A walk would get the blood flowing,' Gary said.

Five minutes later, we were strolling along the beside the river. I got quite excited when I recognised the Houses of Parliament and Westminster Bridge. Two more ticks on my to-do list. I got even more excited when we turned off, walked past St James' Park, and found Buckingham Palace. I made Gary take a photo of me next to a guard with the palace in the background. Another tick.

Eventually, he was able to drag me away and we started the walk back to the hotel. It hadn't seemed so far when we were walking out, but by the time we got back, my feet were killing me.

'I think I'll have a shower before dinner,' I said.

'Don't use all the hot water,' Gary replied. 'I know what you're like once you're in a shower.'

I folded my arms. 'I doubt a hotel of this calibre would allow such a thing to happen. It probably has more hot water than even I could use up.'

In the bathroom, I quickly showered and put on my new underwear and stockings. French knickers were surprisingly comfortable; I might have to make them a regular feature of my underwear drawer. Less so was the balconette bra that the saleswoman had assured me would enhance my already generous cleavage and drive my boyfriend wild. I felt as if my boobs had been pushed under my chin. I pulled my dress over my head and checked myself in the mirror. I wasn't accustomed to so much prominence in the chest area. Apart from that, Gary would never guess what I was wearing underneath my dress.

'You look nice,' Gary said when I came out of the bathroom. 'New dress?'

'A girl needs a new dress when her boyfriend takes her to London. I'm glad you like it.' I gave him a little twirl.

'Do you want to eat in the hotel, or should we find somewhere else?'

I didn't want to trail around London on my still-aching feet when there was a perfectly good restaurant and bar downstairs.

'Let's eat in; we can find somewhere else tomorrow,' I said.

Gary offered me his arm and we went downstairs.

The restaurant was all brass, glass and red coloured light fittings. Quite modern with a nod to the old pubs.

Gary chose a steak and chips with all the trimmings while I went for Dover sole with new potatoes and lemon cream sauce. It was delicious. We emptied a bottle of Nuit St Georges which I know, strictly speaking, didn't go with fish, but I enjoyed it.

'Let's get coffee in the bar then go up,' Gary said.

Coffee came with little chocolates on the side. Gary gave me his. He didn't have much of a sweet tooth, which was okay: mine was big enough for both of us. After that, I tried a couple of cocktails. A tequila sunrise, which I liked very much, and a white Russian, which tasted okay, but not as nice as the tequila sunrise. I felt nicely mellow when we went back upstairs.

Someone had been into the room while we were downstairs. The curtains had been drawn and the covers had been pulled back. A gold wrapped chocolate sat on each pillow. I pounced on mine.

Gary held out his chocolate and I scoffed that too.

Gary sat on the bed and unbuttoned his shirt. Taking my cue, I kicked off my shoes and went over to the chair by the window, pulled the dress off, threw it down and turned to face Gary. He was sitting on the side of the bed pulling off his socks. He threw them in the general direction of his bag to join the shirt that he'd already thrown.

I slinked towards the bed just as Karen had shown me, just not as good. I was so focused on Gary that I forgot to look out for my shoes, not that I could see the floor past my uplifted chest, which is how I trod on a shoe, tripped over and sprawled on the floor. I felt one stocking give way at the knee. Yet again, my knee would be hanging out of a hole in my hosiery. I was useless at seduction. Also, those stockings had been expensive, I would have thought that they would be stronger than that. I considered going back to the shop to complain.

Gary leapt up and helped me to my feet. He stayed looking at me for several seconds.

'That's a change from your normal look,' he said.

'Do you like it?' I asked trying to sound sexy but actually sounding like I had tonsillitis. Blame the fall.

'I do like it.' Gary pulled me to him. He kissed down my neck and across my pushed-up breasts which made me shiver.

'Gary,' I said.

'Mmm,' he replied from my cleavage.

'I'm ready.'

He looked up. 'You're ready?'

I nodded and bit my lip.

'No rush, Sam. We can go as slowly as you like and if you change your mind—'

I reached down and cupped him, cutting off his words.

'I said I'm ready.'

*

Karen had been right: sex with the right person was great. I was glad I had waited for Gary. I couldn't have wished for a gentler and more mind-blowing debut. After we got home, maybe I would take Karen up on her offer the loan of a couple of magazines: the milder ones and absolutely no bondage.

We passed Sunday with a spot of sightseeing and a lot of intimacy; it was with some regret that we had to pack up on Sunday night to give us time to eat breakfast, book out and get to Gary's interview the following morning. Then we had to get home and try to relax, until it was time to leave for the 11pm shift.

*

On Monday morning, while Gary was occupied with his

interview I sat in a nearby café minding the bags, reading the paper, drinking tea, and eating cake. The plan was that he'd meet me there, then we'd get a taxi back to Euston

What then? Maybe we'd decide to move in together. Then I remembered why we were in London. I straightened my back. I would not spoil things for Gary, he wanted this posting so we would just have to make a lot of memories for him to take with him and to keep me warm while he was away.

'What are you smiling at?' Gary asked as he took the seat opposite me. I hadn't seen him come in.

'I was thinking of yesterday, and about when we get home,' I answered.

Gary smiled too.

'What can I get you?' a waitress asked.

Gary looked at my half-full cup. 'Two teas please.'

The waitress left.

'How did it go?' I asked.

He shrugged. 'I didn't struggle with anything, so I think it was okay. I can't be certain until they contact me.' He leant forward, put his elbow on the table and rested his chin on his hand. 'So, what were you thinking about when we get home?'

I also leant forward. 'I think I need a few more lessons.'

*

At 10.45pm I went into the parade room to prepare for the start of my shift. I hoped it wouldn't be too onerous; I was feeling rather tired.

It had only been that morning that we had been in London, but it felt like weeks ago. We had caught the train home and, after stopping off at my home to collect my uniform and exchange a few words with Mum, we had gone back to Gary's flat, where we had spent hours honing my newfound skills. I had managed about an hour's sleep, but I really needed a good long rest.

By 10.55pm Steve still had not shown up, which was not

like him at all. Ken was still off sick, so I had an empty seat on each side. I felt quite alone for the first time since I had arrived at Wyre Hall. A preview of what was to come. I forced myself to think of London; I would not be forlorn after our weekend.

Alan and Shaun came into the parade room and began parade without Gary. Normally, parade was the one time during the shift we were all together. Afterwards, we went off to our own patches, and refs was divided into two sittings. Even at the end of the shift, often someone would be tied up with prisoners or an ongoing incident. Something must have come up when the afternoon inspector was handing over to him. Things felt different, too much change happening at once. I felt uncomfortable.

I jotted my duties down in my pocketbook and listened to the observations and extra attention requests that were being given out. No mention of Steve, or Gary.

Once parade was over, I collected my radio and spare battery, did my test call then nipped upstairs to see Gary before starting patrol.

'Hey, Big Bird,' I said. He waved me in. I noted the strained look on his face. 'What's wrong.'

'Nothing for you to worry about,' he said.

'Okay.' I was accustomed to him having things he couldn't discuss with me. It was probably connected to the fireman's strike. As well as our usual duties, we had to support the army's fire engines, nicknamed the "Green Goddesses", which were covering instead of the usual big red engines.

'Where's Steve?' I asked.

Gary groaned and put his head in his hands. 'He's got himself arrested in the Isle of Man.'

'What?!'

'He and Desmond Monaghan have been arrested for smuggling drugs into the Isle of Man.'

I slumped onto the visitor's chair in shock. 'I don't believe it! What'll happen to him?'

'Sam, it doesn't look good. The drugs squad over there had had a tip off and were waiting for them on Saturday. They kept them in custody, and they appeared in the Summary Court before the High Bailiff this morning. They've been remanded in custody pending trial.'

The Manx system was bit different from ours. I guessed the Summary Court was the equivalent of our Magistrates' Court. I wasn't sure of the equivalent of a High Bailiff: Stipendiary Judge perhaps. All that aside, the offences were considered so serious that Steve and Desi were not given bail.

'Steve wouldn't do that,' I said.

'Sam, you have to wonder: where's he getting the money for his flying lessons?'

'He's staying at home and not buying a car. Also, he's out of his probation now so he gets more money,' I said.

'He doesn't earn that much more than you. Could you afford them?' Gary said.

I thought for a moment. 'If I swapped my car for a moped or something cheap to run and didn't go out, then I might, and that's all Steve has been doing.'

'I hope you're right,' Gary said.

I couldn't—wouldn't—believe that Steve was bent. Not my mate, Steve. All the euphoria from our weekend away left me.

'Does anyone else know?' I asked.

'Not yet.' Gary rubbed his hand over his head. 'I don't want to believe that Steve would do this either. His judgement is sometimes lacking, but even he would understand the consequences for something like this.'

'The problem is, when he's found not guilty, some mud always sticks,' I said.

'*If* he's found not guilty,' Gary corrected me.

'No, *when*,' I insisted. 'There has to be something more to this.'

Gary frowned. 'Sam, I know that look. You must butt out; this is a Manx job. They only let us know as a courtesy, because our officers are involved.'

'How can I interfere with a job on an island in the middle of the Irish Sea?' I asked whilst pondering how I could gather evidence that would release Steve who was incarcerated on an island in the middle of the Irish Sea.

Gary shook his head. 'Just don't, Sam.'

Chapter Seven

I was glad the first night was quiet. The shock of Steve's arrest meant that I was no longer tired, but I couldn't concentrate. I hardly saw Gary all night; he was busy doing whatever it was an inspector had to do when one of his block had been arrested.

After work, I went home and slept fitfully in my own bed until two in the afternoon. I longed to be able to speak to Steve.

I decided that the first thing to do was to pay a visit to his mother. She would be going frantic with worry. I got up, showered, and went downstairs. I didn't bother with a cup of tea; Mrs Patton would force-feed me tea and biscuits.

'Back later, Mum,' I called. 'I'm going around to Steve's. I'm not sure I'll be back for tea, so don't worry about me. I'll sort myself out.' I didn't tell her about Steve's arrest.

*

Fifteen minutes later, I knocked on the door of Steve's house. Mrs Patton opened it. I was immediately struck by the tense lines around her red rimmed eyes.

'Oh, hello, Sam. I wasn't expecting anyone to call around. Have you heard?'

'Yes, that's why I'm here. I want you to know that I don't believe it for one second,' I told her.

She showed me into the sitting room and made us both a cup of tea.

'It's kind of you to pop in.' A single tear leaked from her eye and ran down her face. 'They say the drugs were in the plane;

how could they not know about that?'

'I can't figure out how it's happened, but I think I know Steve well enough to know he wouldn't have had anything to do with it. I wish I could think of a way to prove it.' I took a sip of tea and sighed.

Mrs Patton looked at me for a few seconds. 'I like you, Sam. When you went with Steve to Ken's engagement party, I had hoped…' her voice trailed off.

'I have a boyfriend, Mrs Patton.'

'Yes, Steve mentioned it. Maybe if things don't work out there…?'

I put my cup on the coffee table. 'Steve and I are good friends, but I don't think we'd be compatible that way.'

Mrs Patton looked disappointed, but didn't press the point.

'Tell you what, while I'm here, why don't we put our heads together and start to plot events leading up to the arrest. Maybe we'll spot something that would help,' I suggested.

Mrs Patton brightened. 'Well, I can't tell you very much about what happened after he left the house, but I can tell you he loves flying. I'll get a writing pad and some cake then we can list things.'

I got a pen from my bag and took the pad Mrs Patton offered. Mrs Patton went to the kitchen and returned with a Victoria sponge cut into generous slices. She was used to feeding hungry men and I wasn't complaining. She put a slice on a plate and handed it to me with a fork.

I took a couple of mouthfuls of heavenly sweetness and then picked up my pen. 'Right, tell me how Steve began flying lessons.'

Mrs Patton thought for a moment. 'I'm not sure how it started. Perhaps he saw an advert as he passed Hornthorpe Dell airfield. Anyway, he rang up and asked about them. They're not cheap so he had a chat with us about how he could afford them. He had been planning to get his own place, but we said he could remain at home for as long as he wanted. He went through his statements and worked out that he couldn't afford a car and lessons, so he's kept his motorbike.'

This tied in with what Steve had already told me, but I jotted it down anyway. It showed he had considered his finances and had made adjustments.

'What happened Saturday morning?' I asked.

Mrs Patton dabbed a tissue under her eye. 'Same as normal really. He packed a small bag with things for an overnight stay in case they couldn't fly back, and I made him some sandwiches. He put them in the bag and that was that. He left for the airfield.'

'What time was that?' I asked.

'He was meeting Desi there at ten, so it must have been about quarter past nine.'

'How long has he known Desi?' I asked.

'Not long. Desi offered him some tips and they seem to have become friendly.' Mrs Patton dabbed a handkerchief to her eyes. 'Do you think Desi had anything to do with it?'

That was a thought. I had only met Desi Monaghan once. He was from another division and his hobby of flying was unusual even some local undesirables had heard about his hobby and referred to him as "the flying pig". Maybe doing some digging around Desi would be a good move, and I should certainly go to the airfield.

'I suppose it is possible Desi knew about it, but I think the first thing is to is to visit the airfield and see what I can learn there.'

Mrs Patton smiled. 'I feel better already. Will you stay and have your tea with us?'

I stood up. 'Thanks Mrs Patton, but I'm meeting my boyfriend.'

'Oh well, another time then.'

'Certainly,' I said. I wasn't actually meeting Gary, but if I hurried, I might catch someone at the airfield. I knew I should let Gary know what I was doing, but then he'd be obliged to tell me not to interfere It was for a good cause so I decided it would be better to seek forgiveness than permission.

*

Hornthorpe Dell had once been RAF Hornthorpe, but it had since been sold off and most of the buildings had been demolished. The MOD housing remained, but that too had been sold off then remarketed as Hornthorpe Dell along with a few newly built additions. The airfield was used by private pilots and the flying club now. A heavy, wire fence separated the estate from the airfield. There were notices everywhere warning people to stay away from the airstrip. The last thing a pilot needed to worry about was a curious child wandering across his landing area.

Despite this, the estate was popular with families. The nearby school had a good reputation, the sturdy semi-detached houses were a decent size, and the estate was accessed along a quiet road. I knew nothing about any of the families there, which was exactly how I liked it. As far as I knew, the only time police had attended there was for a burglary a few months previously.

I pulled up in the car park. Large banners advertised flying lessons and plane storage. Three hangars lined the land along the runway. Probably there had been more when it belonged to the RAF. I walked to what looked like a clubhouse off the car park, but nobody was about to direct me. I walked towards the first hangar, which was open, where I could see two small aircraft parked up. I wasn't certain if "parked" was the correct phrase for aircraft; maybe they "moored" like ships. It didn't matter: there were two stationary aircraft in the hangar, and I was going to see them.

Nobody was around in the hangar either. I looked around for a moment to get a feel for the place. There was room for three small planes. There weren't many places to hide things—a few cabinets and lockers and an office off to the side—but when it came to drugs, a little was worth a lot. The drugs that led to Steve's arrest were on the plane, so that's where I decided to begin my investigation.

I went over and walked around the planes. According to the markings, one plane was a two-seater Cessna, the other a Piper. I remembered Steve had told me he was learning in a Piper, so that's where I started. There were several little hatches, I opened one and saw the mouth of a petrol tank. I peered into the cockpit, but I was too short to see much. I couldn't tell how much room there was behind the seats or underneath. It occurred to me that it would have been useful to try to find out how large the contraband had been.

I went over to the Cessna, which didn't seem too different from the Piper. In fact, if they hadn't had markings on them, I would not have been able to guess what they were. I tried to open a door to peep inside but a loud voice made me jump backwards.

'Oi, what are you doing? Get away from there!' A man, fortyish with short hair, strode towards me waving his arms. 'What are you doing there?'

'I'm sorry,' I stammered. 'I just wanted a look.'

The man looked around the hangar. 'Where's Johnny?'

'Who?' I asked.

'The man who's supposed to be here watching out for trespassers and thieves.'

I put my hands on my hips. 'I am not a thief, I told you I just wanted to see inside the plane. I haven't taken anything or damaged anything. I wouldn't do that.'

The man focused on me. 'Who are you and why are you here?'

I'd anticipated that question. 'I'm Samantha Barrie. I saw the adverts, so I came to make enquiries about flying lessons. There was nobody around so I came over here thinking I might find someone, but again, there was nobody here. Not very professional if you ask me. If everyone here is as unfriendly as you, I don't think I'll bother.' I made to walk off.

'Wait.' I turned back. The man exhaled. 'We have to be

careful here. These planes are worth a lot of money.'

'Right.' I resumed my retreat.

'I do lessons.'

I turned and stared at him for a moment. 'No, I don't think so.'

'Okay, I'm sorry. We do sometimes get dodgy characters hanging around here.'

Did I look dodgy? I would have to update my wardrobe so I looked merely a little suspicious.

'I wanted to ask, how much and how many hours to get a pilot licence?'

'Tell you what, that's my plane that you were looking at. I'll let you sit in it and we can talk about flying.' He pulled open the door and indicated inside.

I hesitated. 'What's your name?'

'Pete Flinders. I'm a qualified instructor and also the club secretary. Don't worry, I'm harmless most of the time.' He grinned.

Not Steve's instructor, which was a good thing. Pete had kind eyes and, now he was convinced I wasn't about to make off with his plane, a friendly and open manner. Sitting in the plane would give me a chance to have a good look around and check out the space. 'Okay then, Pete,' I said. I climbed inside and made myself as comfortable as was possible in the confined space.

I looked around, as far as I was able. There wasn't a lot of room in the back; enough for a couple of bags or suitcases perhaps, but that was sufficient to doss small packages and where drugs were concerned, a small package could be worth a lot. Not good news for Steve. I would have to concentrate on how the drugs got onto the plane and how to prove Steve had not been aware. I would try to question Pete about carrying cargo.

*

Half an hour later, I was on my way home, much better informed about learning to fly. I had been sitting in a Cessna 150L. I didn't have a clue what that meant but Pete seemed pleased with it. I had felt a little cramped and there were least three engines fewer than I would have liked. Flying was costly but not prohibitive. It was quite feasible that Steve could afford a couple of lessons a month if he economised. Most importantly, I had asked Pete about carrying luggage. Unsurprisingly, a Cessna was not meant to be a cargo plane, a person could take a little personal luggage only. Assuming the bag with the drugs had been placed on board before Steve had got to the airfield, Steve probably would have assumed that it was Desi's luggage. Desi, however, would have known if a strange bag was aboard; also it would have been impossible for the drugs to have been sneaked in while Desi was sitting in the pilot's seat.

The next question was: had Desi been a willing party to this or was he being forced into it, which could make a good argument for his defence. That would remain to be seen. I decided to have a chat with Gary.

Chapter Eight

There was uproar that night when Gary revealed Steve's predicament to the block. Some, like me, refused to believe Steve had been aware, but Frank Morton had said, 'Not another one.'

This easy acceptance that Steve could be bent had elicited angry responses from Phil and Trevor. Others joined in and all the voices had merged into one horrible racket as everyone shouted their opinions and defended or condemned Steve. I couldn't stand it. I clamped my hands over my ears. 'Stop it!' I yelled.

'You two are always together, how do we know you're not involved?' Frank shouted back.

'You're dragging me into this?!'

'Leave Sam alone,' Phil shouted.

'She's always nosing into things,' Frank replied. 'And don't think we don't know she talks to the cows on the docks.'

'Gathering information and intelligence and preventing crime! Isn't that what we're supposed to do? Would you prefer me to follow your lead and coast my way to retirement?' I shouted back.

Gradually, we became aware that the Inspector was banging on the table in an effort to restore order.

'Shut up, all of you, or I'll shove a fizzer up all your arses!'

It took another couple of minutes for calm to be restored; even then, the atmosphere was tense. Two camps had emerged: people on our side of the room largely supported Steve. The other side didn't. It was even worse than when Brian had been arrested;

we'd all been on the same side then. Everyone now looked at everyone else with suspicion. I was uneasy about Frank's attack on me; if he thought I might be inclined to criminal activity, others would as well. What would that mean for me?

After parade, people began their patrols with none of the usual banter and friendly jokes. I told Ray that I had to see the boss for a while, so he was to mark me as occupied until further notice.

The door, which was normally always open, was shut when I got to the Inspector's office. Whatever he was dealing with had to be confidential or serious, or both. I hovered for a moment, debating whether I should wait, when the door opened and DS Finlay came out.

'Oh, hi, Sam. Are you waiting to see the boss? I'm done, so he's all yours.'

'Come in, Sam,' Gary called from the office.

I went in and shut the door behind me.

Gary raised his eyebrows. 'Is this about parade?' he asked.

'Not directly,' I replied. 'I have a confession,' I sat on the chair in front of the desk. 'You know how you keep telling me to stop going off on my own missions?'

'Don't tell me you've gone *off piste* again.' Gary didn't sit at his desk, he paced around behind me.

'I was thinking about Steve's predicament, so I went to visit his mother this afternoon. She told me that on Saturday he didn't leave the house until quarter past nine because he was meeting Desi Monaghan at ten. This ties in with what Steve told me.'

'Steve talked to you about it?'

I wouldn't normally worry about that question, but after Frank's insinuation on parade, I was a bit sensitive.

'He invited me to go to the Isle of Man with him but we were going to London. I did tell you.' Gary nodded, so I continued. 'Desi would have got there earlier to do all the checks and logging the flight beforehand. I think this gives Desi time to load up the drugs and the more I think about it, the more I think he probably had help.'

Gary cocked his head. 'That doesn't sound too bad at the moment, but I have a feeling there's more.'

'I wanted to help Steve, so I went to the airfield to mooch around. I pretended I was enquiring about lessons, and a trainer—a Pete Flinders—let me sit in his plane. I had a good rummage around the available space. If the plane had been loaded before Steve arrived, it's quite likely that he didn't know anything about it. If he did see a bag, he probably assumed it was Desi's.'

'Bloody hell, Sam!' Gary exploded. 'You've been told so many times about rushing in, but you just don't listen. Don't make me have to extend your probation.'

'You can't do that!' I cried.

'Don't test me,' Gary warned. 'At work, I won't tolerate behaviour from you that I won't accept from anyone else on the block. I will put in the recommendation if it is going to be the only way you'll learn to keep yourself safe. Yet again, you've gone half-cocked into a situation without telling anyone and without the means to call for backup. What if you had uncovered something of note? You could have put yourself in danger and also we probably could not have used the evidence. WHEN ARE YOU GOING TO LEARN?' he shouted.

I jumped up. 'Don't you raise your voice at me! I know you're upset, but what happened on parade was not my fault. I haven't done anything terrible; I was trying to help my friend and now I've seen a plane like the plane Steve and Desi were in, I know what it can carry and how.'

'So what?! It isn't your show. It isn't even our force dealing; it's the Manx police who need to follow this up. This is their investigation, and we only carry out investigative tasks at their request.'

Gary had once described one particular incident as "The Sam Barrie Show", as in "This isn't…". That wasn't, and neither was this, but I had to try to help my friend.

'You should be taking action instead of sitting around waiting for instructions from some dot of land in the sea!' I said. 'Am I the only one trying to help Steve? What do you care; you're going to Hong Kong so none of this affects you anymore.' I paused. 'I'm sorry. That was uncalled for.'

Gary said nothing for several seconds. 'You said you didn't mind.'

'I don't. Not really.'

'Sam, if you didn't want me to go you should have said.'

'I don't want to stop you doing anything. I'll miss you.'

Gary reached out and I gave him my hand. 'I'll miss you too, but I'm just a phone call away and it won't be forever,' he said.

'I'm not sorry I went to the airfield, but I am sorry I made you feel bad about Hong Kong. You should go, I'm just being silly.'

'I have to be accepted yet,' Gary said.

'You will be.' I felt it deep in my heart.

'Sam, I'm sorry I shouted,' he said. 'I want you to promise me, no more snooping around by yourself. Not at this stage of your career anyway, and not while I'm still your inspector. I cannot be seen to treat you more favourably than the others. You have put me in an awkward position, but as you found nothing of evidential value, I won't inform the Manx police. If anyone says anything I'll just put it down to a young officer seeking information about a potential off-duty hobby.'

'If you think that's best,' I said.

Gary was having to fudge the truth because I'd rushed in again. I knew how that would grate on him. It dawned on me that I had learned my lesson: I had to let people know where I was going so Gary wouldn't be put in this position again.

'You might want to tidy yourself before you go back out; you resemble Rudolph.' Gary opened his door and I trailed out.

Mike Finlay was sitting at his desk in the CID office as I walked past on my way to the ladies' toilet.

'Did I hear the boss shouting?' he asked. I turned to him and he pursed his lips. 'Oh dear. I hope it's all sorted now.'

I nodded and hurried on to the ladies. My reflection in the mirror confirmed that my cheeks and nose glowed deep red. Rudolph would be jealous. I was beginning to see another reason why relationships such as ours were frowned on. It wasn't just concern for the junior officer; Gary would sometimes have to pull rank at work, and I would have to accept it.

I touched up my make up and went to resume patrol.

I heard voices coming from Gary's office as I passed.

'…she's crying in the toilet,' Mike said.

'Okay, Mike, leave it with me,' Gary said.

Mike came out of Gary's office and I pretended I hadn't been standing there eavesdropping.

'Hi, Sam,' Mike said as he walked past. Not a word about talking to Gary.

'Hi, Sarge.' I replied.

Gary put his head out of the office and gestured for me to go in. I went in and sat down again.

'Are you all right?' Gary asked.

I nodded. 'In the spirit of openness, I know it's not our job, but I'm going to the collator's office to check if there's anything on that airfield, or the name Peter Flinders,' I said.

Gary rolled his eyes. 'If you must, but if you find anything, you have to pass it on.'

I nodded. 'I'll go now, before I go out if that's okay.'

'Okay. Dismissed.'

*

In Irene's office, I looked around the rows of little drawers packed full of cards, pondering where to start. There was so much information on those little cards, I was sure I'd find something significant. I decided to do a general search on the airfield itself. I went to the relevant drawer and flicked through until I found a card. Actually, it was several cards sellotaped together that opened out in a long concertina. I pulled out Irene's chair and sat down to read through all the information.

Some of the information went back to the 1950s. A couple of airmen got into trouble for fighting in the town and were handed over to the military police. I didn't recognise either of the names. Then as the RAF moved out, the tone changed, and local kids were often found damaging buildings

In more recent times, there was concern that a known burglar was working as a groundsman. He had been questioned about the burglary at the old MOD housing, but nothing could be proved. He moved on and there hadn't been a problem since.

So that was that. There was nothing of great interest. I moved on to search for the only name I had—Peter Flinders—without success. It was time to go out and start my patrol.

I went into the control room, mainly to let them know I was going out, but I also thought I could pick their brains.

'Ray, can you tell me anything about Hornthorpe Dell airfield?' I asked.

'I can't think of much happening there apart from burglary a few months ago,' Ray said.

'A parachutist was killed there, just after the war, when it was still RAF Hornthorpe,' Derek said.

'That's right,' Ray said. 'His parachute didn't open.'

I shuddered at the thought. 'What a horrible way to go. He must have known he was doomed all the way down.'

'There was an investigation, but it was recorded as misadventure,' Ray said.

'Horrible. Anyway, I'm off out. Anything I should know?' I asked.

'Nothing of note,' Ray said.

'I'll see you later, then.' I left the building to start patrol.

Chapter Nine

I headed for Karen's house, hoping I'd catch her before she left for her night's work. I wanted to collect Mum's scarf. I spotted one of her neighbours smoking a cigarette on his doorstep as I arrived. Even the poor street lighting couldn't hide the stains on his ratty vest. He didn't acknowledge me, nor I him.

I knocked on the door and waited for her to answer. All the time I was aware the neighbour was watching me.

When she answered I immediately said, 'You called to report an incident, Miss Fitzroy.'

Karen glanced across the road to where the neighbour was lighting another cigarette. 'Yes, that's right. Come in.'

I went inside and she shut the door behind me.

'I hope your neighbour won't give you any trouble because I've called here,' I said.

'Don't worry,' she said. 'I'll just say I had a frisky client if he says anything.'

'Good idea; you need to have a reasonable story. Nobody around here would tolerate you being friends with a copper.'

She went to her sewing box and brought out the scarf. It was exquisite. Ivy curled around perfectly embroidered roses and snaked up the edges of the scarf. Each rose petal was picked out in a slightly different shade of red making it look so realistic, I felt I could pluck them from the material.

'It's so beautiful,' I exclaimed.

Karen preened. 'I'm so glad you like it.'

'Mum's going to love it.'

Karen wrapped it in a paper bag and gave it to me. 'I don't

want you to get ink or something on it.'

I put it in my bag and paid her. 'That seems so little for work this good; people would be clamouring for this stuff.'

'You're not going to nag me again, are you?' Karen asked.

'No,' I sighed. 'But you know I'm right.'

'Maybe one day,' Karen said.

'Hello, is that a small breakthrough?' I asked.

Karen laughed and went into the kitchen where a kettle was whistling. She came back with two mugs of tea and passed one to me before settling in her armchair.

'How was London?' she asked.

I grinned. 'Wonderful.'

'About time!' Karen cried. 'Details?'

'You know what sex is, Karen. You don't need me to describe it to you.'

She laughed. 'I meant the Great Seduction.'

My turn to laugh. 'I wore stockings and a push-up bra with French knickers.' Karen nodded in approval. 'However, I was a bit tipsy. I fell over my shoes and put a hole in my stockings, but he got the message.'

Karen laughed again. 'So, how about those books?'

I thought for a moment. 'Okay, just a peek, but no bondage or S&M.' I might have made a major breakthrough, but some things would never feature in my life. Too many bad memories.

Karen went to a box under her stairs and brought out a *Razzle* and a *Fiesta* and plonked them on my knee.

'Pretty tame stuff, but you might get some ideas if you read the story,' she said.

I read the story, and a load of tripe it was too, but it did give me a couple of ideas for when I was next alone with Gary.

After about twenty minutes, I left. The neighbour was still on his doorstep.

'Any further problems ring the station.' I said loudly enough for him to hear.

Karen cottoned on. 'Thanks for coming.' She shut the door

and I walked away as if resuming patrol.

I meandered towards the park, intending to walk through to check nobody was making a nuisance of themselves; then from there I could check out Kensington Road in case Boyle was hanging around.

It's never completely dark in a park in a well-lit town. Some light always bleeds through the trees. Once my eyes adjusted, I could see a fair bit but I was still glad there were lampposts dotted around the footpaths. The trick was not to look directly at the light; it ruined your night vision and plunged you into total darkness until your eyes readjusted.

I was somewhat surprised to see Leonard Jackson from Kensington Road out with his dog. He was standing close to the duckpond staring towards a thicket. I remembered that he was diabetic and his wife insisted that he stuck to a routine. I wondered why I hadn't seen him out so late before.

'Hello, Mr Jackson, how are you feeling?' I asked.

He jumped. 'Oh, hello. Err, Constable Barrie, isn't it? I'm fine thank you. You're on the night shift?'

'Yes.' I nodded towards the trees. 'Have you been looking for something?'

He chuckled. It sounded strained to me. 'I was walking the dog before bed and I thought I heard a cat in distress. I thought it might be stuck in a tree but was a squirrel.' He rolled his eyes at his own foolishness. 'Did you hear it too?'

I smiled. 'No. Oh well, let's hope Mrs Jackson doesn't mind sewing.'

He looked down at the hole pulled into his jumper; a twig was still attached to it. 'She'll probably scold me.'

I heard a noise from the thicket and caught a movement between the leaves. 'Is someone else in there?' I asked. I took a step towards it.

'No. That's the noise I heard, but it was a squirrel. There's loads of them here.'

The glance I had caught seemed bigger than a squirrel, but I nodded. 'Good evening then, Mr Jackson.'

'Good evening, Constable.'

He dragged his dog towards Kensington Road, and I walked on. After half a minute, I dodged behind a bush and looked back towards the thicket. Nothing seemed amiss so perhaps it had been my imagination.

I turned back towards the gate and in the distance, walking swiftly towards the small gate near Windsor Close, I saw a figure with long hair. From the shape I was sure it was a man. It was a bit hard to tell in the meagre light but I thought he looked like Boyle. If it was, and he'd been talking to Mr Jackson, he'd be breaching his bail conditions and I would have legitimate grounds to arrest him. He'd be sure to have bail refused this time. I hurried after him but by the time I reached the gate, he was gone from sight.

I walked to Kensington Road and despite it being after midnight the lights were still on, so I knocked at number ten. Mr Jackson would only have been in a short time.

'Hello, Mr Jackson, I saw your light on,' I said when he opened the door. 'After we talked I saw the man who assaulted you in the park. I just wanted to make sure he hadn't been bothering you.'

'Goodness me! I didn't see him but thank you so much for checking.'

Mrs Jackson came to the door dressed for bed. 'Leonard, what's happening?'

Mr Jackson turned to her. 'That dreadful man has been seen in the park. The officer saw our light on and was checking that he hadn't been making a nuisance of himself.'

Mrs Jackson smiled at me. 'That's so kind. Leonard, you must stay away from the park until all this is over. Sandy can do his business in the garden.' It wasn't a request.

'I'll leave you to it,' I said. As I walked away, I decided to leave a message for Irene. I wasn't sure quite what was going on, but something was off, and I wanted it logged in the system until I could figure it out. Meantime, I would find somewhere quiet to make up my pocketbook. Back to the park would be a good call, I could sit at one of the picnic tables near the playground. There was a streetlight nearby so it was lit well enough for me to see what I was writing and far away from the area preferred by drunks. I didn't want to bother with a D&D, or D&I at present.

The homeless also gathered in the park. They slept in little groups between the trees, for safety I assumed. I could hear them whispering as I walked past. I never encountered any problem with them, so I never disturbed them in what was effectively their home.

'Hey, lady.'

I stopped and looked around for the source of the voice. A man stepped out of a clearing where a few homeless people were gathered. I had met him before. Little Billy was educated but chose this lifestyle and had fiercely resisted my attempts to direct him to the social services or even the night hostel in the town. He made no attempt to look after himself, so I kept my distance in case his fleas decided to look for new accommodation.

'Tell her, Billy,' said a woman I couldn't see.

'That man you spoke to earlier, he was speaking to someone else. I heard the other man say he was going to go to the police,' Billy said.

'Was the man I was talking to threatening him in some way?' I asked.

'No. I think he owes the other man some money but can't pay so the other man is going to go to the police. I thought it was odd that he told you he was chasing squirrels.'

Interesting. 'Can you describe the other man?' I asked.

'You saw him. I thought you were going to catch him,' Billy said.

I hadn't even known I was being watched. 'Why did you think I was trying to catch him?'

Billy shrugged and grinned. He knew much more than he was letting on.

'Do you know who the other man is?' I asked.

'No. I've seen him around a bit, but I don't know him.'

'He's a southerner,' the female said from the trees.

I was now even more convinced that the man I had seen was Boyle. I resolved to speak to Mr Jackson about owing money; it might explain why Boyle had started to hang around Kensington Road.

'Billy, would you be willing to make a statement about what you just told me?' I knew the answer, but I had to ask.

'Lady, I didn't tell you owt.' His eyes twinkled and I knew that it was pointless to pursue the matter any further, without a statement from Billy, I would never prove that Boyle had breached his bail. However, a note in Irene's basket would make sure that information got onto the system. I might just add it to my notebook too, when I got around to making it up.

I walked back to Kensington Road, but number ten was in darkness. I would try again tomorrow night.

Chapter Ten

I wasn't able to catch Mr Jackson on nights and as far as I knew, nobody from the CID visited him. Back on lates, I had been busy during the first half of the shift, and now I was covering the control room while Derek had his refs. I would call on Mr Jackson after Derek had come back. I was also covering the front desk. It wasn't a problem, it was tranquil. The rush-hour had passed, and the fighting and domestic disputes wouldn't start until the pubs closed. Sitting in what was normally Derek's chair by the phones, I had the best view through the glass partition to the enquiry office so I would see any visitors.

'Make the tea, love. The kettle's not long boiled,' Ray said.

The kettle had never gone cold as far as I knew. I went into the cupboard-sized room behind the control room, selected the least stained of the mugs, and made tea for us and Alan and Gary.

Ray and I were sitting in companionable silence, drinking our tea and enjoying the peace when the front door crashed open. Vincent Boyle strode into the enquiry office carrying a large, buff envelope.

'Oh no, It's Boyle,' I said.

'Want me to deal with him?' Ray offered.

'No, I'll go,' I said. I fixed a smile and went into the front office. 'Hello, Mr Boyle, how can I help you?'

'You!' He eyed me for a moment and said, 'Is there someone else?'

'I'm afraid not for now. You're welcome to wait for someone else to become available, but that might be some time.' I pointed to the hard, plastic seats that lined one wall in the foyer.

Vincent Boyle peered past me into the control room. 'What about him?'

'He's the radio operator; he can't leave the radio unattended.'

'You can do it while he speaks to me,' Boyle said.

'I'm sorry, but I'm still in my two-year probationary period so he wouldn't be allowed to leave me unsupervised in the control room,' I half-lied. Actually, I couldn't be left for a full shift, but that wouldn't have been good practice for anyone. Leaving me for a few minutes would have been okay; however, after my last dealings with Boyle, I wasn't going to make things easy for him.

Boyle exhaled heavily. 'I suppose you'll have to do then.' He slapped the envelope onto the counter. 'I want to report a murder and here is the proof.'

I almost wished that I had asked Ray to take over for me. I would have to get a detective down from CID to speak to him in more detail.

'Do you want to tell me briefly what happened?'

Boyle looked around the empty foyer then said, 'Leonard Jackson killed my father in 1945. I have pictures as proof. He emptied the envelope onto the desk. I picked up an old newspaper cutting about a tragic accident where a parachutist had fallen to his death on a training exercise. I looked at old black and white photographs of parachutists leaving a plane, and of an airfield. I recognised the hangars; they hadn't changed much. This had to be the incident Derek had talked about. On the back of each photo was a department and date stamp.

'Are these Hornthorpe Dell?' I asked.

'RAF Hornthorpe in those days,' Boyle replied.

I shuffled through the photographs. 'Which photos do you say provide the proof of murder?'

He handed me a photo of a man about to leap from a plane. 'That's my father. James Summerskill, about to take his last jump.'

I examined the photo. Everything looked normal to me; he

even had a parachute on his back.

Boyle handed me a rather nice photograph of open parachutes taken from above. 'If you look to the right of that parachute,' he tapped the photo. 'You can see my father's parachute hadn't opened properly. His reserve parachute failed too.'

I peered at the photo and could make out a white smudge next to the perfect circle of an opened parachute. At first glance, it could have been a cloud, but a man was facing his last seconds under it. Suddenly, the photo didn't look so nice anymore, but I still couldn't see evidence of murder.

'Mr Boyle, so far, this just shows that your father died in a horrible accident, exactly as the newspaper reported.' I tapped the newspaper clipping.

Vincent Boyle threw down another photo in triumph. 'There: that building is the stores. Can you see Leonard Jackson? Why was he there, eh? He wasn't a storekeeper, he wasn't aircrew, and he wasn't a parachutist. Also, I have been told that he previously attacked my father.'

I looked closely at the indistinct figure in the picture, standing outside a building, apparently smoking. It could have been a young Leonard Jackson, but it could equally have been the recently deceased Elvis Presley in full Las Vegas stage attire.

'I'm sorry, but this could be anyone. Being seen by a building is circumstantial evidence at best.' I picked up another photo. It showed the same building from a different angle. A WAAF was holding a door open apparently going inside. She was looking over her shoulder as if the photographer had called to her. There was no sign of the figure alleged to be Mr Jackson in that photo.

'I also have this.' Boyle shuffled through the papers and pushed a document towards me. 'I got hold of archive material. Proof that Leonard Jackson spent a night in the brig and was fined a week's wages for assaulting my father.' Boyle sighed. 'My father was a womaniser. They got into a fight over Jackson's sister. She alleged that he was the father of her baby. That sort of thing was important in those days.'

They were still quite important, but I remained silent. It could provide a motive for murder, but so far we had no proof worthy of the word.

'So far, I think the evidence is purely circumstantial,' I eventually said. 'It's certainly nothing that we could take to court. However, I will ask a detective to come and speak with you and decide how to take this forward. Please take a seat.' I pointed to the chairs.

Mr Boyle gathered his photos and documents and sat down.

I paused before I returned to the control room. 'Mr Boyle, does Mr Jackson owe you money?'

Boyle frowned. 'I haven't loaned him anything. This is irrelevant. I'm trying to report my father's murder.' Boyle's voice rose in righteous indignation.

'It was just a thought.' I smiled. 'Never mind, I'll go and make that phone call.'

'Something interesting?' Ray asked.

'He wants to report a thirty-year-old murder, but the photos he showed me prove nothing much in my opinion. I'm going to ring CID to speak to him.'

Ray lit another cigarette. 'Makes a change from the normal stuff we get.'.

I picked up the phone and dialled the number for the CID office.

'Wyre Hall CID.'

I recognised Eamon Kildea's lovely Irish accent. 'Hello, Eamon, it's Sam.'

'Sam m'darlin', how can I help you?'

'There's a man in the front office wanting to report a historical murder. He's got pictures and documents but it's all circumstantial as far as I could see,'

'How historical?' Eamon asked. 'Do we need an archaeologist?'

I laughed. 'Just over thirty years.'

'Okay, m'darlin', I'll be right down.'

I returned to the front office. 'DC Kildea will be down to see you shortly,' I called to Mr Boyle. A phone rang so I returned to the control room and took a call about people parking their cars inconsiderately.

Eamon came down with DS Mike Finlay and came into the control room. 'All right, Ray, Sam,' Mike said.

'All right, Mike,' I replied. 'Mr Boyle is in the foyer.'

Eamon looked through the glass partition. 'That's the gobshite who almost blinded Ken.'

'The very same, but he's playing nicely today,' I said. 'Oh, by the way, it might be coincidence, but I met Mr Jackson in the park when I was on nights last week and I'm almost certain I saw Boyle making off. I put a note in for Irene.'

'I saw it. He'd be breaching his bail conditions if he were there with Mr Jackson,' Eamon said. 'It's a shame you're not totally certain.'

'I can't be certain enough to arrest him for it.' And Little Billy wasn't for making a statement. He'd just deny everything. I shrugged.

'We'll keep it in mind. He might let something slip,' Eamon said.

Mike and Eamon went into the foyer and I stood in behind the front desk in case I was needed, or as Ray said, being nosy.

'Just to clarify, Mr Boyle, your father's name was James Summerskill,' Eamon said.

'Yes, my mother gave me up when I was born and Boyle's my adopted family's name. I got in contact with my birth mother earlier this year and she told me James Summerskill was my father. I've since found out he was murdered.'

I returned to the control room and Vincent Boyle went with Mike and Eamon to the interview room.

'Do you think they'll be able to do anything with it being so old?' I asked Ray.

He drew on his cigarette and blew a stream of smoke down his nose. 'They'll have to investigate it, but I think they're on a hiding to nothing.' Ray stubbed his cigarette out in the battered ashtray beside him. 'It'll be a case of no cough, no job.'

Exactly what I thought. Without a confession from someone, this case was going nowhere, especially as there had been an enquiry at the time that had not found anything suspicious.

*

About half an hour later, Boyle stormed out of the interview room.

'Fucking morons,' he shouted.

Mike, who had followed him out, pointed a finger. 'Any more of that and I'll have you in the cells.'

'I know what this is; you're ignoring evidence because of your mate, who attacked me first,' Boyle shouted.

'Your evidence is not good enough. We'll have to speak to Mr Jackson before we make a decision on how to proceed with this.'

'He should be under lock and key. I bet if he'd complained, I'd already be in the brig.'

'Brig. He's ex-navy,' Ray whispered to me.

'Like I said, we'll speak to Mr Jackson then make a decision. Now I suggest you leave before my good mood evaporates.' Mike pointed to the door.

Muttering to himself, Boyle left. Mike and Eamon came into the control room.

'Seems like tit for tat,' Eamon said. 'He's hitting back because he was charged with assault on Jackson.'

'He does have a lot of photos,' I commented. 'Do you think he would have gone to so much trouble if he didn't believe what he was saying?'

Eamon cocked his head. 'I would believe him capable of anything if it fitted his agenda.'

'I suppose so. Hornthorpe Dell is featuring a lot recently with one thing and another but I didn't see anything unusual when I was there—' I tried to suck the words back, but Mike seized on them.

'When were you there?'

'A few days ago,' I admitted.

'Why would you expect to see anything unusual?' Mike asked.

'Steve and Desi flew to the Isle of Man from there,' I mumbled.

'So, why were you there?' Mike asked.

Remembering the cover story Gary had told me to use, I took a deep breath. 'I went to the airfield to make enquiries about flying lessons. I didn't see anything out of the ordinary.'

'What did you see?' Mike asked.

'I met someone called Pete Flinders. He let me sit in his plane while he explained what I needed to do to get a pilots' licence.'

'You've been inside the hangars at the airfield?' Eamon asked.

I nodded.

Eamon moved closer to me. 'Have you been off making your own enquiries again, m'darlin'?' He was using that deep, syrup-sweet voice he used when he was trying to charm people he was questioning. I normally enjoyed listening to it, but today it irritated me. I hadn't done anything criminal.

'I am entitled to a life outside the police, Eamon,' I snapped.

'Okay, okay,' Mike said. 'So, what was your impression of the place?'

'There's not many people around. Someone called Johnny was supposed to be looking after the hangar, but he wasn't there. Those planes are really small. I can't see how Desi wouldn't have been aware someone had put stuff on board,' I said.

'Interesting. Thanks, Sam,' Mike said.

I knew they'd guessed my true motive for going there but let them prove it; it was about time that knowing-versus-proving problem worked for me.

'Does the boss know you went there?' Eamon asked.

'Yes, he knows,' I answered. 'Haven't you got a murder to investigate?'

'An alleged, historical murder,' Eamon clarified.

Derek came back down. 'I heard that Ken is coming back on

the Monday of earlies. He'll be going part time, no nights.'

I relinquished the seat and moved into the enquiry office with Eamon.

'That's fantastic,' I said from the doorway. Everyone agreed with me.

Derek sat down. 'He'll be on light duties until the New Year.'

'That's to be expected until the hospital gives him the all-clear,' Ray said.

'You know what this job's like. One ruckus and he'll be blinded for life,' Derek said.

'Like Derek could remember anything about life outside these walls,' Eamon whispered.

'At least the enquiry office problem will be solved, temporarily at least,' I said.

'That's a point,' Ray said. 'We'll be able to stop taking foot patrols off the street if Ken's here. That'll be good with the water fairies on strike. I won't have to scratch around trying to find a patrol to find a hydrant for them.'

'We'll still be one man down. He won't be operational outside where we need him,' Derek complained.

Eamon rolled his eyes. 'Every silver-lining has a cloud.'

Mike thumped Eamon on the shoulder. 'Come on, let's get this started.' They went upstairs.

The good news for Mike and Eamon was that this incident had already been logged as a tragic accident long ago, so if no further evidence turned up, they could write it off as malicious or, if they were feeling kind, a plain mistake, and the original findings would stand.

I replaced the batteries in my radio and resumed patrol.

Chapter Eleven

As I walked past The Capstan, a pub near the docks with a tough reputation, a young man ran from one of the houses opposite. He spotted me, paused for a moment, half turned as if returning to the house, then turned back and hurried towards me.

'My friend is sick. I was going to the phone box to ring and ambulance,' he gasped.

I followed him into the house. It looked like a typical terraced house from the outside, but inside, it had been divided into bedsits with a communal kitchen downstairs and a bathroom upstairs.

A girl peeped out of the room to my right and jumped back when she saw me.

'I thought you were that man back again.'

'What man?' I asked.

She shook her head and closed the door.

'What man?' I asked.

'Dunno, there was no man here when I arrived.' He led me into one of the downstairs rooms. Heavily flowered wallpaper peeled off in parts, and damp patches stained the ceiling. It was cluttered but not dirty. I had been in worse places. A male, possibly still in his teens, lay on the bed. It was evident even from where I was standing that he was beyond help.

I went over and felt for his pulse. Nothing. His chest was still. A little vomit had dried on the pillow and a dot of dried blood on his arm told me he had injected something. There was nothing I could do.

Blue Sky

'I'm afraid he's gone,' I said to the man, who crouched on the floor and rested his back against the peeling wallpaper. 'Tell me what happened.'

'We arranged for me to come over, I arrived and got no reply. That girl you saw let me in. Funny, she thought I was that man too. Anyway, I came in and found him like this.'

I looked around before I called it in. A syringe lay on the floor beside the bed and drugs paraphernalia, including a small plastic bag of powder, sat atop the chest of drawers beside the bed. I had learnt not to make assumptions on what the powder might be. It would have to go for testing. I know in television programmes the police would dip a finger in to taste the drug, but this wasn't telly. I didn't want to finish up high or dead. I radioed the incident in and asked for supervision to attend and for a doctor to attend to confirm "life extinct". There was no doubt, but I wasn't medically trained and therefore my opinion on the lad's status of existence counted for nothing.

As I waited I got out the sudden death form and questioned the young man who had summoned me.

'Who is he?' I asked.

'Lee Hatton,' he replied.

'How old is he?'

'Eighteen.'

'Who are you?'

'Do I have to tell you?' he asked.

I waved the form I was holding. 'I need it for my report. It makes me wonder what's going on if you don't tell me,' I replied.

He chewed his lip then said. 'Dave Tully. I'm eighteen too.'

'So, Dave, do you want to tell me what the story is here?' I could see he was reluctant to talk. 'It will save a lot of time if you just tell me what led up to this.'

Dave rubbed his hand over his head. 'Lee phoned and told me he'd got hold of some junk. He said it was good stuff and said if I came around we could… Well, you know.'

I knew. Lee had got some heroin and invited Lee to share it.

'Where did he get it?' I asked.

Dave shrugged.

'Oh, come on, you must have some idea.'

'He used to score from Kev Lynch, but I heard he's done a runner. I don't know where Lee got this. Hey, maybe the man the girl next door is talking about is a dealer.'

'Possibly. I need to speak with her afterwards.'

Shaun Lloyd, our patrol sergeant arrived. I went to the front door and let him in.

'Lee Hatton, eighteen years,' I said. 'His friend here is Dave Tully. He found him. I've requested a doctor.'

Shaun nodded to Dave and went over to Lee. 'OD?'

'He has a puncture mark and there's a syringe on the floor and a bag of powder by the bed, so it looks like it.' I noticed that the bag was missing. I turned to Dave and held out my hand. 'Thank you.'

Dave handed back the bag of powder back. 'I was only minding it in case someone came in and took it while you were busy.'

I cocked an eyebrow at him.

Shaun said, 'We've had too many ODs for it to be a coincidence.'

'There are always ODs,' I said. 'It doesn't mean they are connected,'

'Not this many. It could be there's a tainted batch in town.'

'You mean that he was poisoned?' Dave had gone white. 'That could have been me.'

'When we send that powder for testing we should get some clue what's going on,' I said. I also wanted to go through his pockets; who knew what else he had lifted in the thirty seconds I had been at the door. I spotted the doctor arriving. Shaun could deal with him; I needed a quick statement before we sent him on his way.

*

Blue Sky

The doctor was happy to confirm life extinct and, unsurprisingly, was unable to provide a death certificate. Lee was going to have to go to the mortuary for a post-mortem.

It niggled at me that someone had supplied the drug to Lee. Would they have been aware there was a problem with the batch? Would they care if they did? I wanted to see whoever had sold that drug to Lee charged with causing death with their poison. Manslaughter maybe. I'd have to check through the charge book to see what fitted best in circumstances like this.

Meantime, I had to have a chat with next door before Lee was removed to the mortuary.

*

The girl next door wasn't very forthcoming on the subject of the man. I learnt that he had arrived a few hours previously and was older than Lee's usual visitors. He had short hair—unusual, especially in that area—but she couldn't tell me why he had visited.

I spotted the undertaker's van pulling up and excused myself. I needed to go to the mortuary and collect Lee's belongings but I had no idea who they would be sent on to. Shaun had been having a rummage around to find any information on family, but there was nothing. The belongings would have to sit in our property office until it could be claimed.

The undertaker and his assistant went into the flat and looked at Lee's body.

'He's not a big lad, is he?' the undertaker commented.

'Drugs,' I said. It seemed to be a feature with druggies that they were thin: stunted, almost.

The undertaker and his assistant quickly manoeuvred Lee into a body bag and carried him out to the van. I spotted the girl next door peeping out as they passed.

'If you think of anything else, call the station,' I said to her.

She nodded without speaking, her eyes never leaving Lee as he left the house for the last time.

*

Ken was in the front office when I arrived at Wyre Hall for the early shift. He was wearing a pair of glasses with a side piece that made them look more like goggles. His eye still had bruising around it but the eyeball looked a whole lot better, but still not quite right. I wondered if he had returned too soon, but he must have had the all-clear from the hospital.

'Great to see you back,' I said.

'Good to be back,' he said. 'Although earlies have come as a bit of a shock. I had forgotten there were two seven o'clocks in a day.'

'Not my favourite shift either.' I pointed to his eye. 'You might be on light duties, but you should still take it easy.'

'There's a counter between me and the customers, which should prevent most of them trying to have a pop at me.'

'I hope so,' I said. 'Any trouble, shout for Ray: he used to box in the Merchant Navy. He's got fists like piledrivers.'

'It's not the same without Steve here,' Ken said.

'I still don't believe he was part of it,' I said.

Alan came out of the sergeants' office, carrying the parade book. He stopped when he saw Ken and me.

'Sam, I hear you've been to Hornthorpe Dell.'

'Yes Sarge,' I said. Blooming heck, was it really anyone's business what I did off duty? Okay, I was snooping for evidence that would free Steve if not Desi, but it wasn't as if I had flown to the Isle of Man with a file in a cake.

'Can you go and see DS Finlay in the CID office after your refs, please. He needs to speak about something with you.'

'Alan,' Derek called from the control room. 'Is the boss in your office?'

'He's gone upstairs,' Alan called back.

'We've got another death.'

Ken and I glanced at each other and, being typical nosy bobbies, followed Alan to the control room.

Derek handed a job sheet to Alan. 'Man found dead. Mike Four's area. It seems to be an overdose. There's a syringe by him. Doctor has been informed.'

The latest death was nowhere near where I worked, so I took myself off to parade before Alan got cross.

*

After refs, I went to the CID office, which was unusually quiet. Only Eamon was there, and a stranger. A man in his late forties, silver-streaked hair, sat at one of the desks, eyeing me curiously. I stared back.

'Oh, great, you're here. DI Corlett, this is Samantha Barrie. Sam, this is DI Corlett,' Eamon said.

'Good day, sir,' I said.

'Good day, Samantha.' A northern-sounding accent but not local. There was something else in there: Irish maybe.

Mike Finlay came over from DI Webb's office. I wondered why Webby wasn't around. He normally liked meeting newcomers.

'Thanks for coming,' Mike said to me. 'Eamon, have you done the introductions?'

'Aye,' Eamon replied.

'Good, good. Would anyone like a cup of tea before we start?' Mike looked around but DI Corlett shook his head. I decided to follow his lead.

'No thank you, Sarge,' I said. The last time these two had buttered me up like this, I had been sent undercover before I had really been ready. Gary had been furious.

'How do you feel about taking a flying lesson?' DS Finlay asked.

I was taken aback. 'I can't afford flying lessons, I'm still a probationer,' I replied.

'You didn't say she was a probationer,' DI Corlett said to Mike.

'Yet you made enquiries about them at Hornthorpe Dell,' Eamon said.

'For when I finish my probation in February and my pay goes up a bit,' I retorted.

'The job would pay,' DS Finlay said,

'The Isle of Man police to be specific,' added DI Corlett.

Honestly, I would rather eat horse manure than take a flying lesson. However, if I was being prepared to gather evidence, that evidence might be disallowed if it became known I had I had been nosing around the airfield for any other reason than exploring an off-duty hobby.

'What does DI Webb say about this?' I asked.

'He's away for a few days, but he's aware and has authorised us to ask you. DI Corlett has come over from the Isle of Man to follow up enquiries into the incident where two of our officers have been detained,' DS Finlay said.

'I know Steve, he wouldn't have known anything about the drugs,' I said.

'Is he her boyfriend?' DI Corlett asked Mike. 'If he is, this won't work.'

I turned my full attention to DI Corlett. 'With respect, sir, it is possible for a woman to have a male friend without it being a romantic relationship. Steve is my good friend and a good police officer, and I do not—will not—believe he knew anything about the drugs on the plane.'

DI Corlett smiled a genuine smile. 'When someone says "with respect", it usually means the exact opposite. You seem angry, Constable Barrie.'

'I am angry on behalf of my friend, who has been dragged into something that will ruin his entire life.'

'Can you be sure he's so innocent? Can you trust his word?' DI Corlett asked.

'I would trust him with my life,' I declared. 'He'd never do such a thing.'

DI Corlett chuckled. 'Those of us with a few more years in, can tell you that there have been people in this job who were trusted and liked who turned out to be bent as a paper clip. I personally have had that happen to me. It leaves a bad taste.'

DS Finlay and Eamon nodded their agreement.

I sighed. DI Corlett had been sent here on a mission. He probably hadn't chosen to come over, and he seemed a decent enough bloke, and he was the one I had to convince of Steve's innocence.

'I apologise if I have spoken out of turn, but… it's Steve, he wouldn't…'

'No offence taken, Samantha.'

'Sam is fine, sir.'

DI Corlett turned to Mike. 'She's spirited, just as you said.'

They had been talking about me. Was being spirited a good thing, or was he saying I was obnoxious and gobby?

'Mike, why don't you explain things to Sam?' DI Corlett continued.

'Very well, sir,' Mike replied. 'DI Webb is in the Isle of Man; he's assisting them as DI Corlett is making enquiries here. He'll speak to both Steve and Desmond and hopefully we can look forward to the release of at least one of them.'

I smiled, feeling real hope for the first time since I had heard of Steve's arrest.

'It wasn't just Steve and Desi who were arrested; a couple of Manx ground crew were also involved,' Eamon said.

'We also got the gang that the drugs were going to,' DI Corlett said. 'From them we got the information that someone from Hornthorpe Dell airfield was involved. Nobody knows names, or so they said, so I came over to try to get as much information as possible. I can't just barge in and start asking questions without alerting those involved, and if any of the CID from here go in they'll be recognised and word will get out to the suppliers, so you might be my way in there.'

'But word has probably already got out from the arrests in the Isle of Man,' I said. 'A plane flies out, then doesn't return? You can't hide that, even those not involved in the drug smuggling will miss a plane.'

'She's quick,' DI Corlett commented to Mike and Eamon. He turned his attention back to me. 'Possibly, but we believe we have prevented that as far as we are able. Each part of this chain seems to be independent; nobody is told anything beyond their own link.'

'DI Corlett thinks it's a good idea, seeing as you've already been asking about lessons, that he goes to the airfield with you and pretends to be your dad. He wants to have a nose around and if he acts the affluent, doting father paying for his little girl's hobby, he'll have plenty of time to mooch while you're at your flying lesson,' Mike said. 'We're calling this Operation Blue Sky.'

I really, really didn't want a flying lesson.

'Blooming heck, Sam, I don't know why you're hesitating; most people would jump at this chance. It's not something that comes around every day. It will just look like you're following up your last visit. You'll be the distraction while DI Corlett does the snooping.'

I didn't have a choice. 'Sure.'

Mike clapped me on the shoulder. 'Good decision. You only get one lesson though, no asking for more.'

I seriously doubted that I would ever ask for another lesson, I didn't even like a big dipper at the fairground. I perched on the edge of a desk, feeling more relaxed in DI Corlett's presence now that I was an official part of an operation.

'As I said, each link in this chain seems to be independent,' DI Corlett said. 'Someone on this side gets the drugs from wherever they get them from. They then load them onto the plane with or without help from the airfield staff. That's them done; they have no further involvement until they are called again. The pilot travels to the target area. It isn't always the Isle of Man; it just happens that this is where they went this time. That's the pilot's job done. They might or might not be used again. The ground crew at our airport unloads while the pilot has a coffee or is otherwise occupied, then they pass them on to a gang for distribution on the island.'

'That's the part that's been shut down?' I asked, just to be sure.

'That's right,' DI Corlett said.

'Someone had to have tipped you off that the drugs were being taken to the Isle of Man,' I said.

'I expect so,' DI Corlett answered.

And that was that; he wasn't giving me any more information. 'I'm not going to have to try to infiltrate the gang, or smuggle anything, am I?'

DI Corlett laughed. 'No.'

'That sounds okay. Has anyone spoken to Inspector Tyrrell?' I asked. 'We're a bit short-staffed on B Block.'

'I had a chat with him earlier,' Mike said. 'He's fine about it.'

Nice of Gary to tell me. 'When do we start?' I asked.

'Tomorrow,' DI Corlett said. I'll ring the airfield and make sure this Pete Flinders is available.'

'Yes, sir,' I said.

'Bring civvies.'

'That's understood, sir.' I would treat myself to a fish and chip dinner on the way home to make up for the horror of flying.

Chapter Twelve

My stomach churned as DI Corlett, dressed in an expensive-looking camel-coloured overcoat with a maroon, paisley-patterned silk scarf around his neck, drove our rented Aston Martin to the car park. He parked up and flexed his leather clad fingers as he looked around.

'It's quite small,'

'They sold a lot of land off, but Derek, in the radio room, told me it was never a major base,' I said. In the distance, I saw someone on a ride on mower. 'Dammit.' I ducked down.

'What is it?' DI Corlett asked.

'The bloke on that mower. It's Vincent Boyle. I didn't know he works here. We've had dealings. He injured Ken Ashcroft and is going for trial. Also, Mike and Eamon are dealing with him over the alleged murder of his father, thirty years ago, right here when this airfield was RAF Hornthorpe.'

DI Corlett looked over to the mower. 'Has he seen you off duty, with your hair loose?' I shook my head. 'I think in that case he's far enough away not to recognise you, and he doesn't know me, so no problem. Just don't look over there while we're walking to the clubhouse or the hangar.'

We went into the clubhouse, where DI Corlett had arranged to meet Pete Flinders.

It was a large room with a bar at the end closest to the door and tables and chairs arranged around a raised platform at the far end. Framed photographs lined the walls and clustered behind the bar. A large, well-stocked Christmas tree filled one corner.

'Samantha, you're here,' Pete said. He advanced with his hand held out.

I shook hands. 'Pete, this is my dad.'

Pete held out his hand to DI Corlett, who shook it vigorously.

'I'm pleased to meet you, Pete. Samantha has been looking forward to her first lesson,' he said.

'Pleased to meet you, Mr Barrie. It's not often we get young girls interested in flying,'

'Samantha is a unique girl.'

'She's got your eyes,' Pete said.

That was going to come as a shock to Dad.

DI Corlett beamed. 'And her mother's beautiful face.'

That was true, but pass the sick bucket.

Pete shuffled his feet. 'Did Samantha mention the cost?'

'Yes, it's no problem,' DI Corlett declared. 'It gives me the chance to spoil my special girl for Christmas.' DI Corlett smiled at me, every inch the doting, wealthy father.

He followed Pete into an office while I remained in the bar. A second later, Pete popped his head out of the door.

'Barbara, the manageress, is due in anytime now. Would you tell her I'm busy for a few minutes, please?'

'Of course,' I replied. I wandered around, looking at the photographs of the airfield when it was RAF Hornthorpe. Behind the bar, I recognised one photograph. It was the one Boyle had shown me of James Summerskill about to take his last jump. I looked closely, but there was nothing on the photo that could offer any new evidence.

'He died a few minutes after that was taken,' said a woman from a doorway. Around fifty, bottle blonde, too-tight, pink, crimplene dress. This must be Barbara. I hadn't heard her come in. Careless. Fortunately, it didn't matter this time.

'Is he the one whose parachute didn't open?' I asked.

She came over to stare at the photo beside me. 'That's right. How did you hear about it?'

'Someone at work mentioned it when I told them I was coming for lessons here,' I replied.

'You're with the flying club?'

'This is my first lesson. Dad's in the office with Pete sorting out the fee. I think I'll see how this goes then think about it. By the way, if you're Barbara, Pete says he'll be a few minutes.'

Barbara nodded. 'Thanks. They're a decent bunch, the flying club. My bloke, Johnny, is an honorary member. He has to be: if they don't treat him right, I won't serve them.' She laughed and so did I.

'Isn't it a bit morbid having a picture of someone's last jump on display?' I asked.

Barbara quirked her mouth. 'Perhaps. But for those who were there, it's a sort of memorial. Those lads tend not to be sentimental; dark humour is more their thing, so this is just the ticket. I still see some of the old faces, they live local and like to pop in for a drink and to talk about the old days.'

DI Corlett and Pete came out of the office and saw us looking at the photo.

'Is Barbara telling you about our unfortunate parachutist?' Pete asked.

'He must have known he was going to die all the way down.' I shuddered.

'Is all the old RAF stuff here or has that been destroyed now?' DI Corlett asked.

Pete scratched his head. 'The RAF will have taken all the important stuff.' He turned to Barbara. 'You were a WAAF here. Do you know where they took all the old stuff?'

'There were some old files left behind when the RAF moved out about twenty years ago, but nothing important. I believe the council took those, but whether they archived them or incinerated them I couldn't tell you.' She gestured around the room. 'They left the photos, so when we found them, we made a display of them.'

'It looks great.' DI Corless looked around nodding his approval. 'I'm ex RAF. I like to relive the old days.'

'Why don't you go to the local RAFA club or the British

Legion? There's a few from RAF Hornthorpe days who drink there. They'd probably enjoy swapping a few stories,' Barbara said.

'I might just do that,' DI Corless said.

Pete turned to me. 'Are you ready, Samantha?'

My heart thudded, but I said, 'Oh yes, let's go.'

'If you need anything, ask Barbara, or Johnny,' Pete said to DI Corlett.

'Is he the one we just saw on the mower?' DI Corlett asked.

'No, that's Vince. He just looks after the grounds and cleans up the hangars. Johnny is a jack-of-all-trades. He's an ex-RAF mechanic and the nearest thing we have to security.'

'Righto.' DI Corlett said. 'Have a wonderful time, sweetheart.'

Bastard. He knew I was dreading this. 'Thank you, Daddy,' I called as I followed Pete out.

*

The lesson was every bit as awful as I had expected. We did a brief orientation session then went straight on to flying, with Pete piloting. Pete said I'd understand the theory better if I had time in the air. I'd be expected to take theory exams alongside practical lessons.

Scooting along the runway wasn't too bad, but I hated the way the ground dropped away, taking my stomach with it. I hated how the little plane moved. I hated feeling the bumps that Steve so loved, and I absolutely loathed the feeling that a metal door was all that stood between me and certain death. And I had to remain smiling and enthusiastic throughout the lesson, even when Pete told me to take the controls and complete some basic manoeuvres. They might have been basic to him, but they scared the living daylights out of me.

Eventually, Pete brought us down and we taxied to the hangar. I saw DI Corlett walking towards us. I was somewhat surprised that my legs didn't give way as I climbed down from the cockpit.

Thank goodness it was over.

'Did you have a good time, sweetheart?' DI Corlett asked me as he wrapped an arm around my shoulder.

'Wonderful! Can I do this again, Daddy, please?' I gushed, confident that there was no way the job was going to fund another lesson.

DI Corlett chuckled. 'I know we're getting close to Christmas, but do you have any free slots, Pete?'

'Let's go back to the clubhouse, Mr Barrie and I'll check the book.' Pete smiled at me. 'The second lesson is easier. Everything was new today and there seems so much to think about. Next time, you'll start to get a proper feel for it.'

'I can't wait,' I said. I hoped DI Corlett was just making things look realistic. 'I'll wait for you in the car, Daddy.'

I flumped into the comfy seat of the Aston Martin and slammed the door shut. I needed something to calm my jangled nerves. Chocolate would be good, lots of chocolate. I'd ask DI Corlett if he'd stop on the way back to the station. I could buy myself a family-sized bar and scoff it all myself. That would make me feel better; a bit sick but less jangled.

DI Corlett arrived back and eased himself behind the steering wheel. 'You have a lesson next week.'

'Yeah, but that's not going to happen, is it?'

DI Corlett raised one eyebrow.

'No! Please tell me the booking was just for show.'

'I need to go back,' DI Corlett said.

'Nooooo!' I wailed.

'Aren't you going to ask me what I did while you were flying?' DI Corlett asked.

'Did you find anything interesting, sir?' I asked without enthusiasm.

'I did, in fact. I met Johnny. His name is John Poulter, and he is indeed ex RAF; we spent a happy time chatting. I think we bored Barbara, she disappeared somewhere.'

'You really were in the RAF?' I asked.

'Don't look so surprised. Yes, I was at Collinstown, which is now Dublin airport, but I wasn't a pilot. It seems that Johnny is often left alone for long periods, which would give him the opportunity to load anything he wanted on to the plane. He's in demand as a mechanic, so nobody would question him tinkering with a plane.'

'You suspect that he's the link on this side?' I asked.

'It's possible. I need to do a bit more digging,' DI Corlett said. 'I would like to find out who is supplying the drugs to the airfield.'

'Which is why we have to come back?'

'Exactly. I was able to have a quick root through the office Pete uses, but there was nothing of interest there.'

'Could Pete be involved?' I asked.

'Uncertain,' DI Corlett said. 'However, I think if they had their own pilot, they wouldn't have to use people like Steve and Desmond. Let's keep an open mind on that.' He started the engine and pulled away.

'Can we stop at a shop on the way back, please?' I asked. I needed a lot of chocolate.

Chapter Thirteen

A couple of days later, I spotted DI Webb walking across the yard. I wanted to run over and quiz him about speaking to Steve and Desi, but I guessed that wouldn't be appreciated. However, I knew someone who would know what was happening. I hoped he would be able to tell me about it.

I nipped upstairs and looked into Gary's open office. 'Are you busy?'

'Yes, but I could do with a break,' he replied.

I went in and sat down. 'I saw Webby going across the yard.'

Gary's chair squeaked as he leant back. 'So you're here nosing. I'm going to speak to everyone at knocking-off time.'

'So, you do have news,' I bounced in my seat. 'Is it good? Are they coming home?'

'Wait until later,' Gary said. 'Haven't you got work to do?'

'Yes, sir.' I pouted.

'Then make me a cuppa, then get out and let me get on.'

Outside his office, I resisted the urge to call into the CID office, however I could go to speak to the collator. It had to be good news; Gary looked lighter than I'd seen him since our return from London.

I hurried downstairs and peeped into the collator's office. 'Hi, Irene.'

'Hi, Sam. Come on in.'

I shut the door carefully, not wanting to incur Irene's wrath by causing a breeze that could scatter the scraps of paper from her information basket: the place we put scribbled notes about any information or intelligence that we heard of so Irene could then transfer it to the system.

'If you're here to ask about the murder, I can't discuss anything,' Irene said.

I stared. 'What murder? The last death I heard of was another overdose on Mike Four's area.'

Irene gritted her teeth. 'Forget I said anything.'

'Is it that one?' I asked. 'Are the other overdoses suspicious too?'

'I can't say.'

'So they are the same MO as the one I went to by The Capstan?'

'You're a persistent little bugger. No, this one had the needle still in his arm.'

'Like the one found in the park when we were on rest day?' I asked.

'No, that was an accidental overdose.'

'The needle was at the wrong angle, like Kevin Lynch?' I asked.

'Stop trying to make me talk about stuff I can't talk about,' Irene said.

That told me all I needed to know. Someone else had injected the victim. 'You know I'm trustworthy; I never reveal confidential stuff.'

'You shouldn't know about it at all,' Irene replied. 'Now, as you evidently had no idea until I let it slip, what were you really coming to see me about?'

'I see DI Webb is back from the Isle of Man,' I said.

'Yes, and you want to know what I know about it,' Irene said.

'Busted! Are Steve and Desi coming home?'

'Gary will talk to you all later. Be patient.'

Yeah, I'd find out soon enough, but being patient was hard. Meantime, there was that cup of tea to make. Ray and Derek would be sure to want one too, and while I was about it, I might as well make one for myself.

*

At the end of the shift, as usual, we gathered outside the charge office for the inspector to address any issues that had come up over the shift and to sign off our pocketbooks, which was a great incentive to keep up to date with it. So much could happen so quickly, it would be easy to forget something that might be crucial in a later court case. This little measure ensured we logged things whilst they were still fresh in our memory, and was one of the reasons it was considered safe for us to use our books in court where necessary.

'Before you all shoot off, I have some news,' Gary said.

Everyone stopped chattering and turned to him.

'Steve has been released without charge,' Gary said.

I gave a cheer, along with a few others. 'Is he coming back to work?'

'Yes, after a little time to decompress,' Gary replied.

'We don't want another bent copper here,' Frank said.

I turned to face Frank. 'How can you say that? Steve's not like Lewington. He'll be coming back with a clean record.'

'So, the Isle of Man couldn't prove anything against him. Even with your short service, you should understand that knowing and proving are different—'

'I bet I've done more in my short service that you have in the last ten years, judging by your narrow mind,' I cut in.

Frank continued talking over my interruption. '—like I know that you and he are thick as thieves.'

'Explain what you mean by that!' I demanded. 'Are you suggesting that Steve and I are both bent?'

A collective gasp went around the crowd.

'Handbags at dawn,' said someone I couldn't see.

'Enough!' Gary shouted over the clamour. 'Frank, I'd like a word before you leave.'

We shut up, but shot each other filthy looks.

'I don't know full details,' Gary said. 'Desmond Monaghan

asked for a meeting with his legal representative. He told them that he knew he was transporting something on the plane. Steve had been completely unaware of everything.'

I wondered if DI Webb's visit had had anything to do with Desi's sudden desire to confess.

'Not Desi Monaghan. I worked with him in Tynvoller division. He's as straight as they come. Patton must have conned him somehow,' said Frank.

'That crook conned Steve, not the other way around,' I snarled. Several others murmured their agreement.

Gary coughed and continued. 'It's always hard when we find one of our own is bent, especially if they are a personal acquaintance. Desmond Monaghan remains in custody and Steve has been released with no stain on his character, and I for one will welcome him back to the block.'

Steve's supporters cheered, while Frank looked sick.

Steve was no longer facing charges, but Desmond Monaghan was another matter; however, that was not my problem. He'd admitted his guilt and justice would be done. He would serve his time and lose his job, and pension. Despite that, I found it hard to feel sorry for him. His actions would reflect badly on us all when the papers inevitably got hold of the story.

*

Next day, Pete and I left DI Corlett, aka "Daddy", in the bar at Hornthorpe Dell and walked over to the hangar for my lesson. In the distance, I saw Vincent Boyle raking up leaves or something. Although we weren't close, I turned my face away in case he looked in our direction.

As we approached the hangar, a man in oily overalls called out to Pete and hurried towards us.

'All right, Johnny, what's up?' Pete asked.

'I'm expecting a delivery of parts that needs a signature. I can sign for it if you're busy.'

'Okay, get Vince to help with shifting if you need it,' Pete said.

'Will do, Pete.'

'Oh, Sam's dad is in the clubhouse. Try not to bother him,' Pete said.

Johnny nodded. 'He came over for a chat the other day. Nice chap. Ex RAF. I'll go and speak to Vince now.'

Time for me to get out of there. I followed Pete to the plane and climbed in.

'You can taxi us out to the runway today. Can you remember how to get started?' Pete asked.

'I think so,' I answered.

Under Pete's guidance, I got us going and managed to leave the hangar. Just in time too: I saw Vince walking back with Johnny. Another couple of minutes and he would have been close enough to recognise me, even with my hair loose.

*

The second lesson was as horrible as the first lesson, except I now knew what was causing some of the movement of the plane. I still hated the take-off, although I was better once we were at our designated altitude and Pete handed over control to me.

'Do you want to take the plane down?' Pete asked after a while.

'You mean land it?!' I could barely keep the plane steady.

'You'll need a few more hours before you can land.' Pete laughed. 'Take us to five hundred feet then I'll take over.'

I was surprised to find that I was able to do that without too much guidance from Pete.

Pete took over and changed channel on the radio. 'Returning to base,' he said.

'Roger,' a male voice replied. 'All clear.' Was that Johnny? I was accustomed to listening to voices on radios and could pick out individual voices and accents that might not be so clear to a non-user.

Pete changed the channel back and began the landing procedure. I hadn't noticed him doing that last time. I had been so terrified I wouldn't have noticed had a pigeon done a fandango on the wing. I made a mental note of the second channel in case it was useful to Operation Blue Sky.

'Why did you change channel?' I asked, just as a good student should.

'I have the channel for air control.' Pete pointed to the radio. 'But we also have a receiver in Hornthorpe and when I'm ready to land, I find it useful to switch channels for a few seconds and radio ahead in case of problems.'

'What sort of problems?' I asked.

'Oh, things on the runway, ice, vehicles, people.'

I understood the reasoning. 'I would imagine ice will be a problem over the next couple of months.'

'It might be, but don't leave it too long between lessons,' Pete cautioned.

'I won't.' I hoped I sounded enthusiastic.

Pete did a running commentary of everything he was doing as we landed, pointing out what to look for on the instruments and how to keep the plane steady in the weak but persistent wind. It was quite interesting, but I was looking out for delivery vehicles. A dray was parked by the clubhouse and someone was rolling large metal barrels down a ramp ready for the thirsty customers, but nothing was parked by the hangar.

We touched down with barely a bump and I saw DI Corlett coming out of the hangar to greet us. Pete brought the plane to a stop and watched as I did the checks before leaving the cockpit.

When Pete was satisfied the plane wasn't going to roll away or the battery wouldn't be drained, we climbed out. DI Corlett came around and stood close to me. I glanced up at him, wondering what was going on, but he didn't move and smiled at Pete.

'How was it?' he asked.

'She's coming along fine. Just to let you know, Mr Barrie, that

I'm taking a break over Christmas. I won't be doing lessons again until the New Year,' said Pete.

'Do you want another lesson before Christmas or wait until New Year?' DI Corlett asked me.

This student pilot thing was supposed to have been a one-off, now it seemed that the job would fund another lesson if DI Corlett requested it. I didn't want another lesson.

I sighed. 'I have work to think about. Perhaps we'd better leave it until the New Year.'

'Nonsense!' boomed DI Corlett. 'They work you too hard. There's nothing wrong in taking time out for yourself, darling.'

'Thank you, Daddy, but work is important. I would prefer to wait until New Year,' I said.

'You can't complain at her work ethic. Let's go to and get next year's diary out.' Pete led the way, but DI Corlett stopped me.

'You wait in the car and I'll sort this out.'

I hesitated for a second, wondering what he was trying to tell me. 'All right, Daddy.' I would ask later why he wanted to keep me away from the hangar.

In the car, I looked morosely out of the window as I waited for DI Corlett. Movement by the hangar caught my eye. Johnny appeared to be arguing with Boyle over something. Their agitated arm waving told me that this was not a friendly discussion. As I watched, Boyle started to walk away, pausing to jab his finger in Johnny's direction. Johnny responded by raising two fingers to Boyle.

DI Corlett opened the door and sat in the driver's seat. 'Sorry to chase you off, Sam. Vincent Boyle was in the hangar.'

'Thank goodness you did.' I pointed towards Boyle who was stamping off towards the far end of the field. 'He was arguing with Johnny. It's a shame I couldn't hear them.'

DI Corlett started the car and reversed out of the parking spot.

'Hang on,' I said. 'Pete's gone over and is talking to Johnny.'

We watched for a minute as Pete and Johnny spoke, their

heads close together. Then they both turned and stared towards an oblivious Boyle.

DI Corlett pulled away. 'Interesting little exchange.'

'Mm,' I said. 'While you were in the hangar, did you see if anything was delivered?'

'A van arrived from *Andrew's Flight Spares and Accessories*. Vincent Boyle was dispatched to deal with him while Johnny chatted to me.'

'Do you think that's who brings the drugs? They deliver them with parts and Johnny stows them on the plane. We probably got in the way a bit today, so they had to bring in Boyle to help.'

DI Corlett inclined his head. 'It had occurred to me, actually. I managed to see Johnny open some boxes, but they really were all just parts. It doesn't mean that isn't how they get the drugs in. I think we need to share our findings and think about making our move.'

'Does that mean I won't have to have another flying lesson?' I held my breath in hope.

'Perhaps. It's too late for us to intercept this batch if it is drugs at all. I suppose every airfield needs parts from time to time, without it being dodgy. If Vincent Boyle was involved, it might mean that this was a legitimate delivery.'

'Or he's involved too,' I said.

'Maybe they're all at it,' DI Corlett said. 'We aren't sure who the courier is over here. Like I said, every link is separate. Let's get back and have a think.'

'I could go back after hours and have a mooch around, find out what other deliveries they have,' I offered.

DI Corlett chuckled. 'They warned me you might do this.'

'Who warned you?' I asked.

'Do you want the full list or the abridged version?'

My reputation preceded me. 'In my defence, it was all work related. This time I would have taken a radio with me.'

'You went without means to call for assistance?' DI Corlett shook his head.

I felt I had nothing more to add to the conversation, so I sat back in the comfy seat and watched other drivers admire our car.

Chapter Fourteen

DI Corlett stood in front of a whiteboard and listed our—well, DI Corlett's—findings.

'It doesn't really give us much to go on,' DI Webb commented.

'I have enough to bring Johnny in. Maybe we can get him to talk.' DI Corlett said.

'We also saw Johnny apparently arguing with Vincent Boyle,' I offered.

'Could have been about anything,' DI Corlett said.

'Yes, but Pete told Johnny to use Vince to help him with a delivery. Surely that would give us grounds to bring Vince in for questioning. Pete too.' I cocked my head.

'Helping with our enquiries,' DS Finlay mused. 'I'm not sure now is the time. If we bring one or two in now, it's not going to take any time before they all know and that'll bugger everything up. We need to get more evidence, then hit the airfield hard and bring them all in.'

'Yeah, you're right,' DI Webb said. 'We can't risk alerting them before we move in.

'Mike, you and Eamon trace the offices of *Andrew's Flight Spares and Accessories* and find out anything you can.'

'Will do, boss,' DS Finlay said.

'Sam, would you go to see Irene and see what she has on anyone and anything that has come to our notice?'

'Yes, sir,' I replied.

'I've already done checks on Poulter,' DI Corlett said. 'There's two in the system but I think one is a bit too old for our man.'

Anything interesting turn up?' DI Webb asked.

'Apart from a couple of D and Ds in the sixties, nothing.'

'Okay, thanks, Sir.'

'And on that note, I wish you all a Merry Christmas. I'm flying home tomorrow. I might be back in the New Year, depending on how enquiries go.'

We all wished DI Corlett a Merry Christmas, and I obediently went to Irene's office. I would check on Poulter again, too; a fresh pair of eyes never hurt.

*

'I thought you went off duty ages ago. Gary's already gone,' Irene said when I entered her office.

I looked at the dusty, ancient clock on the wall. 'I hadn't realised what time it is. I've been out with DI Corlett,' I replied.

'What can I do for you, seeing as you're here?' Irene asked.

'I need to check some names and locations for DI Webb.' I looked down at my hastily scribbled note. 'Specifically: Peter Flinders, John Poulter, and *Andrew's Flight Spares and Accessories*. Vince Boyle is also connected and Hornthorpe Dell, but it's not been long since I checked those out.'

'Wouldn't hurt to check again; you never know what's been added since you last looked.'

Irene was right, things could have happened while I was off duty. 'Okay then, Vincent Boyle and Hornthorpe as well. Also, can I use your phone, I'd better let Mum know I'm late.'

Irene pushed the phone towards me. 'She's still worrying about you?'

'Not as bad as before. I believe she's finally getting used to the idea that I'm all grown up, but I think she'd still really like to come to work with me so she can keep watch. I try not to get too exasperated with her.'

Irene chuckled. 'She's been through a lot as well.' She stood up. 'I'll start with Poulter and Flinders while you make your call.'

BLUE SKY

I dialled home and explained to Mum where I was, without giving too many details. It had taken her a while to accept that I couldn't, or chose not to, share some things with her, but she seemed to be okay with that now.

Call over, I searched through the system for *Andrew's* and Hornthorpe.

Irene said, 'I've got two John Poulters, one's almost seventy the other is in his fifties. I wonder if they're related?'

'It'll be the younger one,' I replied. Related or not, the older one was of no interest to me.

Irene slammed shut the drawer and carried a small concertina of cards to her desk.

'Flinders is clean, but I have a little on John Poulter. A couple of D and Ds from a while back.'

Just as DI Corlett had said. I held up the larger concertina of cards relating to Hornthorpe Dell. 'I got nothing on *Andrew's* and nothing new has been added to the Hornthorpe Dell entry. I'll check on Boyle next.'

'We know he's an aggressive little swine,' Irene said.

I put the Hornthorpe cards back. 'Yeah, I've also noticed that he's most aggressive with people he perceives as weaker. He was as good as gold around Phil and Mike.'

'I would be too if I were a prisoner.' Irene said.

I pulled Boyle's cards from the system and scanned them. 'Nothing new here. He's got nothing relating to drugs, just the harassment and the assaults.' I put the card back. 'I'll draft a report for DI Webb.'

'Is *Andrew's* the only company that delivers there?' Irene asked.

'I don't know,' I said. 'Maybe it depends on the parts needed. I'll make sure I mention that to DI Webb.'

I went to the report writing room and settled myself behind one of the ancient typewriters. I quickly typed out what I had learnt then sat back to think for a moment. Someone could do with staking out the place to see who exactly goes in and out. I added my recommendation at the end of the report. Ken would be ideal if B Block did the watching. He was on light duties, so someone fully operational wouldn't be taken off the street, and he would only have to log deliveries and some registration numbers. Also, he wasn't known to anyone there. I pulled the sheet from the typewriter, signed it then hurried up to the CID office to leave it for DI Webb.

As I crossed the yard to my car to go home, it occurred to me that I could spend some time watching the airfield. I could park in my own car on the road to the housing estate and simply log cars coming and going. Instead of going home, I turned towards Hornthorpe Dell.

The days were short now. The field and hangars were in darkness when I arrived, but there were lights on in the clubhouse. I didn't want to get out and wander around because I could see cameras overlooking the car park and I wasn't sure if they were operating, so I drove in and parked up, confident that nobody would recognise my Triumph Herald. I jotted down the registrations of the cars in the car park then left and parked outside. A couple of cars left but nobody entered. I waited a while longer but there was no more movement apart from a woman walking a dog. She watched me as her dog did its business in the gutter, then, when it had finished, she walked on to the estate.

I shivered. I had kept the engine and the lights off and it was freezing. No point in hanging around any longer, there probably wouldn't be any deliveries now. I started my engine and drove home, relishing the warm air around my feet.

*

Next morning, Gary called me to his office.

'Where were you last night?' he asked.

I could sense this was work related and he was being the boss rather than my Gary, but I trusted him enough to know he wasn't being controlling.

'At home,' I answered.

He looked down at a piece of paper in front of him and rested his chin on his hand. 'Before that?'

'I was working with DI Corlett and I did some checks with the collator.'

'After that?'

I sighed. 'I stopped off at Hornthorpe Dell to gather some info. I took registrations in the car park and watched the clubhouse for a while.'

He pushed the piece of paper across to me. It was a job sheet from the previous day.

'Suspicious person in a blue Triumph Herald. Ray recognised the number and passed it on to me' Gary said. 'You gained an entry into the parade book for observations! Ray has deleted it, seeing as we know who and where you are. I bet you didn't have a radio with you, or that you didn't tell anyone where you were going.'

The call probably came from that woman with the dog. It was good that the neighbours looked out for each other there, but it was damned inconvenient for me at the moment.

'It wasn't like the other times. I never got out of my car. I took some numbers, which I intend to pass on. It's not a secret,' I protested.

'No, it isn't.' Gary picked up the job sheet and waved it at me. 'I suppose I should be grateful you didn't try to break in and steal a plane.'

'Now you're being silly. I promised you I wouldn't put myself in danger again,' I said.

'It's still embarrassing when you appear in our systems. Listen, next time you get an idea, any idea, run it by me first.'

My cheeks burned. 'I didn't mean to embarrass you.'

'I know you didn't; you don't think that far ahead.' Gary gave a wry smile. 'When you do get your own investigation, you'll be great at it. But until then, don't go off anywhere on your own: wait to be asked.' I nodded. 'Now, go and get those cars checked and pass them on to the DI,' Gary said.

I went downstairs and into the control room. A new computer, the PNC, had been installed in the force control room. It meant that, instead of filling in cards, sending them down to Swansea then waiting days for a response, we could make a phone call and get an answer in minutes. Criminal records were being transferred onto it as well. At this rate, Irene would be out of a job.

'When you get a minute, would you ring through to the force control room and check on the PNC for these cars, please. It's for Operation Blue Sky.' I handed the sheet of paper to Derek.

'Any rush?' he asked.

'No. I'll get them when I come back for refs. I'm going out now.'

*

Gary was looking pensive when I arrived at his flat after our shift. 'Sit down, I have something to tell you.'

I spotted paperwork scattered across his dining table. The pretty Christmas centrepiece I had put there had been pushed to one side to make room.

'You've been accepted,' I guessed.

'Yes, the letter was waiting for me when I got home,' Gary drew in a long breath. 'The posting is not six months. It's three years.'

My jaw dropped. 'Three years!' I was close to tears.

'I would be able to travel home on leave once or twice a year, and you could come to see me,' Gary said.

Yes, it wasn't impossible, but could we maintain a long-distance relationship for three years? I had no point of reference on that. Gary was my first proper boyfriend.

'It's the other side of the world,' I said, as if he hadn't realised that.

'There are planes,' Gary said. 'You wouldn't have to swim

it.' He sighed. 'We have time to think about it. I don't have to accept.'

'You should.' I would not stand in his way.

'Come with me,' Gary said.

'You know you're not allowed to take girlfriends to these postings,' I pointed out. The penny dropped. 'Oh!' I gulped. Marrying Gary was something I hoped for in the future, but this seemed so sudden. 'I don't know…'

Gary sat beside me. 'I didn't expect the first proposal I ever made to be greeted with such a lack of enthusiasm.'

'Call that a proposal?' I couldn't laugh at my quip. I rested my head on his shoulder and stared at the brightly coloured tree in the corner. 'In different circumstances, the answer would be a definite yes. Now, I'd have to leave everything to come to a strange country with a completely different language and culture. Gary, I don't have enough service in to take a career break. I would have to resign.'

'Okay, but you could rejoin when we come back. If we come back,' he argued.

'But that means I'd have to start all over again. And what do you mean *if* we come back?'

'Apparently it's a rather good life out there. I'd earn enough so you wouldn't have to work and when the children came along, there are English speaking schools they could attend. Some people send their children back to England to attend boarding schools. We'd be able to afford a good one.'

'Hang on, hang on.' I stood up and paced up and down his fireside rug. 'This is moving too fast. Five minutes ago, I was a police constable soon to finish her probation and considering what direction to go in. Now you're talking about getting married, moving to Hong Kong and sending our future children to boarding school thousands of miles away while I sit around doing nothing.'

'Okay, we could send them to an English-speaking school in Hong Kong, if you don't like the boarding school idea,' Gary said.

I shook my head. 'I don't know, Gary. I need time to think. I love you and I'm happy for you that you've been accepted. I want to get married and have children, eventually. I hadn't ever considered emigrating.'

'It's not emigration, it's a posting,' Gary said.

I flapped my hand at him. 'Irrelevant. This is life-changing, and I need time to think.'

*

We spent hours talking through all options, and the only thing we managed to agree on was that Gary would take the posting. Not ideal, but it would do for now.

He rang them the following morning, confirming his acceptance.

'That's it, then. I just need to get my starting date.'

I nibbled on my toast and marmalade and took a sip of tea. 'Did they give you any idea when it would be?'

'March. I need to sort out a visa and they advised me to have a yellow fever vaccination.' Gary came up behind me and wrapped his arms around me. 'Stop stuffing your face and let's make some memories.'

I gladly followed him into the bedroom.

Chapter Fifteen

Steve's return to work was a subdued affair. Ken and I welcomed him, as did Phil and several others, but not everyone was pleased to see him. When duties were given out on parade, I got my usual patch but Steve didn't. I wondered if they wanted to move him away from his usual stamping ground in case a member of the public had heard about events in the Isle of Man and would give him a hard time, but it wasn't the public Steve had to worry about.

'I don't want him in my area,' Frank declared.

'You'll take whoever I put in your area, Frank,' Alan said.

Frank ignored Alan and said to Steve, 'I don't know how you did it, but I know Desi's taking the fall for you.'

'Rubbish!' I exclaimed. 'Desmond Monaghan almost ruined Steve's life.'

'And you can shut your face.' Frank barked. 'You're always creeping around the CID office. Are you sleeping with someone to get information to pass on to your boyfriend? Is that how he was able to dupe Desi?'

'You're insane!' I cried.

The room erupted, in my defence I'm glad to say. Alan and Gary stood up trying to restore order.

Steve strode over to Frank and stood in front of him.

'Now, stand up and say that again.'

It was a challenge, and everyone fell silent and held their breath as Frank stood up.

'Steve, don't,' I said. 'He's a moron and it's not worth risking your job for a moron.'

'Listen to her, Steve,' Gary said.

Alan moved beside Steve, who glanced around then turned back to Frank.

'She's right: you are a moron and you're not worth it. Desi *is* bent and you're in denial.' He turned on his heel and returned to his seat. Frank sat down and the room collectively exhaled.

'Frank, consider yourself on a disciplinary. We'll discuss the details afterwards,' Gary said.

'What about him?' Frank jabbed a finger in Steve's direction.

'He was responding to your unwarranted comments. You need to apologise, Frank. To Sam and Steve.'

'Fuck that.' Frank stood up again. 'I'm twice their age and I'm being treated like a playground bully? I'm going home.'

'If the cap fits…' I said.

'You can't just leave because you lost an argument,' Alan said.

'I've got a migraine.' Frank walked towards the door.

'Very well, but I'll need a doctor's note from you,' Gary said.

Frank stopped. 'I'm entitled to self-certify for a few days.'

'I repeat: when you return, I expect to see a doctor's note from today. I'll also draw up your disciplinary while you're off recovering from your migraine.' Gary didn't raise his voice; he didn't need to.

Frank slammed the door behind him as he left.

We all sat stunned for a minute. I had never seen such a display from anyone and I really didn't know what to say.

Steve stood up. 'Sir, I'll say this in front of everyone. Maybe it'll be best if I'm not here. I think I should put in for a transfer to another division.'

'No!' I exclaimed. 'You're the innocent party. Why should you be forced out?'

'In the interest of block harmony, it might be for the best,' Steve replied.

Gary neither agreed nor disagreed. 'Come to my office after parade. We'll have a talk.'

'Yes, sir.' Steve sat down.

Blue Sky

*

I didn't get the chance to speak to Steve during the first half of the shift. We walked out to our beats after refs in virtual silence, at once familiar and awkward.

Eventually, I said, 'So, are you staying?'

'I think so,' Steve said.

'Have the air force made contact?' I asked.

'They have,' Steve replied. 'I've been invited for interview, but I won't be going.'

'After all your planning and agonising about it? You said you love flying,' I said.

'Yes, I do, but I can do that off duty. I'm not going back to Hornthorpe Dell. I'll go to Forest Dene airfield.'

'You shouldn't let what happened interfere with your plans. Desi's the criminal, not you.' I reminded him.

'Remember when I was asking you and Ken about it, and Ken told me that I'd have to balance what I have now against what I'll gain if I move?' Steve asked. I nodded. 'Well, I've balanced it and the scales tipped towards the police. Besides, who else will look out for you when the boss goes.'

'Do you think I'm getting special treatment?'

'I'd look out for my girlfriend and I don't suppose he's any different. Maybe you're just not aware of it.'

When I thought about it, Gary had covered for me when I had rushed into things. He had omitted things from reports that would earn me criticism. He would turn up as backup in potentially serious incidents, but wouldn't we all back each other up? Yes, we would, but Steve was right, my probation had had some rocky moments, but it would have been worse without Gary. I had mixed emotions. On one hand I was pleased that Gary had been quietly looking after me and touched that Steve felt he wanted to step in when Gary moved away, but then I was also a bit resentful that they felt I needed to be protected by a man like some pathetic fairytale princess.

'This is my stop,' Steve said. We stopped walking to continue our conversation.

'You and Ken are my best friends. We're the three musketeers. It was daft to think about moving away.' Steve paused. 'I would miss you; miss you both.'

'But that's the way of things. This time next year we could all be scattered all over.'

'Maybe.' Steve thought for a moment. 'I think we'd have drifted apart. Lord knows where in the world I'd be sent, and we'd be so busy with our lives, we'd lose touch. I don't want that.' He took a few steps towards his beat. 'Hey, this means we'll all be taking our sergeants' exam at the same time next year. We'll have to be study mates.'

We waved to each other and began our patrols.

I pondered on Steve's words as I walked the quiet streets. I wasn't sorry he'd changed his mind about the RAF, but this idea Steve had about protecting me, disturbed me, especially as his mother had told me straight that she hoped we'd get together. Steve hadn't had a girlfriend in all the time I had known him, and from time to time, I still wondered if he preferred men. I had always considered it none of my business, but perhaps it was my business. I resolved to have a chat with him. It would be a little awkward, but I needed to know what he was thinking and, if necessary, to set him straight.

*

I didn't get a chance to speak to Steve for the rest of the shift. He was busy with a couple of prisoners and I ended up on hospital watch, sitting with a mentally disturbed woman who had been admitted to the General. So, the following afternoon, I called around to Steve's house with a box of chocolates for his mum and a pot of stilton, which I knew his dad enjoyed.

'Come in, Sam.' Mrs Patton took the gifts from me and

ushered me into the living room, where Mr Patton was playing cards with Steve.

'Hi, Sam,' Steve said.

'Steve told us that your boyfriend is going to work abroad for a while.' Mrs Patton said.

'Yes, he leaves for Hong Kong in March.'

'Such a long way away,' Mrs Patton said. 'If you're at a loose end anytime, just call in, you're always welcome.' She turned to her husband. 'Would you come and help me in the kitchen, dear.'

Mr Patton looked up in surprise. 'What? Oh, coming.' He stood up and winked at us then followed his wife.

Steve waved at the newly vacated chair. It was still warm, and I made myself comfortable.

'I wanted to talk about what you said yesterday. I thought your parents would be out.' I had thought his dad would be at work and his mum would be visiting her sister, as was her habit on Tuesday afternoons.

'Dad's on leave this week and my aunt is staying with my cousin for a few days; but no, this isn't a bad time.'

At that point, the door opened, and Mrs Patton brought in a tray of tea and biscuits. 'Here you are,' She put them on the coffee table and poured two cups of tea. She popped a couple of bourbons on the saucer and handed it to me.

'Thank you,' I said.

'Thanks, Mum,' Steve said.

Mrs Patton left, and Steve sighed. 'She's determined to get us together.'

I picked up a biscuit and crunched on it. Perhaps the sugar rush would quell the butterflies in my stomach. 'That's what I wanted to talk about. I didn't get the chance to see you after you told me you were not joining the Air Force. Steve, please tell me you haven't turned your back on something you've been dreaming of because of me.'

'It's because of a lot of reasons.'

'Your mum knows I'm spoken for, and so do you.'

'How long for though?' Steve stared down into his tea.

'Gary and I are solid,' I said. 'We can survive a few months apart.'

'It's not just a few months though, is it. I looked up these overseas postings, some can be for years.' He caught my questioning look. 'I was curious when you told me about it, that's all.'

'Right, so we're friends. Just friends,' I said. I needed him to answer that.

'Best friends,' Steve grinned.

That would do. We both knew where we stood without awkwardness.

Mrs Patton came in to collect the tray. 'Have you told Sam about Richard's good news?'

'No, Mum,' Steve said. 'My brother wasn't the first thing I thought of while we were conversing.' Steve turned to me. 'Dick the Berk's finally found someone who can bear to spend more than one night with him, so he's getting a ring on her before she realises what a wazzer he is and escapes.'

'Don't be unkind about your brother,' Mrs Patton said. Turning to me, she said, 'They're not bothering with an engagement party, they're just going to marry in March so she can move around with him and they can get a house on base,' said Mrs Patton. 'You and your boyfriend will come, won't you?'

'I'm sorry but Gary will be in Hong Kong by then,' I said.

'You'll still be here though. You'll have to be Steve's plus one. I'd really like you to come.'

I smiled. 'Thank you.'

She picked up the tray and left us alone again.

Steve snorted. 'It won't last; Richard's a skirt-chaser. Besides, it's too fast. I bet she's pregnant.'

It was faster than normal, but it was being done so she could accompany her man. The same decision I had to make. If I said yes, we would just have time for a quick visit to the registry office to fulfil legal requirements and paperwork to allow me to go with him. I suddenly realised that I wouldn't need another couple of days, I was certain at that moment what my decision was.

'Maybe she is pregnant, but I wish them happiness. People do change,' I said.

'This is Dick the Berk we're talking about.' Steve eyed me for a moment. 'So, you don't mind being my plus one?'

'I look forward to it.'

'Great. It'll shut my brother up. He's decided I'm queer and isn't shy about bringing it up at every opportunity.'

'Are you?' the question was out before I thought about it. 'Sorry, none of my business.'

Steve's eyebrows rose. 'No, Sam, I'm not.' He remained quiet for a few seconds, then said, 'For a few years now, I've watched Richard running after girls and I've seen some of those girls break their hearts over him. I've had girls pretend to like me to get closer to him and I've taken abuse from some because they did get close to him and he used them. A couple have even claimed to be pregnant.'

'Were they?' I asked.

'Don't think so; no babies arrived, anyway.' Steve sighed. 'I'm not like him. I don't want to be like him. I don't want to cause hurt like he does. I want a relationship that will last, not a series of one-night stands.'

'You're not talking about you and me...?' I felt it was important to reiterate our status.

Steve shrugged. 'We're best friends, two of the three musketeers. I'll be Aramis.'

I chuckled. 'Thank you, Aramis.' I stood up. 'I'd better go home; Mum will be wondering where I am.'

'Not seeing the boss?' Steve asked.

'Not until work; he's got a bit of admin sorting out to do before he goes to Hong Kong. You wouldn't believe the bureaucracy.'

'Fancy going out for a drink? You can ring your mum from

here,' Steve said. He caught my expression and put his hands up. 'Best friends remember.'

'Okay, that would be nice.' I went into the hall to use the phone and ran into Mrs Patton coming out of the kitchen. 'Steve said it would be all right for me to phone my mum from here. We're going out for a drink,' I said.

Her face lit up. 'Lovely. Of course, I'll give you some privacy.' She went back into the kitchen and I rang home.

Steve came into the hall as I was finishing and put on his jacket. 'See you later,' he called to his parents.

Mr Patton came out of the kitchen and handed Steve a card. 'Drink's subsidised at the British Legion, and there's entertainment. They do a nice chicken in a basket too. Use my pass.'

'Thanks Dad.' Steve pocketed the pass and opened the door. 'Ready, Sam?'

'Coming.' I called my thanks to Steve's mum and went out.

'Do you want to go to the legion for an evening of crappy jokes, poor singing and fried chicken or do you just want a quiet drink?' Steve asked when we sat in my car.

'I'm a bit peckish, so fried chicken sounds good,' I said.

'To the British Legion then, and don't spare the horses.' Steve dramatically pointed to the road ahead and I complied.

Chapter Sixteen

The British Legion was busy when we got there. The room was decked out for Christmas. Someone had even tied tinsel around the ends of the snooker cues.

'You find a seat and I'll get the drinks and order food,' Steve said. 'They do scampi if you prefer.'

'No, chicken is fine, thanks,' I replied.

Steve turned back to the bar and I scanned the room. There wasn't a free seat anywhere I could see. Steve nudged me and handed me a drink.

'Maybe we can squeeze onto someone's table,' he said.

'Hey, Stevie.'

We both turned to the young man waving in our direction.

'Hey, Donny,' Steve called back.

Donny came over to us and Steve shook his hand.

'Great to see you.' Donny said. 'Who's your friend?'

'This is Sam. Mitts off, she's taken.'

Donny laughed and Steve turned to me and said, 'This is Keith Donald, known to everyone as Donny. His dad served with my dad, and we went to the same schools.'

'Hi, Donny,' I said.

Donny shook my hand then gave me a swift kiss on the knuckles. 'Pleased to meet you, Sam. The place is heaving. Come and sit with us; my dad's here so you'll be quite safe.' Donny led us to a table and a thick set man about the same age as Steve's dad stood up.

'Dad, you remember Steve, don't you?' Donny said.

Donny's dad shook hands with Steve. 'Of course I do. How

are you, lad?'

'I'm well thanks, Mr Donald.' Steve pushed me forward a little. 'This is Samantha.'

Mr Donald shook hands with me, and we all sat down.

'Is it always so crowded here?' I asked.

'It's quiz night and that's always popular, and Christmas is upon us. Have you ordered food?' Mr Donald asked. I nodded. 'Good. We have, too. We might get served before the quiz begins; you won't have a chance later on.'

'So, what are you up to these days, Stevie?' Donny asked. I mentally cringed on Steve's behalf.

'Still in the police, and I've been taking flying lessons. I've got a few hours under my belt now.' Steve replied. If he felt tense about the question, it didn't show.

'Brilliant. Is it expensive?'

'A bit; that's why I'm still living at home. It'll be worth it,' Steve replied.

'Where are you taking them? Hornthorpe?' Mr Donald asked.

'Yes, with a bloke called Tony,' Steve answered.

'I heard someone from there got arrested.. Drug smuggling,' Donny said.

Steve's face never altered. 'Yes, they were caught in the Isle of Man.'

It was clear that neither of the Donalds had any idea that Steve had been involved.

'Someone was killed there just after the war,' Mr Donald said.

'The Isle of Man?' Donny asked.

'Hornthorpe Dell,' Mr Donald replied.

'I heard about that. His parachute didn't open,' I said.

Mr Donald nodded. 'I remember it happening.'

'Were you there?' Steve asked.

'Not personally, but I had a mate who was.' He nudged Donny. 'You remember Tom Minchin, don't you? Everyone called him Minchie.'

'I've never heard of him.' Donny said.

Mr Donald snorted. 'He went for parachute training at Hornthorpe. We didn't have the facilities for that in our place.'

'Did you ever think about doing that, Dad?' Donny asked.

'Hell, no. I'll spend all day on and in the water, but jumping out of planes?' Mr Donald shuddered. 'It's not natural. Anyway, Minchie would come back and tell us tales about things that happened on the camp. One name kept cropping up, Summerskill. He was a right one. Always after the ladies and a right b—' Mr Donald glanced at me. 'Not very nice to anyone who wasn't RAF.'

'Was he the one who died?' Steve asked.

'Yes. Minchie told me that the straps got caught around the canopy then he left it too late to deploy his reserve chute. It got tangled up or something.'

A waitress brought over four baskets of chicken. We each claimed one and passed around the salt cellar.

I popped a chip into my mouth. 'You were telling us about that parachutist, Mr Donald.'

'I was.' Mr Donald bit a piece of chicken and chewed for a moment. 'Minchie told me that nobody was really upset when Summerskill died, so when the report concluded that it was a tragic accident, nobody bothered with it anymore.'

'Do you think there might be something more?' I coaxed.

'Not really; nothing concrete anyway. Some people talked about one of the airmen who had had a fight with Summerskill. Apparently he had been around the equipment before the jump, but Summerskill had upset so many girls, would one of them have been able to do something to his rig? You know what they say about a woman scorned.' He chuckled.

'They'd all have been questioned for the enquiry though?' I asked.

'I suppose so.' Mr Donald took another sip of beer.

'Wouldn't a woman hanging around a parachute in those days look out of place?' Steve asked.

Mr Donald shook his head. 'The WAAF packed the parachutes, then they were stored before they were brought out for use.'

'Don't they check their own parachutes before they jump?' Donny asked.

'Not normally; the WAAFs were specially trained to pack the parachutes. Minchie would be the one to ask about that. Buy him a pint and he'll talk until your ears bleed.' Mr Donald looked around. 'He drinks in here sometimes; I can't see him tonight though.'

A man walked to one end of the room and tapped the microphone. 'Has everyone got a quiz sheet?'

A low murmur went around, and a few waved their sheets.

'Great, let's get on then.'

I'd pass what I'd been told to Irene, or Eamon later on at work. It might be nothing but speculation, but it would give them something else to look at in their investigation.

*

'Is anyone in the CID office?' I asked when I went to collect my radio from the control room that night.

'Eamon is still up there,' Ray replied. 'He's on until midnight. Egilsby CID is covering nights.'

That was standard. At night, a small skeleton crew of detectives covered both Egilsby and Wyre Hall in case of serious incidents. Anything else was dealt with by the block then, if necessary, passed on to the morning jacks.

'Perfect. I need to speak to him. I'll be back shortly.' I nipped upstairs and knocked on the CID office door.

'Sam m'darlin', come on in,' Eamon called from his desk.

'Evening, Eamon. I have a little bit of information about that historical death you and Mike are dealing with.'

Eamon rolled his eyes. 'The poor man died in a terrible accident. Mike and I have found nothing to indicate anything different.'

'Well, I went out for a drink at the British Legion with Steve tonight. We met someone called Mr Donald who served in the marines with Steve's dad. He was talking about the accident and he speculated that one of Summerskill's many women tampered with the parachute. The WAAFs on the camp packed the parachutes but I don't know if the parachutes were personal, which would have made it easier to target someone, or if they were allocated ad hoc, which would make it almost impossible. He mentioned a man named Tom Minchin, who was there at the time of the accident, and said he was the one to speak to about how the parachutes were stored.'

'Aye, it's another line of enquiry, but I can't see it leading anywhere.'

'Maybe not, but it would be something different to add to the report.'

'Aye, thanks. I'll chat to Mike about it tomorrow afternoon.'

Happy that I had done my bit, I went back down and left a note for Irene so she could add my information to her system.

'Why are you still in here?' Alan asked me from the doorway.

I hadn't heard him approaching and I jumped. 'I needed to speak to CID, and I've just left some info for Irene. I'm going out now, Sarge.'

Alan nodded. 'It's cold out, have you got a scarf?'

'No, Sarge,' I replied.

'You might want to think about bringing a scarf to wear under your overcoat. Black or Navy only.'

'Thanks, I will,' I said.

He pulled a black scarf from behind his back. 'Here, borrow this for tonight.'

I realised he must have seen me in Irene's office and gone and got his own scarf before coming to speak to me. I felt a little warm glow at his thoughtfulness. I took the scarf from him and wound it around my neck, tucking the ends into my overcoat.

'Thanks, Alan.'

'Don't forget though: if you get into a situation, don't give them something they can use to strangle you. Lose it if you have to.'

'Yes, Sarge.'

'Now, get yourself outside.' Gruff Alan had returned.

I grinned, seeing right through the façade, 'Yes, Sarge. Thanks.'

*

'Mike Two from control.' I heard Ray call just after midnight. The radio beeped as Phil replied. 'Thanks Mike Two, can you make outside the YMCA: report of a hit-and-run. One pedestrian injured. Traffic making and Ambulance en route.' The radio beeped again. Phil was acknowledging.

Road traffic accidents—RTAs as we called them—ranged from a simple shunt when someone hadn't paid attention, to full on smashes where people died in mangled metal. Evidence-wise, hit-and-run accidents were the worst. We had to move quickly to get as much information from witnesses as possible before they forgot. Normally with hit-and-runs, the driver would speed off, even turning off their lights if it was night-time, so their registration couldn't be easily seen. There was nothing I could do from where I was, so I continued patrolling.

I heard a terrible crash that seemed to come from the direction of the park. Noises like that at this time of night were never good. I trotted off in that direction.

'4912 to control.'

'Stand by unless urgent,' Ray replied.

'4912,' I persisted. I considered this urgent.

'4912, can you make the main park entrance, report of a car going into the gates there,' Ray said. 'It isn't known if there are any casualties yet.'

'4912 roger. I was about to tell you that I'd heard something. I'm making from Buckingham Avenue. Is there any back-up?'

'Mike Sierra One is making to assist,' Ray said. 'Mike Three has a prisoner, Mike Sierra Two, Mike Two and Traffic are committed with the hit-and-run by the YMCA.'

'Roger.' I started to jog towards the main gates. Mikes One and Four were on the other side of the division, where they belonged. Sergant Lloyd and Phil were at the hit-and-run, which meant I was it here, until Gary could get to me. I broke into a run, my breath puffing like smoke into the cold air.

As I approached the park gates, I could see a ruined Austin Allegro nose first into the metal rails of the gate which had been bent and pushed right back. Stone pieces had been knocked from a high pillar holding the gate. There was nobody around. I peered into the car in case there was a casualty hidden from view. Inexplicably, there was a steering wheel lock still attached.

'4912 to control.'

'Go ahead,' Ray replied.

'I'm at the scene. One wrecked vehicle, an Austin Allegro. Nobody is with the car. The park gates and one of the pillars have been damaged, so could you inform the relevant authority. I'm not sure they'll be safe when the car is removed.'

'Roger,' Ray replied.

'Do we have an informant?' I asked.

'Anonymous male,' Ray said.

The good thing about an accident happening at night was that there were fewer spectators. The bad thing about an accident happening at night was there were fewer witnesses. I looked about to see if any lights were on in nearby houses that could indicate where the call had come from. A woman in a dressing gown and slippers came from a nearby house and scurried towards me.

'I heard it happen. I was in bed and heard a loud bang; everyone around here must have heard it. I looked out and saw a man standing by the car. He ran into the park.'

'Did you phone in?' I asked.

'We don't have a phone,' she replied. My husband was going

to go to the phone box, but you arrived very quickly.'

Typical, one of the few people left who didn't have a phone. Never mind, she was here now.

'I was only in Buckingham Avenue. Did see anyone get out of the car?' I asked.

'No, but I did see a man by the car before he ran into the park.'

'Can you give me a description of the man?' I got my notebook and a pen out of my bag.

'Not a good one. Average height, average build, dark hair, not long like most men nowadays, dark clothing, it's hard to tell exact colours under streetlights.'

I nodded my agreement; yellow sodium light made everything look different.

'I couldn't see how old he was, he was a bit too far away to see clearly,' she added.

'I need to take a statement from you but first I need to tell control what's happening.' I pressed transmit. '4912 to control.'

'Go ahead,' Ray replied.

'I have one witness who saw a male running from the scene and into the park. It's uncertain if he was the driver, but he was seen by the crash immediately after it happened. Description is: average height, average build, short, dark hair, dark clothing. Can we inform the duty garage the car will need removing, please? I don't think it's drivable because a front wheel's buckled, but they might be able to tow it.'

'I'll phone them,' Ray replied.

'Can you also check your sheet for an Austin Allegro, please.' I passed on the registration number. Ray would ring through to the force control room and ask for a vehicle check on the new PNC, but he also kept a sheet of local cars that had been reported stolen for quick reference.

As Ray gave out the description of our mystery man, I turned back to the woman. 'May I have your details?'

'Mrs Margaret Yale. I live just over there.' She pointed to the house I had seen her running from.

'I know it's late, but would it be okay if I came and took a statement from you when this is dealt with?' I asked.

'I'm wide awake now, so when the car's gone, just pop over and I'll put the kettle on.'

Mrs Yale was just returning to her house when Gary arrived. What have we got?' he asked.

'Abandoned car.' I pointed to the house the Mrs Yale had come from. 'A lady over there saw a man running into the park. I'll get a statement later.'

He nodded and walked around the car. 'This'll be a write off.' He stopped by the driver's door. 'This broken window doesn't look like it was caused by the crash. The quarterlight has a hole punched in the middle, different from the big windows.'

I stood next to him. The windows had been shattered by the impact, and thousands of glass crystals covered the seat. A quirky thing I had noticed with car crashes was that the small side window that featured in so many cars often survived impacts that destroyed everything else. When I had been on my traffic posting, they had explained that it because it was small and therefore stronger and protected by the metal surround.

'It's been stolen,' I said.

'4912,' Ray called. He was starting to sound hoarse. He had more than our accident to deal with; the hit-and-run was ongoing too.

'Go ahead,' I replied.

'Duty garage informed. Also, the car was reported stolen this morning by Mr Leonard Jackson of 10 Kensington Road.'

Leonard Jackson's car. I might have thought this was Boyle upping the ante by stealing and wrecking the car, but from the description, the man seen running away could not have been Boyle, unless he'd had a haircut since I'd last seen him.

'Mike Sierra One,' Ray called.

'Go ahead,' Gary replied.

'For your information, sir, the offending vehicle in the hit-

and-run has been described as a grey or blue Allegro,' Ray transmitted.

I stared at the Allegro in front of me. Under the streetlights, it could pass as grey or blue. Dammit.

'Received,' Gary said. 'The car we have at the park fits that description, so we'll need this car checking for forensic evidence.'

'They're already aware, sir, and they will take appropriate action.'

'Thanks, Ray. Would you also leave a note for SOCO to attend to it in the morning?'

'Will do,' Ray replied. He probably had already done it. He knew when Scenes of Crime Officers were required.

I shone my torch around the car. Any damage caused by a collision with a person would likely have been destroyed by the damage caused by the car ramming into the park gates. I bet that had been the plan.

I spotted something in the driver's footwell. Bearing in mind we now had to consider forensic evidence, I didn't want to touch anything. I shone my torch through the broken window. The carpet mat on the driver's side had been pushed up behind the pedals. A dark stain, possibly a footprint, marked it. Something else caught my attention.

'Is that a brick? It doesn't look like the bricks from the gatepost.'

Gary shone his torch in from the passenger side. 'Looks like whoever took the car, deliberately aimed it at the gates then put a house brick on the accelerator.'

'From how far back?!' I exclaimed. 'That car had to have been doing a fair lick to have caused damage like that.'

Gary pointed to a road a short distance away. Balmoral Rise. The clue was in the name. It was a longish road with a modest but continual gradient, and converged with three other roads at the park gates making it quite a wide carriageway at that point.

'If he started up there, he could have aimed the car, attached the steering wheel lock so it wouldn't deviate, revved the engine then put the brick on the accelerator. He could have jumped out before it got too fast, then the car would have continued to gain speed as it came down the hill.'

'The impact would have slammed the door shut if it were open and possibly caused the car to swing round so it's hard to see a direction of travel.' I continued. 'A bit risky. He couldn't have known that another car wouldn't be in the way, or even a pedestrian. He must have followed it down, because Mrs Yale saw a man by it,' I said.

'He might not have been connected,' Gary said.

'Then why did he run off?'

We both looked up as a car approached. It was Phil.

'What's happening at the YMCA?' the inspector asked.

'The casualty has gone to hospital. Traffic are taking the lead on the investigation. They're still there.' Phil nodded towards the Allegro. 'There's a camera at the YMCA; it picked up an Austin Allegro mounting the kerb and hitting a pedestrian who had just left the building. One of the witnesses said he thought it was a man driving.'

'How's the casualty?' I asked.

'Not good. Boss, it's Vincent Boyle.' Phil said.

'Did anyone see the registration?' Gary asked.

'Only part of it.' Phil pointed to the ruined Allegro. 'And that fits.'

'Ray said that this car was reported stolen by Leonard Jackson this morning,' I said, in case they had missed that transmission.

'If Jackson had been planning something like this, he would try to put distance between the car and himself, perhaps by reporting it stolen,' Phil said. 'We have to inform traffic that this scene links to the YMCA.'

'And CID, especially if Boyle dies,' Gary added.

'We know Boyle is an antagonistic sort of bloke so it's possible he has made enemies who would hurt him, apart from Mr Jackson. There are a few rum characters staying at the YMCA, hence the cameras, so it could be that Boyle upset someone there. They'll all have to be spoken to,' Phil said.

Gary radioed in the information for Ray to pass it on to traffic while Phil and I marked out the position of the car and the fallen gates ready for the investigation. Then there was little else for us to do except wait for the garage to arrive. We stood around shivering in the cold, night air.

'Do you want me to go and speak to Mrs Yale and get a statement?' I asked. In her house was warmth and a nice cup of tea. However, the garage arrived to recover the car. No tea for me.

'Mike Sierra One from control,' Ray called.

'Go ahead,' Gary answered.

'For your information, the casualty from the YMCA is not expected to survive.'

I drew a sharp breath; this was not looking good for Mr Jackson.

'CID will need to bring Mr Jackson in,' Phil said to me. As he finished speaking, the council arrived to deal with the pillar.

'You might as well go and speak to Mrs Yale now,' Gary said. 'Get her statement, do your own then pass them on to traffic.'

I was across the road and tapping on her door like a greyhound out of the trap.

Chapter Seventeen

Mum was up when I got home. I could see that she was tired, but she had heard my car pulling in and had boiled the kettle for tea and popped a couple of slices of bread into the toaster.

'Thanks, Mum,' I said as she put the tea and toast in front of me. I was always hungry after a shift.

Mum sat opposite me. 'Have you given Gary an answer yet?' she asked without preamble.

'It's too soon to be married, I'm still only twenty-two and I haven't come out of my probation,' I chomped into a slice of toast.

'I was twenty-one when I married your father,' Mum said.

'So?'

'So, twenty-two is not too young,' Mum said. 'You have the chance to marry a good man and go and live an exciting life without having to worry about money. You might be twenty-two, but Gary is thirty, he's going to want a family sooner rather than later, so he won't want to hang around waiting for you to make up your mind.'

I swallowed a bite of toast and took a sip of tea before I answered her. 'You think that I should marry Gary and go with him to Hong Kong, even though it will mean giving up everything I've worked for?'

'You're young enough to start again,' Mum said.

'Has Gary put you up to this?' I asked. I'd be having words if he had.

Mum shook her head. 'Of course not. I think you're a fool to turn him down.'

I finished my tea. 'I haven't turned him down.' Mum's eyes brightened. 'I told him I wasn't ready *yet*.'

'You turned him down.' Mum's voice was flat. 'I was hoping I would finally be able to stop worrying about you.'

'Stop that!' I snapped. 'I know you worry about me, but I am not going to be emotionally blackmailed into marrying before I am ready, no matter how much I love him.'

'If you love him, what's the problem? You practically live with him already.' Mum threw her hands up.

'If I marry now, it will be a rushed affair. I want to finish my probation, get established in my career and then think about marrying. In about five years, I might be able to take a career break without having to start again. That would be the time to think about a family.'

'So, you're happy to let Gary go away without you? You'll lose him, you know.'

'Yes, Mum, I'm happy for Gary to go away to follow his ambitions, just as you are happy to let Dad work away. It's called trust.'

'That's different!' Mum exclaimed.

'How? Because Dad's on an oil rig?' I demanded.

'Because we are married,' Mum retorted. 'You won't be. Gary will be a single man far away from home.'

I stood up. 'Mum, I love him and I trust him, but I will not marry him before I am ready. My ambitions are important too. I'm going to bed.'

'You'll regret it,' Mum called after me.

I lay on my bed thinking about what Mum had said. She'd never normally resort to emotional blackmail, so she must feel strongly about it. I didn't think I would regret putting off my wedding day, but the thought that I might lose Gary bothered me. I loved him, and I didn't want to lose him. Did that mean I had to sacrifice my own wishes? What if he did meet someone else out in Hong Kong? I would be devastated, but surely I didn't have to marry him to keep him on the straight and narrow. If he loved me, he would remain faithful, but if he did meet someone with less baggage and fewer inhibitions, I hoped he would be man enough to tell me.

*

Next day, I had a headache. Gary noticed that I was on the quiet side and questioned me after parade.

'Is something bothering you?' he asked.

I shook my head. 'Nothing. I didn't sleep well, that's all.'

'Hong Kong?' Gary watched for my reaction. I exhaled loudly and I felt my lips thin as I pressed them together.

'Okay, let's pop up to my office and have a little talk,' he said. We passed the control room and he put his head in the door. 'Ray, mark Sam as unavailable for fifteen minutes please.'

'Will do, Boss,' Ray answered and scribbled on the sheet in front of him.

In his office, I sat down on the chair and Gary perched on his desk.

'Talk to me,' he said.

I twisted the hem of my skirt for a minute before answering. 'Last night, Mum was trying to persuade me to marry you ASAP.'

Gary held up his hands. 'That didn't come from me, though I'm glad she likes me that much.'

'I know you didn't put her up to it: she told me,' I settled back in the chair. 'I feel so torn. I love you but I'm not ready to give up everything yet. Mum thinks that love is enough, but I have ambitions too, ambitions that I'd have to abandon to be your wife.'

Gary chewed the side of this thumb, a habit he had whenever he was thinking something over.

'I won't apologise for wanting you with me, but I don't expect you to give up your ambitions for me.'

I patted his knee. 'If this were happening a few years from

now, I would be racing you to the plane, secure in the knowledge that I could pick up where I left off. Right now, I'd lose too much.'

'I have a suggestion,' Gary said. 'I fly out there and you stay here and build up your career for one year.'

'One year? I still wouldn't have enough time in to take a career break.'

'No, but that will give you time to think about what you want to do, and for me to think about things also.'

'Marry you, give up everything and fly out to Hong Kong, or we break up? Or for you to decide that you're better off alone? I don't like the sound of that,' I said.

'I don't want us to break up,' Gary said. 'I meant that we could decide if you are coming to Hong Kong or whether I should leave Hong Kong and come home, or perhaps we will decide to let things continue as they are.'

'I stay here, and we marry when you get back in three years?'

'Yes, but we also have to think about what we'd do if I'm given the option to stay,' Gary said.

'I have time to think about that.' I felt pressure lift from me. I stood up and hugged him. 'Did I tell you that I love you?'

'Once or twice.' Gary moved his mouth close to my ear and whispered, 'Back to mine after work?'

I pressed myself against him. 'Absolutely.'

*

I was on my way out to start patrol when I ran into Eamon in the corridor. Vincent Boyle was still hanging on, and I had heard on the grapevine that Leonard Jackson had been questioned the day after the RTAs by the park and the YMCA. As they were already dealing with him over the allegation of murder, DS Mike Finlay and Eamon Kildea had been allocated to the investigation. Apparently, he had been cooperative but absolutely insistent that he had not been the driver and that the car had really been stolen. I wanted to believe it, but this seemed too much of a coincidence.

'Has Mr Jackson been charged with anything yet?' I asked.

'Not yet. We still have a couple more things to gather,' Eamon replied.

'I never thought he'd do something like that,' I said.

'You can never tell what goes on in people's minds,' Eamon said.

'Will it definitely be murder if Boyle dies?' I asked. Sometimes we had to take the pragmatic view and go for a lesser charge to secure a conviction.

'Hard to think how it wouldn't be,' Eamon said. 'It's not like Boyle thumping Ken, anyone with half a brain would know that driving a ton of metal into someone is likely to kill them. Somehow, I don't think if he claimed that he only intended to bump Boyle onto his backside, he'd be believed.'

'Can you be sure he was the driver though?' I asked.

'Therein lies my enquiries. We know it was his car that injured Boyle, we just have to get proof he was driving, because he isn't coughing it. The YMCA said they'd let us have a copy of the CCTV film of the hit and run. Would you call in and collect it for me, please? It would save me a job,' He smiled his twinkly smile.

I grinned. 'You don't have to try to play me. I'll happily collect it for you.'

'Thanks, m'darlin.'

*

As promised, I went to the YMCA to collect the film for Eamon. The reception area was an exceptionally brightly lit space with a small office off it. I tapped on the sliding window that opened into the foyer. A man in a tatty tank-top looked up from the sheet of paper he was reading.

'Can I help you?'

'I'm here to collect the CCTV film about the accident the other night,' I said.

'Oh right. I was expecting DC Kildea,'

'He's busy so he asked me to call in. Is it ready?' I asked.

The man stood up. 'Come around and I'll get it for you.'

I went through the side door into the reception office. The man beckoned for me to follow him to a smaller office behind the reception.

'Do you want to see it before you take it?' he asked.

Eamon hadn't asked me to view it, but I thought it might be useful. Besides, like most bobbies, I had an innate curiosity.

'That would be helpful,' I said.

He set up the reels. I was pleased to see that the part we wanted had been transferred to a small reel. It would save trawling through the whole day to find our clip.

'We're getting a video system next year,' he said.

I was impressed. 'Really? That is bang up to date.'

He smiled, evidently proud. 'Yeah, none of this reel-to-reel any more. Even the council won't have video technology.' He switched on the player.

I saw some people leaving and arriving, then I saw Boyle. He was wearing his customary jeans and leather jacket. He exchanged a couple of words with the person on reception, laughed then walked out the door, took a couple of steps into the street and paused to light a cigarette. Almost at once, a car raced past from the right, far too close to the doors of the YMCA. Boyle didn't see it coming. One second he was lighting his cigarette, the next he was knocked onto the bonnet of the car and thrown into the air and off screen.

'That's pretty conclusive,' I said.

'Yeah. Some of the lads saw it happen. You can't see them on film, but they said the car was blue or possibly grey, and a man was driving. It happened so fast, and it made off with no lights on, nobody got a real good look.' He replayed the film and I saw that the car had indeed been driven with no lights on. This would prove intent in case a court decided that mounting the pavement wasn't good enough evidence. Why would the driver leave the lights off unless it was to make it hard to trace them? Sadly, I couldn't make out anything of the driver. Wrong side,

'I'll pop it in an envelope for you' the man said.

'Thanks.'

*

Back at the station, I took the reel upstairs to the CID office.

'Thanks, m'darlin',' Eamon said as he took them from me.

'The man told me they're getting video technology soon,' I said.

'Video? That'll make things easier,' Eamon tapped the reel he was holding. 'Have you had a look at this?'

'I have. It's all so fast, all you can see is the car hitting Boyle. I couldn't make out anything of the driver and I'm not good at recognising cars, especially in a two second clip.'

'That's disappointing,' Eamon said. 'I'm going to have to bring Jackson back in.'

I hoped it would turn out that someone really had stolen his car, someone who also had a grudge against Boyle, but it seemed pretty hopeless.

I went back downstairs, pausing to put my head around the control room door to tell them I was going out again. Ray marked me as available on the sheet.

I was about to leave the building when I heard Eamon call my name. He was puffed out having chased down the stairs. He was settling into married life a little too well, perhaps he needed to review his fitness.

'Glad I caught you, Sam. How do you feel about going for a drink with me?'

'You're married and I'm seeing someone.' I replied.

Eamon laughed. 'Webby wants me to get into the club at Hornthorpe Dell, and maybe chat up some customers to see if

I can glean anything about the drugs getting in for the Manx police. You'll be my way in there.'

'Like with DI Corlett?' I asked.

'Exactly like that,' Eamon confirmed.

'Who will you be: my big brother?'

'I thought maybe a cousin over from God's own country. It would explain the differing accents,' Eamon said.

'When?'

'I'll tell Webby you're up for it and he can arrange it with Inspector Tyrrell.'

'I wouldn't have to do anything other than make you look less conspicuous?' I asked.

'Not a thing. You get us in, and I'll do the detecting,' Eamon said.

Money for old rope. Bring it on.

Chapter Eighteen

I pushed open the door and stepped inside the Hornthorpe club. The warmth was welcome.

'Are you a member?' asked the man behind the desk in the foyer.

'Samantha!'

I looked across to Pete who was coming towards us. 'Hi Pete, this is my cousin Eamon. He's staying with us over Christmas, and I thought it would be nice to bring him for a drink here.'

'No problem; you can sign in as my guests.' Pete held his hand out to Eamon. 'Peter Flinders, Samantha's instructor.'

'Eamon Kildea.' Eamon took Pete's hand and shook.

'Where are you from?' Pete asked when he heard Eamon speak.

'Downpatrick,' Eamon replied.

'A lovely part of the world,' Pete said. 'When I was a boy, I had some wonderful holidays with my aunt and uncle in Ballycastle. For two pins, I would have moved there permanently, but my uncle died and my aunt came to England to be near us.'

'There's a lot come over here from the old country, with the troubles and all that,' Eamon said. I noticed his accent had thickened as he spoke to Pete.

'Sad times. Let's hope they don't last,' Pete said. 'Anyway, here I am keeping you chatting. Let's get you signed in and then you can enjoy the evening.'

We all signed the book. Pete went into the office, and Eamon and I went to the bar where Barbara was working.

'Hello again. Merry Christmas,' Barbara said.

'Merry Christmas. This is Eamon. He's staying with us over the holidays.'

'What can I get you, Eamon?'

'Pint of bitter and a lager and lime for my cousin please,' he said.

Barbara got us our drinks and we settled on a couple of bar stools that gave us a good view of the room.

'Do you know what you're looking for, Eamon,' I whispered.

'Anything and everything.'

I pointed at the photographs on the wall. 'Recognise that?'

Eamon put his drink down and went over to inspect them. 'I've seen that one before.' I went and stood beside him.

Barbara noticed us looking. 'Have you shown him the one we talked about?'

'We were just looking at it,' I replied.

A man, mid-fifties, silver hair came to the bar. 'Summerskill's last jump,' he called to us.

'The usual, Minchie?' Barbara said.

'The usual, Barbara,' he replied.

'Minchie, Tom Minchin,' I whispered to Eamon. 'The one Mr Donald told us about. He knows about storing the parachutes.'

This wasn't exactly what we had been looking for, but it was too good an opportunity to pass up. We returned to our drinks.

'I couldn't imagine anything more horrible,' I said.

'You wouldn't get me jumping from a plane,' Eamon agreed.

'Oh, it's not so bad,' Minchie said. 'I was nervous at first, but you get used to it.'

Barbara put a pint in front of him and he chugged half of it straight down and smacked his lips.

'You were in the air force?' Eamon asked.

'I was a marine. Commandos trained in parachute jumping, it was necessary for some missions. We had to train with the RAF.'

'I suppose it makes sense to pool resources,' I said.

'Exactly,' Minchie said. 'I was here on that day. I watched

Summerskill fall.'

I edged closer. 'I heard about it when I started flying lessons here. His parachute didn't open.'

'It deployed, but the straps had got wrapped across it so it couldn't open properly,' Minchie said. 'He left it too late to cut away the canopy and had to deploy his reserve chute while the main canopy was still attached. They got tangled.' He banged his glass on the bar. 'Same again please, Barbara.'

Barbara put another glass in front of him and again he drank half straight off.

'Don't get him started on the old days,' Barbara warned. 'Once he's had a pint, he's hard to shut up. In fact, he's probably had a couple before he got here.'

'There was an enquiry, wasn't there?' Eamon asked, knowing full well there had been.

Minchie nodded as he took another long mouthful of beer. 'We all were questioned, even Jacko and the packers because that shouldn't have happened if they had packed it properly.'

'Surely that would be negligence and not an accident in that case,' I said.

'Packing is a specialist job. The WAAFs did it here. The supervisor confirmed that all the packers had been trained, and the packed parachutes were checked by the supervisors before being passed to go to the stores, so they were blameless. It was deemed an accident. The enquiry thought that Summerskill might have opened the rig himself and had a furtle around because it was coming to the end of its shelf life.'

'What does that mean?' I asked.

'If they hadn't been used for a while, the canopies had to be unpacked, rechecked and repacked. It was all quite strictly controlled.' Tom took another huge mouthful of beer.

'I thought the parachutists always checked their own parachutes,' I said.

'We didn't have our own parachutes; they were allocated to us per jump,' Tom said.

There was no way I could see that a particular parachutist could be targeted, so could this have been someone sabotaging parachutes indiscriminately and Summerskill just happened to be the unlucky one? If there had been a psychopath trying to kill random parachutists, why had there been no more since Summerskill?

'Barbara told me she had been a WAAF,' I said.

Tom shook his head. 'Not when this happened. Barbara had left the WAAF by then.'

'Had she been a packer too?' I asked.

'Yes, most were,' Tom said.

'Who was Jacko?' Eamon asked.

'He was an airman, but he didn't fly,' Tom answered. 'He had been on cleaning detail. Everyone knew Jacko hated Summerskill, and the feeling was mutual. They'd got into a fight because Summerskill had got Jacko's sister pregnant. Jacko ended up on jankers.'

Well, there was an interesting little morsel. It could provide a motive for tampering with Summerskill's parachute, but I really couldn't see when he would have had the chance.

'Can I get you another, Tom?' Eamon asked.

'Thanks, lad,' Tom pushed his glass towards Barbara, who paused for a moment, her eyes on him, before refilling it.

'It makes you wonder if Summerskill had upset someone and they got at his parachute,' Eamon said.

Tom raised his eyebrows. 'It would be very difficult to tamper with any parachute. Nigh on impossible to tamper with a particular one, there wouldn't be any way of knowing who would get which parachute beforehand. Like I said, the rigs weren't passed for use until a supervisor had seen them, so any shenanigans like that would have been picked up at once.'

'So, it was a terrible accident.' Eamon said.

Tom nodded as he took another swig from his pint. 'Everyone thought it was the right decision. We were all shocked at what happened, but nobody was really upset for him, egotistical sod he was. Once the enquiry was over, life moved on.'

'Don't speak ill of the dead, Tom,' Barbara said from behind the bar.

'You remember him, Barb. He was a nasty piece of work. Often late and hungover. In fact he was late the day he died and almost missed the jump. Conceited and condescending. He treated girls appallingly.' Tom laughed softly. 'You must remember that; you were one of his harem, weren't you?' Tom tapped the side of his glass meaningfully. He could certainly put away his beer.

'I think you've had enough,' Barbara said.

'I'm fine,' Tom retorted. He lowered his voice and turned back to me. 'She hadn't been at the base long when he seduced her. She got pregnant. It was why she had to leave the WAAF.'

Barbara stood before us with her hands on her hips. 'Tom, stop airing my dirty laundry, it's nobody's business. No more booze for you. Go home or I'll have to bar you.'

'I'm a member, you can't bar me,' Tom replied.

'I'm the manageress, I can bar anyone who doesn't behave,' Barbara retorted. She moved away to serve another customer then turned back to Tom. 'You still here?'

'Evidently,' Tom replied, a distinct slur in his voice.

'I told you I'm not going to serve you again and I'm not going to serve anyone else you con into buying drinks for you.'

Tom stood up. 'I'm not staying where I'm not wanted. I'm going to the legion.' He turned to us. 'Thank you for the pint.'

'I enjoyed the craic,' Eamon said.

We watched Tom weave his way to the door.

'Do you think he's going to drive like that? We should go and check,' I said.

'And blow our cover?' Eamon whispered.

Oh, yeah, that. Eamon went off to use the phone booth and I ordered a couple of coca colas. Barbara plonked them in front of me and immediately went off to serve someone else. I turned and faced the room.

Everyone seemed to be enjoying themselves. No rowdiness and no evident drunkenness. Barbara ran a tight ship, as my dad would say. The lady herself came from behind the bar and started to gather empty glasses.

She caught me watching her carry them back to the bar and smiled. 'I'll be glad when the barmaid's back off leave. It can get a bit busy for one person.'

I decided to grab the proverbial bull by the horns. 'Did you really go out with him?' I nodded towards the photograph on the wall.

Barbara let her gaze rest on it for a few seconds. 'I did. That man had a silver tongue. It wasn't for long, none of his girls lasted long. When I found I was in the family way, my dad gave me a hiding and there was no question of me keeping it. He'd have killed James if he'd known it was him. I told James but he wasn't interested. He made out I was the town bike who had probably had so many men, I didn't know who the father was. Bastard, I was only nineteen and he had been my first.'

A memory tickled at the back of my mind, something Boyle had said about Summerskill and Mr Jackson fighting over Mr Jackson's sister's pregnancy. 'Are you related to a Leonard Jackson?' I asked.

Barbara smiled, a little sadly I thought. 'No. I know who you're thinking of though, June Jackson. She was a lovely girl; James Summerskill always went for the nice girls. She died young; blood poisoning I heard.'

'Oh, how sad.' There was little more I could say but I noticed that she hadn't mentioned June's pregnancy. Perhaps Barbara hadn't known because she was off dealing with her own problem. I wondered how many more illegitimate children Summerskill had fathered without consequence for him.

'I bet Minchie told you about her,' Barbara said.

'Actually, no. I know Mr Jackson and his wife.' And I wasn't going to explain how I knew them. 'Tom was out of order,' I said. 'And I want you to know, I don't judge you.'

Barbara smiled. 'I try not to hold stuff against him. He's an alcoholic. It's a leftover from when he was sent to Malaya in the fifties. He doesn't talk about that unless he gets really soused. I usually send him on his way before he gets to that state. I don't think he means any harm; his tongue runs away with him. He'll keep the stories coming if it gets him a free drink. Sometimes they aren't always accurate; he's prone to exaggeration.' She looked over my shoulder and waved at someone. I looked around and saw Johnny coming in. 'Thanks for coming in,' she called to him. She looked back at me. 'It was my lucky day when I met Johnny. I'm short-handed this week, and my son's in hospital after a car accident, so I need to spend time there as well as run this place. Johnny's got his own job, but he still comes in to help me.'

'It sounds awful for you. I hope your son isn't too bad,' I said.
'He's in a coma.'

My neck prickled. 'I read about a bad accident in the paper. A hit-and-run.'

'That's the one. We'd only just met up again since I'd had to let him go as a baby. He'd traced me a few months ago. I got him a job looking after the grounds here.'

'Your son is the baby Tom was talking about?' I asked.

Barbara nodded. 'I never had any more. I never trusted anyone enough until Johnny, but by then I was too old to be thinking of a family.'

'That must be so hard for you,' I said. I did have some sympathy for Barbara; she wasn't to know her son, Vincent Boyle, was a violent criminal.

Eamon reappeared and picked up his drink. 'Coke?'

'We don't want to overdo it,' I said.

Barbara moved to the other side of the bar and loaded the glass washer.

Eamon leant in and whispered to me, 'I alerted Ray about Tom. I saw him get into a car and leave. Ray's going to circulate the details.'

'Sneaky,' I said.

Eamon smiled. 'Learn anything new while I was gone?'

'Nothing relating to the Isle of Man thing, except that Johnny is her chap. I'm not sure if they're married or living over the brush. The barmaid is on leave and Johnny has come in to help. Tom Minchin is an alcoholic with a tendency to exaggerate but what he said about Barbara is true.'

'That could be a problem if we need him for evidence. The defence would put anything he said down to the ramblings of a drunkard,' Eamon said.

'The interesting thing is, the child she had adopted is Vincent Boyle: our Vincent Boyle. He traced her a few months ago. She visits him in hospital, but I don't think she has any idea about his activities.'

'She doesn't seem the type to tolerate criminal activity,' Eamon said.

'No, this is a well-run place. I can't see Barbara tolerating drugs in here, or anywhere else,' I said.

'But Steve and Desi flew from here, so the drugs have to be getting in somewhere.'

'Maybe they bypass the club, and the drugs go straight to the planes,' I suggested.

'Lord knows.' Eamon finished his drink. 'Shall we call it a night then?'

'May as well.' I agreed. I finished my drink and followed Eamon out, waving goodbye to Barbara as I passed.

*

It was cold and damp outside as we started towards the car. Christmas lights flashed in the windows of some houses on the estate, casting colour into the dark. I stood looking towards the deserted hangars. It would be good if we could check them out. I wasn't sure what we'd find, but it was worth a peek.

'Eamon,' I said.

He was a few paces ahead of me and turned back.

'What is it?'

'Those hangars are deserted and dark.'

He looked over. 'Yes, they are.' He looked back at me. 'You've been told about this, m'darlin'.'

'I know, but I wouldn't be going off on my own; you'd be with me.' I smiled my brightest, hopeful smile.

'We haven't been authorised to conduct a search,' Eamon warned, but he was walking back to me.

'But we could if we saw criminal activity, and I'm sure I saw someone over there. Maybe they're breaking in,' I said.

'Is that so, m'darlin'? Perhaps we'd better check it out.'

We ran across the wet grass, keeping to the shadows as much as possible. It had been tacitly agreed that if we were challenged, or if we had been picked up on the car park cameras, we had seen someone trying to break in.

We ran once around the nearest hangar to see if there were any windows left open. There weren't. We came to a halt at the rear.

'I can't see a way in,' I panted.

'Me neither.' Eamon leant against the wall to catch his breath.

'Perhaps we could force a window?' I suggested.

Eamon shook his head. 'Without a warrant or evidence of a crime being committed, that would be crossing the line into burglary.'

Had I been alone, and had I not promised Gary I wouldn't go off on my own enquiries, I might have been tempted to go ahead and do that, but Eamon was right. Bad Sam.

Eamon looked around. 'Let's look at the other hangars.'

'They're only used for storage, hardly anyone goes there, Pete told me,' I said.

'Perfect for hiding stuff, then,' Eamon said.

We ran to the next hangar and made a round of that too. Again, it was secure.

'Let me catch my breath before we go to the last hangar,'

Eamon wheezed.

We both froze as we heard whistling coming towards us. We shrank back into the darkness and held our breaths. I peeped around the corner of the hangar and saw Pete pulling a low trolley with two stainless steel kegs on it coming towards the hangars. He was not trying to conceal himself.

He walked past hangar two and on to the last hangar. Communicating by hand signals, Eamon and I crept after him. We found a window, secure unfortunately, but enough to allow us to peep in.

Pete opened the door and switched on a light, not the main light but enough for him to find his way around and for us to see what he was doing, which did not appear to be anything interesting. He pulled the trolley past the planes that were stored there and stopped at the rear. He unloaded the two barrels and left the way he had come.

'They must keep the empties here,' I whispered.

Eamon scratched his chin. 'It's a bit of a trek. The delivery guy would normally collect them after they'd dropped off the fresh delivery, so I'd have thought they would want to keep them near the club.'

We shivered in the dark until we were sure Pete had gone, then hurried back to the club. Instead of going straight to the car park, we walked around the club building. There was an enclosure at the rear surrounded by a high, wooden fence. Access from the outside was via a padlocked gate, a double door led into the building.

I peered into the pen and saw a number of barrels.

'Here's where the empties go,' I whispered to Eamon. 'So, what was that at the hangar all about?'

'Sam, m'darlin,' I think I know how they get the drugs onto the airfield, and your friend Pete is involved.'

Chapter Nineteen

My time in the police had not cured my hatred of early mornings, but working earlies over Christmas wasn't so bad. Some effort had been made to decorate the station: Ray had tied tinsel to the radio aerial and an artificial tree appeared in the public area of the enquiry office.

On Christmas Day, everyone on the block brought in some food, a cheese and onion hedgehog and a cheese and pineapple hedgehog in my case, and a load of shop-bought mince pies in Gary's case. While we were all out on patrol, Ken, who was still on light duties, left the front office in the charge of Ray and Derek and spent the morning preparing the refs room. He divided the food into two, one lot for first refs and another for second refs, and set out our Christmas feast. A couple of days previously, he had suggested to Gary that we did mulled wine, but Gary vetoed that one. Drinking on duty generally wasn't allowed. It wasn't as if we were trying to fit in at a bar and had little choice but to have a drink. He couldn't justify it, but he still felt mean for refusing.

Patrol was damp, cold and quiet, and every second dragged on and on. I couldn't even dodge into the paper shop for a cup of tea because they were shut. Eventually, it was time for first refs. Cold and famished I hurried back to the station, where I dumped my overcoat in the drying room and raced up the stairs where I met Steve.

'I am so ready for this,' Steve said.
'Me too, my stomach has been rumbling for hours,' I said.
Together, we went into the refs room. I paused by the door.

Ken had really pushed the boat out. He had the radio tuned to a station that played nothing but Christmas carols and had pinned a tinsel star over the archway to the kitchen where the food for seconds refs sat under tin foil. He had brought a Christmassy table covering and laid out paper plates, and on each plate was a party hat, and beside it was a Christmas cracker. When we'd finished, he would have fifteen minutes to clear the table and set it up again before second refs came in. Together with the shabby, tilting, silver tree in the corner of the room by the snooker table, the effect was very cheery. Gary was there too, instead of going for his usual scoff time run.

'Hey, come on you two, you're standing under the mistletoe,' Trevor shouted.

I looked up and saw that Ken had pinned a sprig of mistletoe over the doorway.

'Give her a smacker then, Steve.' Trevor was one of the block who remained convinced that Steve and I were an item.

I turned to Steve and said, 'He's not going to shut up about it if we don't.'

Steve bent down and we pecked. Out of the corner of my eye, I saw Gary laughing.

'Call that a kiss? Speak to me later, you obviously need lessons,' Trevor cried.

'That's all you're going to get,' I said.

'Everyone's here now, so let's eat,' Ken called.

We made a beeline for the table, donned our party hats, and tucked into the food.

'What did you bring?' I asked Steve.

'The cocktail sausages,' he replied through a mouthful of mince pie.

'I bet your mum cooked them,' I said.

'Yes, but I brought them,' he answered. 'Which is yours?'

'The hedgehog. All made by my own fair hand.'

'Cheese and onion, my favourite,' he said. 'I can't be doing with cheese and pineapple, it tastes weird.'

Blue Sky

'Second scoff are getting that,' I said.

'Glad we're first scoff then,' Steve said.

We got forty-five minutes for scoff, so by the time we'd finished eating there was no time for party games. Instead, we all sang along to the Christmas carols on the radio. Just as well there were no bosses in apart from Gary; what we lacked in talent, we made up for in enthusiasm, and noise.

*

After refs, I took my overstuffed stomach back out on patrol and hoped I wouldn't encounter anything too strenuous. The shops were shut so it was unlikely we'd get any shoplifters. The inevitable domestic disputes wouldn't start until later. The pubs shut at two and by the time the landlord or landlady managed to get them out of the pub, and the well-oiled customers made their unsteady way home, we would be going off duty and the late shift would be the ones to attend. I considered calling in on Karen, but then I remembered she had invited a couple of the working girls around for the day. Karen might be police friendly, but I couldn't be certain about the others.

I wandered past the Jackson's house, where all was tranquil, as it should be, and down to the park. To my utter dismay, I saw two men—youths really, judging by the acne—standing together. One passed the other a pound note and the other passed back a small piece of foil. A blatant deal in the park, practically under my nose. Professional pride wouldn't allow me to pretend I hadn't seen it. I hurried towards them, reluctant to run.

The buyer spotted me and alerted the dealer, who ran, damn him. I took off after him, ignoring the buyer. Buyers were everywhere and it was the dealer I wanted. My stomach objected to every step, but I was determined to have him.

'4912 to control urgent,' I radioed. I didn't want to call a scramble, but I needed someone to head him off.

'Go ahead,' Ray ricocheted back.

'Male dealer making off from me in the park, headed to the main gate. White male, jeans, red hair, black duffle coat.'

'I've switched you to Talkthrough, repeat the description,' Ray said.

I did as Ray requested, happy that I was now broadcasting to everyone.

'Mike Three making from Micklestane Hill,' Trevor shouted up.

'Mike Two from town,' Phil called up.

My dealer suddenly veered off and ran towards the railings. I could see he was going to go over the rail, where I wouldn't be able to follow easily.

'4912, he's making towards the railings by the "King Streets". I won't be able to follow him.' If anyone wanted to challenge me on that, I would challenge them to go over eight-foot-tall, spike-topped railings with a skirt, a handbag, and an overfull stomach.

Sure enough, over he went. I watched him disappear into Henry Street. If one of the others didn't get him, I would get him some other time when he wasn't expecting it. He was distinctive enough with that red hair.

'Sighting, Charles Street,' Trevor shouted. 'He's making off towards James Street.'

There was a lot of indistinct noise and I began to see why our chief preferred one voice on the radio, it was all a bit confusing.

'Got him! One male detained, James Street,' Trevor shouted.

'Thirty seconds,' Phil called up to let Trevor know he was backing up. 'What's the charge?'

'Supplying drugs. I saw him deal in the park,' I replied as I trotted to the park gate.

A few seconds later, Trevor shouted, 'Control, please inform the bridewell that one is coming in for supplying drugs. Steve is travelling with me.'

'Roger that,' Ray replied. 'Turning off Talkthrough.'

Phil must have picked Steve up as he came in from town. The

arrest belonged to Trevor and I would be a witness. I would still have to do a statement, but that could wait a while. I felt a bit sick after running on a full stomach. I needed to find somewhere quiet to go to wait for the nausea to pass. I saw Phil slowly drive past the park, evidently looking out for me. Good man, he was saving me a walk. I waved at him and pointed towards the gate.

'Did he put up a fight?' I asked when I reached Phil's Panda.

'No, he just claimed to know nothing about it, but when we turned out his pockets, he had about a dozen little bags and several wraps and a roll of notes in his waist bag. Hop in, I'll take you back so you can liaise with Trevor and do your statement.'

I got in and Phil drove us back.

Trevor was waiting for us when I arrived at the bridewell.

'His name's Jason Harper. He's saying it's mistaken identity. Will you confirm that I got the right person?' Trevor said. 'It doesn't matter if it isn't, he was carrying enough on him for a charge of supplying drugs, it's just a bonus if he is your man.'

I went to his cell and peered through the hatch. White male, red hair, jeans, acne.

'Yes, that's him. No doubt.' I put the hatch back up. 'He needs to dye his hair if he's going to pull that one. How old is he?'

'Eighteen as of last month,' Trevor replied.

That made life a little easier. As it was Christmas, the courts wouldn't be open for a couple of days unless it was an emergency. As Jason was an adult, we wouldn't have to involve social services unless he proved vulnerable in some way, and he could remain with us if he was refused bail.

The bridewell sergeant phoned Eamon, who had drawn the short straw and was a duty jack for the division, and asked him to come down to interview the prisoner.

While that was going on, Trevor and I dealt with the paperwork. I wrote out my statement and handed it to Trevor.

'You may as well do the rest of it,' Trevor said, pushing the file towards me.

I pushed the file back. 'You're the arresting officer; the file is yours.'

He pushed it towards me again. 'You saw the offence take place.'

'You made the arrest.' I shoved it back.

'You're the sprog,' Trevor countered. 'I need to be back out on patrol.'

'But I'm not green. Stop trying to sound noble, it doesn't suit you. I know you will just go to one of your brew spots and drink tea for the rest of the shift.' I ended the conversation by standing up and walking out, leaving him no choice but to deal with the paperwork.

Steve and Eamon came out of the interview room. Jason was escorted back to his cell. Eamon pretend coughed to let everyone know the prisoner had admitted everything.

'He's low level,' Eamon said.

'Aren't they all,' I said. 'Where does he get his merchandise from?'

'Someone named Fergal Tiernan. Fergie, he called him. He's terrified of him and has asked that we don't tell him how we got his name. Tiernan has several underlings around the town.'

'So are we going to find the other dealers?' I asked.

'We could, but I'd prefer to climb higher up the tree, go for this Fergie and try to find who he gets the drugs from,' Eamon said.

Trevor would be elbow deep in paperwork for a while, so I volunteered to find out what I could about Fergal Tiernan from Irene.

'Do you want the information, or should I pass it to Trevor?' I asked.

'Let me have the information. Trevor's dealing with the prisoner, so leave him to that, we don't want to overwhelm him.' Eamon said making us all chuckle.

I went to Irene's office. Because it was Christmas Day, she wasn't there. The perks of being office-based, unless you're in the control room. I checked everywhere I could think of for Tiernan, even reversing his name and checking the nickname, but came up with nothing. However, when I checked on Jason Harper, I found that he had quite a history. His card started when he was around twelve and was caught riding shotgun in a stolen car. The driver had been fourteen. From there, every few months, he got caught doing something illegal, usually connected to drugs. He eventually spent time in Wetherby Borstal.

When he was released, he went to an address in town. It looked familiar to me, but I couldn't immediately place it. Curiosity piqued, I went to the addresses section of Irene's system and looked it up. Westbourne Road, and there was the birdseed incident I had attended with Phil. Jason Harper must be Joan Fletcher's grandson, the one that had green fingers and helped look after his grandmother's greenhouse.

I went back to Eamon. 'Nothing on Fergal Tiernan, but Jason Harper was a borstal boy. What's more, a little while back, I attended a job where a pensioner had grown cannabis from birdseed,' I added.

Eamon laughed. 'I remember that one. The Godmother.'

'It's Harper's nan. He was released to that address from Borstal.'

'I'll talk to Irene about Tiernan, she might know something. She can do a ring around when she comes back on the 28th,' Eamon said.

Irene had a good relationship with the collators in other divisions, so they wouldn't mind when she phoned them to ask them to check their systems. She did it for them often enough.

'This sort of thing will be so much easier when the records are all on the PNC,' I commented.

'You're not wrong there, m'darlin',' said Eamon. 'But I think there will always be a need for local knowledge.'

Eamon went to the charge office and conferred briefly with the custody sergeant. When he returned, he said, 'We'll offer him bail on condition he resides at his nan's address and stays away from the park. When he goes to court, it's up to them what they do about bail then.'

'Will he be sent down?' I asked.

'Probably,' Eamon said. 'Maybe the magistrates will feel kind seeing as it's his first time in adult court and will suspend it.'

I didn't know how I felt about that. Jason was guilty, no doubt, but he was selling for someone else, and I felt strongly that this Tiernan should also face justice.

Chapter Twenty

Next afternoon, I was patrolling close to the docks when Ray called me on the radio.

'Go ahead,' I responded.

'Report of a female, apparently drunk, causing a disturbance by the supermarket on High Lake Road.'

'Roger. On my way.' It was less than five minutes' walk from where I was. As I approached, I could hear shouting and screaming.

'4912 to control,' I radioed in.

'Go ahead,' Ray responded.

'I'm half a minute away. I can hear screaming and shouting. Is anyone backing up?' I asked.

'Mike Two is making. Mike Three is engaged.'

'Roger. Thanks for that.' I ended my transmission and approached the crowd.

It was Ruthie Pritchard. Everything Karen had told me was true; Ruthie was in a right state. I could smell her unwashed body from where I stood. Greasy hair hung in rats' tails across her pale, spotty face. Dark circles surrounded her eyes and she had lost a front tooth since I had last seen her. Scuffed boots flapped against her bony legs as she kicked and wriggled in the arms of the man restraining her, whilst a woman screamed into her face. I checked out how he was holding her, and I couldn't fault him. No excessive force or inappropriate touching.

'Let her go,' I ordered.

'Best not, love, she'll only go for him again.' Ruthie's captor nodded towards a man a few feet away.

The woman stopped screaming at Ruthie and turned to me. 'About fucking time. I want her arresting,' she shouted.

I held my hands up. 'Right, before I do anything I want to know what happened,' I said.

I was almost deafened by shouting from all sides. I held my hands up again and pointed to the man holding Ruthie who seemed to be the most reasonable one present.

'You first: tell me what happened.'

'I've seen her here before but never so bad as she is now. She's pissed out of her tree, I think. She's been grabbing at passing men, including me.' He nodded towards the loud woman. 'This one took exception when she grabbed her fella.'

I turned to the loud woman, 'Is this true?'

'It certainly is. The dirty mare tried to get his dick. I'm not having that.'

I then turned to the man next to her, who so far had not said a word. 'She tried to grab your penis?'

'Yeah.'

It looked like Ruthie was coming in for indecent assault. Next the all-important question.

'Do you want to make a complaint?' I asked the quiet man.

'Yes, he bloody well does,' shouted the woman.

'Do you?' I asked the quiet man, ignoring his loud companion. I knew the answer before I asked the question. He wouldn't dare not make an official complaint.

'Yes.'

'What happened to you?' I asked the man holding Ruthie.

'Same as him. I was off to the pub when she propositioned me but I told her no. She kept lowering the price and trying to undo my fly. I pushed her away and she latched on to our friend there.'

'Do you want to make a complaint?' I asked.

'The missus might get a bit shirty if she hears I've been manhandling women in the street. I suppose I'd better, seeing as he is too.'

I went over to Ruthie and put my hand on her face, forcing her to look at me.

'Ruthie?'

She stopped flailing and tried to meet my gaze, but her eyes wouldn't keep still long enough.

'Ruthie!' I snapped. 'Are you listening?'

She bobbed her head, so I took that as affirmative.

'You're under arrest on suspicion of indecent assault. You do not have to say anything unless you wish to do so, but anything you do say may be taken down in writing and given in evidence.'

'I don't normally do women, but I'll give you a good price,' Ruthie slurred.

I didn't want to put that reply to the caution into my pocketbook, but it might be evidence of her behaviour if I had to go to court over this. Also, one of the witnesses might mention it so I had no choice. Dammit. I'd have to put it in my statement too. I'd never hear the last of it if one of the lads read that.

A Panda arrived and Phil and Steve got out.

'What have you got?' Phil asked me.

'Indecent assault.'

'It's Ruth Pritchard. Can she give a description?' Steve asked.

'She's the offender,' I replied.

'Who's the victim?' Phil asked.

'The man holding her and that other fellow over there.' I pointed to the quiet man with the loud woman. 'Can you get details for statements later while I 'cuff her and get her into the car, please, Steve?'

Steve went to speak to the quiet man and the loud woman while Phil and I went over to take custody of Ruthie. I got the handcuffs on her and the man let go.

'Please make sure you give your name to the officer over there before you go. I'll need to get a statement later on,' I said to him.

Ruthie looked over at Steve. 'I can do special rates for policemen,' she shouted.

'No thanks, Ruth,' Steve replied, deadpan.

Phil and I got Ruthie into his Panda and I sat in the rear with her. Steve, armed with contact details for the two men, got into the front.

'Do you think she should go to the hospital?' I asked Phil.

'Nah, she'll come out of it. Then she'll want her next hit. If it gets too bad you can ask the police surgeon to attend the bridewell. Back to the office?' Phil asked.

'And don't spare the horses,' I replied, the smell from Ruthie was starting to make me feel nauseous.

By the time we reached the bridewell, Ruthie had woken up a bit. She answered questions put to her by the custody sergeant and allowed me to take her to the female cells without too much of a fuss.

DS Mike Finlay came down to see our prisoner. 'She looks rough.' He closed the little viewing hatch in the cell door. 'I take it she's still doing heroin?'

'Yes. It seems she's not coping since her mum went to prison and has gone out of control,' I replied.

'I'll need a female in when I interview her. Are you free?'

'The control room know I have a prisoner; they won't expect me to respond to anything for a while.'

'May as well do it now, she seems awake enough.' Mike went and sat in the interview room while the bridewell officer and I brought Ruthie from her cell.

She sat on the hard plastic chair and looked around the dismal surroundings. Finally, she looked at Mike and smiled a gappy, simpering smile at him.

Mike reminded her that she was still under caution, for all the notice she took, then said, 'Ruthie, I need to ask you some questions about what happened today.'

She sat up straight and put her hands in her lap, which made her bony shoulders look even skinnier.

'Do you want to tell me what happened?' Mike asked.

'Giz a bifta first,' Ruthie said.

'I don't smoke,' Mike said, correctly translating her request for a cigarette.

'Neither do I,' I said.

Ruthie looked at us as if we'd spat in her eye. I clocked the shaking hands and the knee jiggling up and down. She was going to need another hit before long and perhaps giving her a cigarette would delay that moment.

I went out and explained our problem to the bridewell sergeant, and he kindly gave Ruthie one of his cigarettes and allowed her to use his lighter.

She drew deeply on her cigarette and with evident pleasure, blew the smoke towards the ceiling.

'Right, what did you want to ask me?'

'Why did you go to the supermarket today, Ruth?' Mike asked.

Ruth thought for a moment. 'I had no money, so I thought lots of people will be at the supermarket, so I went there. Dunno why I bothered, it was shut. Hardly anyone was around. Everyone's skint anyway.'

I couldn't disagree with her, that's why more astute beggars homed in on the main shopping centre in the town.

'Do you remember what you did?' Mike asked.

Ruth screwed up her eyes as smoke drifted across her face. 'I started off asking for money, but people just walked past. I thought that if I showed them I wasn't just begging they'd give me money. Anyway, I didn't have anything to sell, so I decided I could offer my services. I tried stopping one man and told him I'd blow him, but I don't think he understood. I tried to undo his trousers, so he'd understand that I didn't expect money for nothing, but he pushed me away.'

'You were in a public place,' Mike said.

'Yeah, perhaps I should have told him to go somewhere private.'

Mike shook his head. 'I don't think you understand what I meant.'

'Do you remember what happened next?' I asked.

'I nearly fell over when he pushed me, but then I saw another man and told him I'd blow him instead. I went to open his trousers, but a woman started shouting at me. The first man grabbed me. I thought he'd changed his mind.'

Ruthie just didn't seem to get how inappropriate her behaviour had been. In her mind, she was offering a service for payment. She was a walking deterrent for drug taking.

'You have just admitted to a crime,' Mike said.

Ruthie adopted an indignant expression. 'I did not! I wasn't asking for money for nothing, I was offering a service.'

I tapped the table to draw Ruthie's attention. 'Do you understand what DS Finlay is saying? It's not about the money, it's the fact that you touched those men's private parts without their permission. You have admitted you tried to undo their trousers in the street.'

'How else was I going to blow them?' Ruthie asked. She just wasn't getting it.

'Imagine if they had tried to take your knickers off. They'd be arrested,' I said.

'Not if they paid for it,' Ruthie said, completely missing the point.

Mike made a coughing sound as he swallowed his laugh. When he was able to speak, he said, 'What you did was indecent assault. Constable Barrie arrested you on suspicion of indecent assault, not for asking for money or anything else.'

Ruth looked from Mike to me, I could almost see the pink birdies flying around her uncomprehending head. She crushed her cigarette end in the ashtray.

I turned to Mike. 'I don't think she understands.'

Ruthie's knee jiggling started to make the table shake. She was definitely going to need another hit soon, which made me think of something else.

'Ruthie, where do you get heroin from?' I asked.

'Jase. It used to be Kev.'

'Jase who and Kev who?' Mike asked.

Ruthie shrugged. 'Kev's gone now.'

'Is that why you needed money, to get more heroin?'

Ruthie nodded. 'And to get a bite to eat.'

'When did you last eat?' I asked.

Ruthie shrugged again.

'Has all your money gone on heroin?' I asked.

'It's good stuff,' she mumbled.

'Okay Ruthie, I think that'll do for now. I'll get someone to take you back to the cell,' Mike said.

In the corridor, I said to Mike, 'This new supplier, Jase, is a new name. Want me to pass it to Irene?' I asked.

'Wouldn't do any harm,' Mike said.

'Have you seen how fidgety she is? She's getting ready for her next hit,' I said. I wished I had insisted that Phil had taken her to the hospital first.

'Yeah. Let's get her checked out at hospital, I don't want to get her formally charged until I know she fully understands what's happening, but you were right to bring her in for indecent assault.'

'She doesn't seem to understand the seriousness,' I agreed.

'That's heroin for you.' Mike said. 'You'll have to go with her. I'll take Eamon and get statements from the victims, but first I'll round up a car for you.'

'I'll go and get her something to eat meantime.'

Ruthie wasn't going to have an anaesthetic so I figured a bite to eat wouldn't matter. A local café supplied us with prisoners' meals, so I thought I'd see if anything remained. I went to find the bridewell sergeant.

Lunch had been sandwiches and I was able to get a plateful of slightly stale but still edible leftover ham and cheese sandwiches for Ruthie.

She wolfed them down and glugged water from the plastic cup I brought with it.

'Better?' I asked when she'd finished.

She nodded and burped.

'Right, we're going to get you checked out at the hospital.'

'An ambulance?' Ruth asked.

I shook my head. 'We'll drive you there and bring you back afterwards.'

'Will I have to go to court? Will you be giving evidence?' she asked.

Ah, she finally seemed to understand that she was in trouble. 'Yes,' I confirmed. 'I'll have to tell them what I saw and what the men told me.' Ruthie remained silent as I acknowledged a transmission on my radio that the car was ready for us in the yard.

'What if I plead not guilty? What if you can't give evidence?' Ruthie asked.

'If you plead not guilty, it will go to trial and everyone will have to give evidence. I can't think why I couldn't give evidence. Come on, let's get you to hospital.' I led Ruthie out of the bridewell.

The door to the bridewell was on the junction of two corridors opposite the control room. One corridor went straight on and would lead to the yard, past the sergeants' office and on to the parade room. The other went to the right that would lead past the control room door, to the front door and to the stairs. Ruthie and I stepped out of the bridewell and Ruthie turned right.

I took her elbow and pointed to the corridor in front of us that led to the yard door. 'It's this way.'

She wrenched her elbow away and snarled, 'Don't touch me.'

She was beginning to feel withdrawal, which was making her cranky. I didn't take offence.

'You were going the wrong way.'

Without warning, she threw herself onto the ground and screamed. 'You've broken my arm!'

'Oh, get up, Ruthie,' I said. 'I did no such thing.'

I spotted Ray peering out from the gap between the maps that were stuck onto the glass partition of the control room. Only his eyes were visible. He came out of the control room.

'What's going on?'

Ruth pointed at me. 'She hit me. She twisted my arm right up my back, then she hit me and kicked me.'

'I didn't!' I cried.

Gary and Alan arrived.

'What happened?' Gary asked looking between me, Ray and Ruth.

'She twisted my arm and bashed me into the floor, then she hit and kicked me,' Ruthie said in a little wavery voice. I caught the malicious side-eye she gave me.

'I witnessed the incident and I can confirm that Constable Barrie did nothing more than take her elbow to guide her in the right direction,' Ray said.

'You weren't there,' Ruthie argued.

Ray pointed to the control room. 'I was in that office, not ten feet away. I could see you clearly.'

'If I begin an investigation and find it's a false allegation. I will have you charged with wasting police time as well as any other charges you face,' Gary said. 'I will also support Constable Barrie if she wishes to take out a civil action against you for defamation of character.'

'Police can't do me for a deformed character,' Ruthie cried.

She seemed more upset about that than the charge of indecent assault.

'Just because we normally don't doesn't mean that as individuals we can't,' Ray said.

Ruthie gulped. 'Maybe I was mistaken. I think I might have tripped.'

'So Constable Barrie didn't assault you?' Gary asked.

'I thought she had, but now I think she was trying to help me up and I misunderstood.'

A thought came to me. 'Did you think that if I were to be suspended, I couldn't give evidence against you?' I asked Ruthie.

She refused to meet my eyes.

'You thought that if I was out of the way, the case would be dropped?' I laughed. 'Even if I couldn't give evidence, which is unlikely, the complainants and the witness could. Besides, you admitted the offence in the interview with DS Finlay.'

'Did I?' Ruthie seemed genuinely surprised.

'Yes, you did. Do you want to make a statement rescinding that?'

She paused for a moment before shaking her head.

*

At the hospital, Ruthie was given something to help her deal with the immediate effects of withdrawal and declared as fit as a malnourished heroin addict was ever likely to be. She returned to our custody in a better frame of mind, and indignant that the doctor had called her an addict to her face. I just let her rant; I wasn't going to wear myself out arguing with someone who was so deluded she refused to accept that she was indeed an addict. As soon as I was free, I would do that referral to drugs services, but I suspected that Ruthie was too far gone for any sort of intervention.

Chapter Twenty-One

Life returned to normal, or as normal as one could expect in that limbo week between Christmas and New Year when everybody is full of mince pies and turkey. Everyone complained about their waistbands getting tighter and moaning about the dieting that was to come.

On the last day of earlies, Alan brought the mood down by announcing his retirement in March, pre-empting Gary's announcement.

'I didn't think he'd actually go,' Steve whispered to me.

'Me neither,' I whispered back. 'But I don't think he has a choice any longer.'

'Has your replacement been arranged yet, Alan?' Trevor asked.

'Not yet,' Alan said. 'I'm sure the boss will be doing very thorough checks.'

'I actually have an announcement of my own,' Gary said. 'I'm leaving too; my last shift will be at the end of February. But don't worry, I'll make sure Alan's successor is arranged before I go.'

'May we ask where to, sir?' Trevor said, voicing the thoughts of everyone except me and Steve.

'I'm taking an overseas posting to Hong Kong.'

The room filled with the buzz of voices.

'Is that part of the corruption investigation I've been reading about, sir?' Trevor asked.

'It's connected to that,' Gary said.

'Who will replace you,' Trevor asked.

'I don't know. I have no say in that,' Gary answered.

Phil stood up. 'On behalf of all B Block, I'd like to say that you two have been the best leaders the block has ever had. We wish you all the best. You'll both be missed.'

Everyone clapped and a few added a 'hear hear'. Gary's cheeks reddened while Alan came over all business-like. I could tell he was pleased but he was chary of sentimentality and public expressions of affection.

'Thank you all. Enough of this now. Let's get on. Sam, DS Finlay wants to see you before you go out.'

'Roger,' I replied automatically.

Then Alan moved on to the duties and everything was normal again.

*

After I had got my radio and done my test call, I went upstairs to the CID office. Irene, Mike, Eamon and DI Webb were all there. DI Corlett was sitting at a desk.

'Hello again, Samantha.' He grinned at me.

'Hello, Daddy,' I replied, which caused a couple of heads to swivel our way. 'I didn't expect to see you back until after New Year.'

'I've been hearing interesting things, so I thought I'd drop in for a couple of days. I'll be home again for New Year then back here in January.'

'Let's go into my office and talk,' DI Webb said.

DI Corlett, DS Finlay, Eamon, Irene and I squeezed into DI Webb's office. Irene took the visitor seat and DI Corlett perched on DI Webb's desk. The rest of us stood against the rear wall.

'It's time to advance with Operation Blue Sky. I'll let DI Corlett bring you all up to speed,' DI Webb said and sat behind his desk.

'John Poulter is indeed one of the contacts in Hornthorpe,' DI Corlett said. 'The current belief is that the drugs are getting in in barrels. Therefore, Samantha and Eamon, I need you to go into the club once more and glean what you can. If possible, have a mooch around the hangars. Samantha, you are going to have to go for another lesson.' He paused and grinned at my dismayed face. 'However, it'll just be a front, you need not actually take off. We haven't set a date yet; we need to know we have covered all lines of enquiry first.'

I sagged with relief. 'Roger that, sir.

'I think Norman and I need to have a chat and decide a timeline for the rest of this.' DI Corlett stood up. 'Thank you gentlemen, and ladies.'

DI Webb also stood up. 'Sam, I'll let Inspector Tyrrell know we need to borrow you again and let you know when.'

'Thanks, sir.' Irene and I went back downstairs to let the men talk.

*

The following evening, Eamon and I were in the Hornthorpe airfield club. I was quite happy because I was on overtime. I was supposed to be rest day, but DI Webb had insisted that it had to be me that accompanied Eamon, seeing as I had been there before.

'Merry Christmas,' I said to Barbara. 'Did you have a good one?'

'Merry Christmas. It was quiet. I spent a couple of hours at the hospital.'

'How is your son?' I asked.

'No change,' she said. 'I don't think he's coming out anytime soon. One good thing, they think that they've found the bastard that got him. He's probably going to be charged soon. It's a shame hanging's been abolished.'

Another customer came to the bar and Barbara went to serve him.

'Jackson?' I whispered to Eamon.

'Mike's looking to charge Leonard Jackson with attempted

murder,' Eamon whispered back.

'I thought the enquiries were ongoing?'

'They are,' Eamon said. 'However, Mike thinks that Jackson had the motive and is keen to go with that.'

'Isn't that a bit dangerous? I mean, it might not be him and we might convict an innocent man. Or, if it is him, he might take it to trial. If he's found not guilty because our evidence is circumstantial, then he'd have got away with it,' I said.

'He owns the car,' Eamon said.

'He reported it stolen hours before the accident happened,' I argued.

Eamon took a mouthful of beer. 'I know you're playing devil's advocate, Sam. Personally, I would prefer to see Jackson charged with section eighteen, GBH. We can prove the intent by the fact the car had no lights on and mounted the pavement.'

'Even so, you might be charging an innocent man. I think it's too shaky yet, you need more.'

Eamon took another gulp of beer. 'Aye, you might be right. It's got to get past Webby first.'

That was one of the many things I liked about Eamon: he listened to me despite my lack of service. He might not agree, but he didn't dismiss me as a silly little girl like some, most, of the other detectives.

Barbara's customer came back to the bar. 'Hey, Barb, this isn't Stella Artois.' He pushed his glass towards her.

'Of course it is, you watched me pull it,' she said.

'I'm telling you that's not Stella.'

Barbara sighed, poured the drink away, got a fresh glass and pulled another pint. The customer watched closely.

Barbara put it in front of him. 'There, that's definitely Stella.'

The customer took a mouthful and pulled a face. 'No it isn't.'

Barbara looked nonplussed for a moment, then annoyed. 'Sorry, I asked the drayman to help me replace the Stella when I was busy this morning. He must have attached the wrong barrel. Will you have something else?'

The customer accepted a glass of cider on the house and went off. Barbara saw us watching and came over.

'The Stella is off in case you were thinking of having one,' she said.

'I'm driving so I'll stick to coke,' I said.

'I prefer bitter,' Eamon said.

'No problem,' Barbara said. 'As soon as Johnny or Pete come in, I'll get them to change the keg over. I'll kill Fergal when I see him.'

I recognised the look that crossed Eamon's face. He had just heard something of interest to him. He chuckled, but it lacked the honeyed quality I was used to. He was in detective mode.

'Is he due soon?' he asked. 'Perhaps I should warn the local constabulary there's likely to be a murder.'

Barbara laughed back. Hers sounded natural. 'It's what the daft bugger deserves for embarrassing me like this. Not to worry though; I've got until tomorrow to cool down, so I think he'll be safe.'

We all laughed, just three people enjoying a joke.

'They do deliveries on the 31st?' I asked. 'I thought everyone stopped work then.'

'It's one of our busiest nights,' Barbara said. 'The last thing I need is to run out of booze before midnight, so I order a lot extra.' Barbara glanced over as another customer came to the bar. 'The Stella is off,' she called and went over to serve him.

Eamon stared at me. 'Is this place ever lucky or what?'

I stared back. 'What do you mean?'

He leant forward and whispered. 'We think the drugs are getting here in barrels, with or without Barbara's knowledge. Your prisoner, Harper, told us he got his merchandise from Fergal, aka Fergie. It's not a common name around here. Fergal the drayman. Drugs in barrels. Fergal the supplier. We need to find out who Fergal the inept drayman is, and if his surname's Tiernan, he's connected to here and to your lad Harper. I can't imagine that he isn't delivering to other places too.'

'We can't ask Barbara for Fergal's surname. If she's in on it, she'll guess we're on to them and tell them,' I whispered.

'We don't ask her; we find out which brewery he works for.' Eamon finished his drink. 'Back in a tick. Mine's a bitter.' Eamon stood up and walked past the bar towards the gents' toilets.

I ordered more drinks and read the drink mats for clues, but they didn't help. Pete Flinders came in. He waved at me and I waved back. Barbara buttonholed him before he came over.

'The Stella Artois needs to be changed. I got Fergal to do it this morning when I was busy, but he's got the wrong barrel on.'

'Don't worry, I'll sort it,' Pete said.

Barbara moved closer to Pete, but with a spot of lip reading, I could still just make out what she was saying.

'He's a dodgy bugger at the best of times. I don't trust him. If he's tried to fob us off with some cheap imitation just to line his own pockets, I'm going to report him and the brewery to trading standards.'

'Calm down, Barb.' Pete said loudly enough for me to hear. 'You know Green Square wouldn't tolerate something like that, he'd be out on his ear. It's probably been an honest mistake but if I see he has given us a rip-off version, we'll ring the brewery and let them deal with him.'

Barbara wasn't impressed and let it show.

Eamon came back and I watched him scanning the pumps that lined one side of the bar. Finally he sat back down.

'I was hoping that I would be able to see a brewery logo as I passed, but there's nothing.'

'Green Square,' I said. 'That is a brewery, isn't it?'

'It is. Where did you see that?' Eamon asked.

'I overheard Barbara complaining to Pete about the Stella and he mentioned it.'

Eamon took a mouthful of his drink. 'Tomorrow morning, I'll give them a ring and see if this Fergal is an employee.'

'Hello again, what are you doing here?' said a voice beside me. I turned and saw Minchie sitting on the barstool beside me, and next to him sat a man I didn't know.

I hadn't expected to see him here again, so I was a bit flummoxed and unprepared. 'Hello, Tom.'

He looked past me to Eamon. 'And this is Eamon, over from the emerald isle.'

'Hello again, Tom,' Eamon said, his accent unusually heavy. If he said a single "begorrah", I was leaving.

'Hello, lad.' Tom tapped his own forehead. 'I've got a memory like an elephant.' He lowered his voice. 'It isn't always a blessing.' Tom watched Barbara dealing with a customer then disappear across the room to collect glasses. He leant towards me and whispered. 'You know, I think she rang the police on me last time we met. I was stopped and breathalysed.'

I didn't bother asking whether it had been positive, I just hoped he hadn't driven his car to the club again. Eamon concentrated on his drink.

'Perhaps she was angry with you for telling us about her past,' I said.

Tom snorted. 'I was only speaking the truth. She was a harlot.'

'Hey! Lay off, Tom. Barbara wasn't a bad lass, there were a few much worse than her. She was unlucky,' said the man next to him.

Tom turned to the man. 'You would say that though, you had a little fling with her didn't you, Wally?'

Wally thinned his lips. 'Briefly.'

'Exactly. You, Summerskill, and how many more?'

Wally flushed. 'There were no more and we weren't lovers. Perhaps we should start counting your dalliances.'

'It's different for men,' Tom said.

The sad thing was, he was right. A man could sleep with dozens of women, but a girl like Barbara, who maybe didn't sleep around but got caught, was labelled a harlot for life. By Tom's double standards, I was a harlot! I shook my head and listened to the two men arguing.

'Women are the gatekeepers. If the gates are open, men will

enter,' Tom said.

'You're an idiot. Just stop shit stirring and shut up,' Wally snapped.

Tom finished his drink in a couple of huge mouthfuls and looked over to the doorway. 'Is that who I think it is? Excuse me, will you?'

'It's been nice chatting,' I said to Tom's retreating back.

'He's a terrible gossip at the best of times, ten times worse when he's had a drink, which is most of the time.' Wally held out a hand. 'Walter Gower.'

'Samantha Barrie and this is my cousin, Eamon Kildea.'

They shook hands.

'Do you know Barbara?' Walter asked.

'I've only met her a couple of times. She seems nice,' I replied.

'She is nice, and bright. Intelligent, you know? Despite what Tom mouth-almighty says, she wasn't a tart. She used to pack the parachutes. I remember she once told me that if she had been born male she would have liked to have been a para.' Walter chuckled. 'Once, I let her try on a 'chute. She got into a bit of tangle trying to get her legs into the harness and gave me an accidental glimpse of her suspenders as I tried to help.' He laughed again at the memory.

'Were you the one in charge of the parachutes?' I asked.

'Not in charge, but I was one of the ones who supervised the folding and packing of the canopies.'

'I thought the jumpers did that themselves,' I said. I didn't entirely trust Minchie's information on that point.

'No, it was the WAAFs. It's a specialised role and it was one of my jobs to train them. That's how I met Barbara. Then James Summerskill came along and that was that.'

'Bad luck,' I said.

'I suppose. To be honest, she was less keen on me than I was on her so we wouldn't have lasted long in any case.'

'Tom told me he had been there when that parachutist was killed. Were you there too?' I asked.

Walter nodded. 'I wasn't a jumper, but I remember that day well and not just because Summerskill died. A photographer was prowling around the base taking publicity photos. I had eaten a dodgy sausage or something and I was really sick, but I had to act normally when he was in the store and smile for a photograph. I had to go to see the MO in the end. One of the men, Jacko, covered for me while I went.'

'What's an MO?' I guessed MO had a different meaning here than in the police.

'Medical Officer,' Walter replied. 'Jacko wasn't really supposed to be left because he wasn't trained, but I had no choice. It was that or puke over the floor. It wasn't for long and because there was a jump already on, he didn't have to do anything other than answer the phone and tell visitors to come back later. A proper relief took over within the hour.'

Walter took a mouthful of his drink and Barbara came back to the bar. I quite liked Barbara, and I didn't think it was fair the way men like Tom had judged her and continued to judge her. However, there was something niggling at my mind from my conversations with Tom and Walter. I couldn't put my finger on it, so I concentrated on our task in hand: information for Operation Blue Sky.

'Shall we go and have a mooch around the hangars?' I whispered to Eamon.

Eamon drained his pint. 'Aye, I don't think there's anything more to be had here.'

We left the bar and stepped into the cold night. I shivered and pulled my coat tightly around me.

'You'll soon warm up if we run,' Eamon said.

We were just about to go over to the hangars, when we spotted Pete Flinders pulling his empty trolley back to the club. He saw us and nodded.

'Evening,' he said as he drew closer.

'Evening,' we replied in unison.

'It's getting cold again. I reckon it might snow,' Pete said.

'You might be right,' Eamon said.

'Reschedule your lesson if it does snow, Samantha. You don't have the experience,' Pete said.

'Okay,' I said trying to sound disappointed.

Pete continued on his way.

'That was lucky: a minute later and we'd have run right into him. He's not trying to hide himself, perhaps we've got it wrong and there is a legitimate reason for storing some barrels separately,' I said.

'Sam, m'darlin' one of the first things you will be taught about undercover work is to look as if you belong wherever you are and have every right to be doing whatever you're doing.'

It seemed to me that I was doing all right without ever having had undercover training, but I could see that Eamon meant well.

'Hide in plain sight,' I commented.

'That's right. It's creeping around that draws people's attention,' Eamon said. 'But sometimes discretion is the better part of valour.'

With that in mind, we scurried across to the fence and kept to the shadows as we hurried to the hangars.

Chapter Twenty-Two

A figure creeping along the side of the far hangar towards a window caught our attention. Eamon was right: furtive behaviour was very noticeable. The figure glanced about, then started trying to force the window open. The cloud briefly cleared, and in the moonlight I recognised Jason Harper.

'What do we do?' I whispered to Eamon. 'We can't ignore this, but he'll recognise me from Christmas Day. Pete's the club secretary and he'll have to be informed and he will realise who we are. He might tell Barbara or Johnny.' We were so close to concluding Blue Sky that I didn't want to risk jeopardising things.

Eamon had it in hand. He radioed in and explained the situation and asked for the response car to come in silently via the emergency vehicles entrance at the rear of the airfield.

While we were waiting for the response car, we tiptoed over to the window and watched Jason move around the hangar. He pocketed a couple of spanners and what appeared to be a chisel. Then he went to the barrels stored against the back wall. He carefully examined one then, unexpectedly to me, tried to pull the top off. I could hear him grunting with effort. Then he used the chisel to try to pry the top off.

'What's he doing?'

I was thinking aloud more than asking the question, but Eamon answered, 'Trying to open that barrel, but I've never seen a barrel opened like that.'

After a few minutes, a Panda arrived.

'Here's the uniforms,' Eamon whispered.

A driver and a foot patrol came over. These were from another block and I only knew them by sight. Half a minute later, Webby and Mike Finlay arrived too.

'What's happening?' Webby whispered to Eamon.

'Jason Harper is in there. He broke in and took some tools. He is paying a lot of attention to a barrel,' Eamon answered.

'Maybe he's thirsty?' the Panda driver joked.

'Shush!' Webby demanded.

'Isn't he still on bail still over the Christmas Day drug arrest,' I asked.

'Well, if he is, that just aggravates things.' DI Webb turned to the two uniforms. 'You two go to the front and make a lot of noise at the door. Mike and I will wait here. Odds are he'll come out this way. Eamon, Sam, bugger off. This call has been logged as anonymous. You won't be needed for court.'

'Thanks, boss,' Eamon said. We slipped off to the emergency services gate. We could walk down the access road and re-enter the car park from the street.

Once on the service road, we looked back. The uniformed policemen shouted and banged on the door demanding it be opened. Jason's head popped out of the window and Mike and Webby grabbed him and pulled him out and deposited him on the grass. In the distance, I spotted Johnny and Pete running towards the hangar. Time to make ourselves scarce.

The river was dark apart from navigational aids, not like the jewel-speckled water by the docks.

'We're not far from where Lynch was found.' He jerked his thumb over his shoulder. 'Far side of those woods near the picnic area.'

I looked back towards the woods at the end of the service road. 'What happened over that?'

'It's still being treated as suspicious,' Eamon said.

'So it could be murder?' I asked.

Eamon waggled his hand to tell me it could go either way. 'There's several odd things that indicate that it could be.'

'Odd things like what?' I asked.

'You know that I can't tell you everything, but the pathologist has committed to paper that it was unlikely that Lynch could have injected himself where they found the puncture mark. The angle was all wrong.'

'Somebody else had to have been with him,' I said.

'Somebody else must have injected him and caused his overdose,' Eamon agreed. 'Because it's unlikely to be suicide.'

'I think you've just talked yourself into accepting it's at least manslaughter,' I said.

Eamon sighed. 'I think I have, m'darlin'.'

*

We took our time driving back to Wyre Hall, then Eamon and I went straight to the CID office. DI Corlett was waiting there and came over to us.

'Norman's downstairs interviewing that burglar that was brought in. What happened?' he asked.

'We were on our way to check out the hangars when we spotted him breaking in. We didn't want to break cover, so I radioed it in,' Eamon said.

'Good thinking,' DI Corlett said.

Eamon continued. 'He's a lad named Jason Harper. He's got a long record and he was arrested on Christmas Day for dealing. Long story short, he's an underling for a man named Fergal Tiernan, aka Fergie. When we were in the club, the manageress commented that the drayman from Green Square brewery had assisted her with changing a barrel but had got it wrong. His name is Fergal. It could be a coincidence, but it's an unusual name around here. We think it's worth checking so tomorrow I'll make a few phone calls and try to find out if Fergal is an employee with Green Square brewery.'

'If he is an employee, we know he'll be making deliveries in the morning of the 31st,' I added so I didn't feel left out.

DI Corlett nodded. 'It would be really good if we could get an address when you make your calls, Eamon.'

'I'll see what I can do,' Eamon said.

Webby came back into the office. 'He will go guilty for the burglary.'

'What about the barrel?' I asked.

'We're letting that go for now,' DI Webb said.

I was astounded. 'But we think that's how the drugs are getting in!' I tapped Eamon's arm. 'That's what he must have been going after. Somehow he knew the drugs were transported in barrels and he was trying to get at them.'

'And that's why we're not going for that yet.' DI Webb said. 'We'll charge Harper as if he broke in to steal the tools. With a bit of luck, the supplier and the club staff won't realise that we're on to the kegs.'

It looked like DI Webb was trying to get higher up this particular tree. I had learned that no matter how high up we went, there was always someone higher, everyone answered to someone. I speculated that one day we would finally get to the very top and find that all the crime in the world was run by one incredibly rich person.

'Eamon has a name,' DI Corlett said.

I thought it was nice of him to give Eamon the credit, a lot of bosses would just claim the information without acknowledging where it came from. It would have been even nicer if he had included me.

'Green Square brewery and Fergal Tiernan,' Eamon said. 'Sam heard the manageress talking about it. I'm going to follow that up tomorrow.'

Bless him. Eamon would be a good boss. I wondered if he had taken his promotion exams. Probably he had.

'Right, you do that and maybe we can get this boxed off by the end of January.'

*

Next day, I was walking out to my beat. The most direct route took me through the main shopping street, but I couldn't be bothered with the street pedlars and entertainers whom I would be expected to check for proper licences. Steve was covering that area, so I decided to leave him to see to them. I walked up the quieter road that ran between the shops and the car park.

I had almost reached the end when suddenly I heard a shout and a woman's scream coming from close by. I ran to the corner; there, I saw a man trying to pull a handbag from Joan Fletcher, who clung on with admirable tenacity. Shouting a scramble, I raced towards her and could see a couple of other people running from other directions.

The man had his back to me so didn't see me. He punched Joan full in the face. She released the bag and fell to the ground. He turned to run, just as I leapt at him and brought us both to the ground. We grappled for a few seconds and he managed to grab a handful of my hair. I screeched in pain as he pulled hard. I could feel hair ripping from my scalp, but I kept my hold on him. Meanwhile, a woman picked up Joan's handbag and handed it to her then sat with her, helping her to staunch the blood running from her nose. A man joined me in restraining the offender. I shouted the caution at my prisoner and told him he was under arrest for robbery. He made no meaningful reply, he was too busy trying to get away.

An elderly woman I hadn't seen previously set about my prisoner with a large, black umbrella.

'You're scum! Attacking women! Attacking police! How dare you!' she interspersed each sentence with a resounding wallop with the umbrella.

'Gerroff you mad old bat.' The prisoner let go of my hair and wrapped his arms around his head to protect himself from the blows.

A man appeared beside me and peered down at the offender. 'So you like robbing old women? Let's see how you like this.' He kicked the prone offender hard in the ribs.

Strictly speaking, I should have arrested the other man for assault, but I was one copper and couldn't do everything all at once. I had some sympathy with his sentiments but enough was enough. I'd probably get the blame for my prisoner's injuries and I could do without hours of writing following a complaint.

'Please don't do that,' I said to the young man as calmly as I could, given that the offender had started bucking to free himself and get at the man who had kicked him. He screamed threats and obscenities, but the man just laughed at him.

'Go screw yourself, loser,' he said and sauntered off. I was in no position to stop him.I heard the sirens approaching and Phil and Trevor drew up. They came over and each took an arm of the offender and hauled him to his feet. Phil handcuffed his hands behind his back, they pushed him into Trevor's Panda and shut the door. I cancelled the scramble but not in time to stop Steve sprinting around the corner from the shopping street.

'Are you okay, Sam?' he panted.

'You missed the fun,' Trevor said. 'You can gather witness details then ride back with the prisoner.'

'What's the story?' Trevor asked when the prisoner was secure.

'I heard screaming and saw him trying to take that lady's bag.' I pointed at Joan. 'He punched her; she fell. I stopped him before he got away.' I pointed out the man who'd helped me. 'He helped me. I've cautioned the offender and told him he was under arrest for robbery. We need an ambulance for that lady.'

'Don't forget, he hurt you too,' said the man who had helped me restrain the prisoner.

'What happened?' Phil asked.

'He just pulled my hair,' I said, trying to ignore my smarting scalp.

'He gave her a damned good woolling,' the man said.

Phil examined my scalp. 'It's bleeding. We can add assault police to the charges.'

I went over to Joan. She would have two black eyes and a very swollen nose tomorrow.

'Hello, Joan. Remember me?' I asked.

She peered at me. 'Oh, you came to look at my greenhouse.'

'That's right. An ambulance is on the way. Is there anyone I can contact for you?'

'There's only Jason, but he's out. I think he went to his allotment,' Joan replied.

I patted her hand then went back to Phil and Trevor.

'I think I should go to the hospital with her.'

Trevor peered past me to Joan. 'Poor woman. Maybe that's best. We'll lodge the prisoner for you to deal with once you've finished at the hospital.

The ambulance arrived and saw to Joan.

'Get the ambos to give you some antiseptic for your head,' Phil advised.

I nodded and climbed into the back of the ambulance for the ride to hospital.

Chapter Twenty-Three

At the hospital, Joan was treated very kindly by the staff, who were appalled at what had happened to her. Her nose was broken, and her eyes were swollen The bruising already looked bad but would be spectacular tomorrow. The doctor told me not to try to get a statement from Joan that night. I wouldn't have tried anyway once she'd been given painkillers. A defence team would use that to suggest that the drugs caused the victim to be confused, and therefore their evidence was not to be trusted.

'I'll ring and see if Jason is back,' I told Joan. She gave me her phone number and I went to the public phones in the waiting area and rang Jason. After about half a dozen rings he answered.

'Is that Jason?' I asked.

'Who's this?' Jason asked.

'It's Constable Barrie—'

'Why are you ringing here? My nan might have answered.' Jason cut across me.

'Calm down, Jason,' I said. 'I'm with your nan at the General Hospital. She's been robbed and she wants to see you.'

I heard Jason's breath catch. 'How is she?'

'She's going to be okay, but she's got a broken nose and a lot of bruising,' I replied. 'Can you get here?' The quicker he was at the hospital, the quicker I could get back to Wyre Hall and deal with my prisoner.

'I'll be there soon.' Jason ended the call.

I returned to Joan. 'Jason is on his way.'

Joan smiled. 'He's a good lad.' She sighed. 'He's made some stupid decisions but that's hardly surprising. My daughter wasn't the best of mothers. A child needs love and some boundaries.'

I smiled at her. Jason was now an adult, but to his nan he was still a little boy. I didn't doubt that Jason loved his grandmother.

I went back outside and waited for Jason to arrive. I shivered in the cold; even with a thick jumper and overcoat I was still freezing.

Jason cycled through the gates and into the car park. He chained his bike to the rail beside the steps and came to the casualty entrance. He stopped when he saw me.

'Tell me everything,' he demanded.

'A man tried to snatch her bag. He punched her in the face, but he's been arrested.'

Jason nodded. 'Good. He'd better hope I never meet him.'

'I think you're in enough trouble as it is. You don't want to make it worse,' I said quietly.

Jason scowled at me. 'Can I see her?'

'Of course.' We walked in together and Jason gasped when he saw his grandmother.

'Nan!' A fat tear ran down his cheek.

Joan turned towards us and held out her hand. 'Here's my boy.'

Jason was beside her in a shot and took her hand.

I felt redundant, so I said, 'I'll go now. Someone will speak to you tomorrow, probably.'

Joan dragged her eyes away from Jason. 'Thank you so much, dear.'

'I hope you feel better soon.'

'I expect I'll be home tomorrow,' Joan said.

'Don't count on it,' said a nurse from behind me. She came to Joan's bedside. 'The doctor wants you to be admitted for a couple of days. You'll be moved to the geriatric ward shortly.'

'Oh, not the geriatric ward, it's full of old people,' Joan objected.

I chuckled. Some of them would be younger than her.

'Look after your nan, Jason,' I said and went to phone for a lift back to the station.

*

When I got back to Wyre Hall, we charged my prisoner with Robbery and Assault on a Police Officer. He was denied police bail.

'You didn't tell me you'd been assaulted too,' Gary complained when he came down to the bridewell to do the prisoner checks.

'He yanked my hair. Phil said it was bleeding.'

'You know you might end up with a bald patch if he's damaged the follicles.'

'You'll still want to marry me, won't you?' I asked.

Gary rubbed his chin. 'In sickness and in health is one thing, but I don't know about with hair or without.'

I slapped his arm. 'You'd better hope you don't go bald then.'

We both laughed. Gary would be gorgeous even without hair.

*

'There's someone here to see you,' Derek said as I went into the control room after dealing with my prisoner. He nodded towards the enquiry office.

I peered through and saw Jason Harper sitting on one of the plastic chairs nursing a small pot plant.

'Did he say what he wanted?' I asked.

'Asked for you by name and won't speak to anyone else.'

Alan came into the control room from the other door. 'Use the office off the front desk; it's less isolated than the interview room. We can keep an eye on things better.'

'Yes, sarge.' I turned to Derek. 'If this is about what I think it's about, Mike and Eamon will need to be informed. But I'll let you know.'

'Give them the heads-up anyway,' Alan said.

Derek picked up the phone and I went into the enquiry

office.

'Jason, you wanted to see me?'

He stood up and came to the desk. 'Yeah. Nan told me what you did. I wanted to give you this.' He pushed the pot plant across the desk. 'I grew that myself.'

'Thank you. I'll have to tell my sergeant; there's rules about accepting gifts.'

Jason was nervous. He glanced around and tapped his bitten fingernails against the desk. 'I need to talk to you.'

'Okay, Jason. Go into through that door beside the desk and I'll join you shortly.'

He went into the office and closed the door. I went into the control room and put the plant on the desk.

'A home-grown plant to thank me for looking after his nan.'

'No problem, Sam. I'll make a note of it,' Alan said.

'He wants to talk so I'm going to interview him,' I said. 'I'll let you know if we need to tell the jacks.'

'Roger that,' Ray said.

I gathered some paper and went into the office. 'My sergeant says no problem about the plant. What is it you want to speak about?'

'Fergal Tiernan,' he replied.

I got my pen out and sat back.

'You won't need that for a while. I'll just tell you what I know then you can decide what to do with it. Just keep my name out of it, because he'll put both my nan and me in the mortuary.'

'Do you think he might have had something to do with the attack on Joan?' I asked.

'No.' Jason thought for a moment. 'I don't think so. No, he had no reason to hurt her.'

'Okay then. Tell me what you know.'

'Right. I first met Fergie a few years ago, when I was about ten. Mum was working in The Capstan and he delivered the beer. He started coming around to ours. He was nice to me at first. Made sure I had enough food and shoes and stuff, and he bought my uniform when I went to secondary school, but it came at a price. He got Mum into drugs, selling and using. Then he told me that my mum was useless because she was always wasted, which she was, and that I would have to take over and sell his stuff.'

I was horrified at what I was hearing.

Jason took a deep breath. 'I wasn't that great at it.' He touched his hair. 'This makes me stand out. People remember me. After I was arrested I told him I didn't want to do it anymore. He told me that if I didn't, my mum would spend a long time in hospital.' Jason paused and gulped. 'Fergie wasn't happy I kept getting caught. He thought that I was doing it on purpose because I didn't want to be part of it, and he kept telling me he'd hurt my mum. She was rubbish, but she didn't deserve to be beaten up, or worse.'

'Were you deliberately getting caught?' I asked.

Jason shrugged. 'Maybe I wasn't as careful as I should have been.'

'Couldn't your nan have helped you?' I asked.

'She and my mum had fallen out, so I hadn't seen her for ages. I found out after I went to live with her that she had sent me a pound note in a card every birthday and Christmas. I never got them. Mum must have kept hold of them.'

My heart ached for Jason. He'd been a neglected child and his mother had denied him contact from his grandmother. No wonder he latched on to Tiernan: he had been the only person who showed him kindness; at least at first.

'I eventually went to Borstal. We had to work there and I found I enjoyed gardening. My nan came to visit me a few times and it was really nice to see her again. It turned out she liked gardening too. When I got out, I went to live with Nan, and it's been great.' Jason's eyes shone as he spoke, this had been a really happy time for him despite the circumstances.

Jason's eyes clouded. 'Then Tiernan found me and told me he wanted me to start selling again. I refused, but he threatened my nan. I had no choice really.'

How would I have reacted in the same situation? I had some sympathy for Jason.

'Where was your mum during all this?' I asked.

'Dead. She overdosed while I was in Borstal.'

'Oh, Jason, that's awful.'

Jason shrugged. 'I wasn't that upset to be honest, too much had happened. They let me out for the funeral. There was only me, a screw, Nan, and Fergie there. Nan and Fergie didn't like each other.'

I bet they didn't. The more I heard of Joan Fletcher, the more I liked her. 'So that's why you went to live with Joan?'

'Nan says she'd have taken me back to live with her in any case. She didn't want to lose me again.'

Hearing Jason's sad story had been fascinating and enlightening, but it wouldn't interest the CID.

'Jason, I need to ask about Fergie in more depth,' I said. 'You said he delivered the beer to The Capstan; can you remember the brewery he worked for then?'

'Green Square,' Jason replied.

So, Fergie was a long time employee with them. I wondered if he answered to somebody in the brewery, or was he so clever he'd been able to hide his activities from his employer? Something to mention to CID.

'How did he transport the drugs?' I asked.

'In bags at first. He hadn't long been working for them when I first knew him, but then he had some kegs modified.'

'Modified how?' I asked.

'He knows people all over: the building trade, motor trade and so on. He got someone to adapt a keg so it could be opened up then put together so nobody would know by looking at it. When I was arrested at Hornthorpe Dell, I was trying to get into one of those kegs.'

'You pleaded guilty to burglary and theft of tools,' I said.

'Would you want Fergie to know that you were trying to

open one of his kegs?' Jason replied.

'I don't suppose I would,' I admitted. 'So, what's the story behind it?'

'That DI helped me see that the only way I'm going to get free of Tiernan is if he's banged up for a long time. It's that, or I move far away, or die. I might still have to move; he has friends everywhere.'

'You agreed to get information for DI Webb?' I asked.

'I told him I'd pass on everything I knew if I could have bail. I knew Fergie was delivering to the airfield and that the modified kegs were kept aside, so I was going to get evidence then bring it to the police. I can't go on like this. I know I'm looking at prison, but I thought if the police would have a word with the courts, I'd maybe get a suspended sentence.'

'It doesn't work like that,' I said. 'The police don't control the courts. We can't tell them what to do.'

'But you hear of deals being made all the time,' Jason argued. 'I made one with the DI.'

'You've been watching too much telly,' I said. 'Your deal with DI Webb was only for bail. The only thing police could do for you is consider what offence to put before the court. Once it's with the courts, they control it.'

Jason sagged in his seat. 'So it was a waste of time.'

'Not necessarily,' I said. 'You tell us about Tiernan, and we can get him off the street. It could be mentioned in the evidence that you have been helpful in the enquiry. Or not,' I added when I saw Jason's horrified expression. 'You'd have to deal with any sentence the court gives, but once that was done, you'd be free to start over.'

'Not around here, and I'd have to take Nan with me,' Jason said. 'She doesn't know anything about this. She thinks I'm this wonderful lad who's put aside his past. I want to be that person for her, but I had no choice: I had to protect her.'

'Perhaps it's time for you to have an honest talk with Joan. She loves you and I can see you love her. When you explain the circumstances, I'm sure she'll understand you had to make a hard choice.'

Jason straightened up. 'Yeah, okay, let's do this. I can tell you where Tiernan delivers. I know his address and where his workshop is, and I can give you the names of some of his other sellers. Is the DI around?'

'He's off duty,' I said. 'But DS Finlay and DC Kildea are here. You've met DC Kildea before. I'd like to bring them down to speak to you. Is that all right?'

'Sure, bring everyone. I'm past caring. I just want out.'

I picked up the phone and dialled the CID office. Eamon answered.

'Hi Eamon, I'm in the office off the front desk. I'm with Jason Harper, he has information he wants to share. Would you come down?'

'We'll be there in five m'darlin',' Eamon said.

I replaced the handset. 'They're coming down. We might have to move to the interview room. More space.'

Jason looked over his shoulder towards the enquiry office. 'Good. I was beginning to feel a little exposed here.'

The door to the front desk opened behind me, and Eamon and Mike crowded into the room. Jason looked alarmed and made a move that I interpreted as him about to flee.

'Don't worry, Jason. I'll stay with you. Just tell the detectives what you have told me about Tiernan, and give them those names and addresses.'

'Before anything, can we go to the interview room?' Eamon said in the soft, friendly tone he used to calm a subject.

Jason visibly relaxed. 'Okay then.'

'Good man. Follow me.'

Once Jason was settled into the interview room, I made everyone, including Jason, a cup of tea and sat down.

Jason slurped from his mug. 'This is a bit different from last time. First class service.'

I laughed. 'I only make tea for honoured visitors and

detectives.'

'Right, let's get started,' Mike said. 'First, give me Tiernan's address.'

'Cornflower Row. I'm not sure what number, but it's at the end of the terrace. It has a grey front door, and all the others are blue. You can't see it, but the door is reinforced. Also, the house next door has a boat parked in the back garden. That's not where he prepares his gear, though; he's canny, he has a place in the garages off Primrose Terrace where he bags things up,' Jason said.

Cornflower Row was in the "flower streets": a labyrinthine estate of back-to-front houses with garages and yards lining the road, footpaths instead of roads at the front and not much evidence of the pretty blooms each road was named after. The estate ran alongside a busy dual carriageway used by vehicles to get to and from the docks day and night. Handy.

'Where does he deliver?' Mike asked.

Jason reeled off a large list of pubs and clubs, including the Hornthorpe airfield.

'Do you know his contact at Hornthorpe?' Eamon asked.

'Johnny Poulter. There's someone else, but I don't know his name. I only heard Fergie talking about him in passing. Something about a stolen car.'

'Fergie stole a car?' Mike asked. 'That seems pretty low level for someone like him.'

'I don't know the story, just that someone was muscling in and had to be discouraged, as he put it. I wasn't part of the conversation and I don't know if Fergie knows I overheard him talking. It's probably best he doesn't know.'

I felt that familiar prickle on the back of my neck. Could this be related to Vincent Boyle? I glanced at Eamon, who raised an eyebrow at me. He was feeling it too.

'The kids he has selling for him, are they connected to these premises somehow?' Mike asked.

'Some are connected, if the pub belongs to family or something, but others have just been sucked in, like I was,' Jason said. He recited a list of names and addresses; I recognised a couple. One I had no doubt would be running the local drugs scene in the future.

'Kev Lynch used to sell for him, too,' Jason said.

'Kevin Lynch who was found dead a few weeks ago?' Eamon asked.

Jason nodded but kept his eyes fixed on the table. 'He wanted out.'

There were so many ways that that statement could be taken. I looked from Mike to Eamon and tried to signal that they should follow it up or allow me a question or two.

Eamon looked at me and paused. 'Sam, do you have a question?'

'I do. Jason, when you said "he wanted out", did you mean out of the drugs business or out of life?'

Jason looked wary. 'He wanted out of the drugs business, just like me.'

'You previously said that the only way out for you was to move far away or to die. Do you think Kev took the second option when he realised how hard it would be to get away?' I asked.

Jason shrugged. 'I just know that people don't leave Fergie, which is why I have to get away with my nan.'

I didn't want to lead Jason too much, but it sounded to me that he thought Fergie had had something to do with Kevin Lynch's death. I left the rest of the questioning to the detectives.

*

The interview went on for some time. Afterwards, Mike arranged for Jason to get a lift home.

'This throws a whole new light on everything, doesn't it? Mr Jackson isn't responsible for Boyle.' I hadn't been comfortable with the idea of Leonard Jackson being arrested when Eamon had mentioned it; surely there had to be sufficient doubt now.

Eamon and Mike exchanged a look.

'We still can't be sure that Jackson was not involved,' Eamon said.

I snorted. 'Jason practically told us that Fergie was involved in that. Surely this casts enough doubt on Mr Jackson's involvement, for further enquiries at least.' I was convinced that Leonard Jackson was innocent of the hit-and-run, although I thought something was going on with him that I hadn't yet figured out. However, until they had something firm, the CID were not letting go. I had to back off and leave Mike and Eamon to deal with it. Maybe I should go into the CID after all; being left on the sidelines infuriated me.

I ran into Frank as I returned to the front office. I knew he'd spoken to Gary, but I hadn't spoken to him since the fracas on parade and I didn't intend to speak to him now.

'About what I said that time.'

I stopped and faced him. 'What about it?'

'It was out of order. I'm sorry.'

I wasn't inclined to tell him it was okay—it wasn't—but I acknowledged what he said with a nod and we continued on our respective ways.

Chapter Twenty-Four

Next day, I was watching the television at home when the phone rang.

'Call for you,' Mum called.

I went into the hall and took the phone from here. 'Hello?'

'Hi, Sam. It's Karen,'

'Hi, Karen.' I sat on the bottom step to continue our conversation and Mum, who had been hovering—probably to make sure work weren't bothering me—went back into the kitchen.

'Can you meet me in the market?' Karen asked.

'Yes. Do you need me on or off duty?' I replied.

'Doesn't matter. I want to show you something.'

'I'm off so I could come now,' I said.

'Fantastic. Meet me in the annex in an hour.' With that, Karen hung up.

*

An hour later, I parked in a nearby street, tied a scarf around my hair to keep it off my face, and walked to the market. It was a large building, probably Victorian. It had a smaller annex and the whole was surrounded by a wide cobbled area where once the horse-drawn taxis would wait for passengers. I could quite happily spend half a day in there, even if I didn't buy anything.

The main hall consisted of large stalls, some almost like conventional shops with wooden walls separating them from their neighbours. Off there was the annex, where Karen was meeting me. It was a smaller hall that had pretty much the same type of stuff that was in the main hall but with more basic stalls. They were smaller and didn't seem to have electricity as in the main hall, but it was still worth a wander around.

Karen saw me coming and waved.

I went over to her. 'What is it you want me to see?'

'This,' Karen said. She led me through the annex and stopped near the rear exit.

'What?' I asked.

Karen held her arms out as if she were a game show presenter displaying the prize.

'A stall?' I was bewildered. We were next to a stall that was little more than a trestle table with a red striped, plastic canopy over it.

'My stall,' Karen said proudly.

I gaped. 'Your stall? You mean you're going to sell your sewing? I've won!'

'I can't afford a stall in the main hall, so this will do for now. I've got a treadle machine so I can sew here, and I can do hand sewing and embroidery. Of course there will be some overlap and I'll have to continue my old job for a while until I can get the business up and running, but, yes, you've won.'

'That's fantastic!' I hugged Karen and we jumped around in joy. 'It won't be any time before you're in the main hall; and who knows, if it really takes off, you could get your own shop. Your own chain of shops.'

'Steady on,' Karen said. 'Let's not get ahead of ourselves.'

'This is the best news, I'm so happy for you,' I said.

'I'm going to get a changing cubicle built, nothing fancy, just some hardboard or something,' Karen said.

'I'm going to recommend you to everyone. It'll be fantastic,' I enthused.

After a short while, I realised that there was only so much admiration a trestle table can elicit.

'Are you staying here or can I give you a lift home?' I asked

Karen.

'I'll stay for a while. I want to get to know the neighbours and find out who can fix up a changing cubicle for me.'

'Okay then. I'll get off. Congratulations, I'm over the moon for you.' I hugged her again and went into the cobbled area outside to go back to my car.

Smaller stalls operated there, trestle tables with plastic overhead to keep off the rain. Vans and lorries lined one side. They backed in from the road, opened the rear doors and set up their tables outside the vehicle. Most stood on the back of their van and shouted their wares to passing customers. Larger stuff was sold there: carpets, furniture, one man juggled with pans to the delight of the couple of old ladies that had stopped at his table. I stopped to watch too; it was entertaining.

Across the road from the parked vans, I saw a familiar name picked out in ornate brick over the entrance to a courtyard between a pub and the auction house. "Smith's Yard". That was the place with the cellar that everyone apart from me seemed to know about. I had never noticed the name before. Driven by curiosity, I crossed the road and nipped through the entrance gate. The access opened into a wide courtyard bounded on two sides by the rear walls of the shops. The far side looked as though, in the past, the whole block had been a stables where carriages had been taken and horses refreshed. It appeared to be used as storerooms now.

Steve had told me that on one of the far corners were steps that led into a disused basement. Remembering to look as if I belonged there, I strolled across the yard and casually went down the steps. I tried the door, but the cellar was secure. I walked to the other corner and went down the steps there. This time, the door opened when I lifted the latch. I slipped inside.

Someone had made an effort to make the place fairly comfortable, but it was filthy. Papers littered the floor and dust clung to everything, but there was an old sofa against one wall and a couple of deckchairs set up. I didn't fancy sitting on the sofa—I could imagine it was riddled with fleas—but the deckchairs looked okay, certainly enough to while away the time until a call went out, catching up with a bit of paperwork in bad weather. I opened a door at the back of the cellar. It was a toilet and wash basin, not in bad condition, and it flushed. Useful to know if I was in the area and got caught short.

I looked out of the street-level window and had a great view of the rear of the pub and the auction house. A police officer sheltering in the building would be able to see someone trying to get into either of those buildings. It would only take a step into the courtyard to be able to see if someone was getting into one of the shops at the side. If a bobby was going to take a few minutes to shelter from the weather, it was a pretty good place to do it.

A dray reversed into the courtyard and manoeuvred behind the pub, blocking my view. It had a green square printed on the canvas sides. Jason hadn't mentioned this pub but maybe Tiernan delivered here too. The problem was, I didn't know what Tiernan looked like and he wouldn't be Green Square's only employee.

The drayman, an average looking man with well-developed biceps, probably from shifting barrels every day, was busy setting up a ramp on which, presumably, the barrels would be rolled directly into the pub's cellar. I wanted to leave but some instinct was telling me to stay put. Once the dray was out of the way, I would get out of the courtyard. I would leave a note for Irene when I got to work.

After a couple of minutes, a familiar red head came into the courtyard with another man. Who was he and why was Jason with him? What were they doing here? They went over to the dray and exchanged a few words with the drayman. It looked as if Jason was making introductions because the drayman and the man with Jason shook hands. Dammit, Gary was going to kill me. I hadn't intended to get myself in a position where I was going *off piste*, as Gary put it, but I was in a cellar with only one door, without a radio or any means to raise assistance, watching Jason Harper chatting with two people, one of whom might be

Tiernan.

Suddenly, the drayman looked over to my corner. He walked over followed by Jason and the other man, came down the steps and stood in the doorway, flanked by the other two.

I fled to the toilet but realised I was trapped in a smaller area, so I came out and faced him. I had to brazen it out and hope Jason didn't let on to me. I thought it unlikely as he stood to lose so much, but it was a worry.

'Hello,' I said, trying not to panic that they had blocked the only way out.

'What are you doing here?' the drayman asked.

'Do you own this cellar?' I countered.

'What are you doing here?' he repeated.

'I'm looking for commercial property to rent, I don't need much so this would be okay with a bit of work. Do you own it?'

The man looked around and smiled, not in a good way. 'Nobody owns this, nobody knows it's here.'

'Well, someone does. It has a flushing toilet and running water. Who's paying the bill?' I asked.

This seemed to confuse the man for a moment. I glanced at Jason, who was looking directly at me. I willed him not to say anything. Maybe he was worried I'd say something to him.

'It doesn't matter,' the man said. 'How come you're here?'

'Someone told me about it, so I came to check it out. If you're not the owner, you can't help me, so I'll leave you in peace.' I moved towards the door, but he didn't shift. My heart rate ratcheted up. I couldn't cope with being trapped by men. Bad memories.

'Excuse me,' I said.

He still didn't move. 'What type of business is it?'

I didn't want to show how nervous I was getting and sometimes offence was the best form of defence.

'None of your business, seeing as you don't own the cellar,' I snapped.

'It's not exactly on the High Street. You won't get any passing trade.' He grinned. 'A little girl, all by herself in a hole like this.' He grinned again. 'Something isn't right.'

He took a step forward and I stepped backwards.

'Move out of the way; I'm leaving,' I said.

'Are you? How rude; we've only just arrived,' the man said.

'Okay, I get it, you're trying to scare me. Mission accomplished; now can I go?' I said as aggressively as possible. I was scared but I didn't want him to think I was cowed.

'Let her go, Fergie,' Jason said. 'I've seen her before; she knows my nan. Nan would miss her calling around.'

Fergie! The drayman was Tiernan, and Jason was trying to protect me.

Fergie eyed Jason for a few seconds. 'Jase, escort the lady to the market.' To me, he said, 'I don't expect to see you around here again. I might not be in such a good mood next time.'

Jason gestured to me. 'Come on, love.'

I sidled past Fergie and the other man and followed Jason into the courtyard. We walked in silence until we passed through the gateway.

'Thank you,' I said.

'Don't thank me. If you've got half a brain you'll get far away from here and from him. He's looking for new premises to bag up,' Jason said.

I watched him for a moment. His quick glances towards the cellar signalled his nervousness.

'Have you spoken to Joan yet?' I asked.

'Not yet, I keep putting it off,' Jason said.

'She's proud of you, you know. She told me how you help her and said you have an allotment.'

'Lots of people have allotments.' He stopped speaking and drew a long breath. 'She was there for me when nobody else was. I won't have her upset.' He spun on his heel and went back to the cellar.

'Then speak to her,' I said to his back.

I crossed the road and disappeared into the market. I hoped

Karen would be there. I wanted people around me so nobody could come after me and grab me. I had to let Irene and the CID know about Fergie. I also had to let it be known that the night staff had lost their hidey-hole, and not just because the sergeant knew about it. I had the feeling that it wouldn't be in their best interests to disturb Fergie there.

Karen had gone, so I walked the long way around to my car, so I didn't have to walk near Smith's Yard again.

*

Back at work, I went to Irene's office and tapped on the door. As usual, she waved me in.

'What can I do for you, Sam?' she asked.

'I saw a Green Square dray delivering to the pub opposite the market. I saw Jason Harper and another man talk to the dray man and I heard Jason refer to him as Fergie.'

Irene folded her arms. 'You know Gary hates you going off on enquiries by yourself.'

'I didn't. I was at the market and saw Smith's Yard. Some of the lads mentioned a cellar there so I went to have a look. I was curious because I never work that area. While I was there, a Green Square dray arrived then Jason and another man arrived, they came to the cellar—'

'While you were there?!' Irene interrupted me. 'Good grief, Sam, what were you thinking?'

'I didn't mean to get caught there. Jason Harper got me out. He told Fergie I knew his nan and Fergie let me go. Jason told me that Fergie was looking for new premises to bag up.'

Irene dropped her head into her hands. 'Oh my God! Have you told Gary?'

'No, and I don't want to. I'm telling you so you can put it on the system.'

'If it goes on the system he's going to hear about it, so it's better coming from you.' Irene stood up. 'Come on, we'll go now. He won't kill you if I'm with you.'

I trailed after Irene, who rapped on Gary's door.

'Do you have a few minutes? Someone here needs to tell you something,'

She cocked her head towards the office, and I went in. Irene came after me and closed the door.

'What have you done?' Gary asked me.

'Before we start, I need to tell you that I didn't go off on my own. Well, I didn't mean to go off on my own.'

'You went *off piste* again, after everything we spoke about?' Gary said.

'It was an accident.'

'To be fair, it does sound like circumstances overtook her,' Irene said to Gary. She nudged me. 'Tell him what happened,' Irene said.

Gary sat behind his desk and glowered at me, which didn't do much for my thumping heart.

'You know I went to the market?' Gary nodded. 'Well, I saw Smith's Yard and went across the road to see the cellar some people had been talking about.'

'You know the one,' Irene said to Gary.

'I know it,' he said.

Everyone had known about it, except me. I continued my tale, making sure to emphasise how blameless I had been.

When I had finished, Gary rubbed his hands across his eyes.

'Bloody Hell! Do you have any idea how badly that could have gone?'

'Yes I do, as it happens, and I know there's stuff happening in the background that I don't know about, but I'm guessing I've somehow jeopardised something. The important thing is that I saw Jason meeting with Fergal Tiernan and another man I don't know. Because of me, we know now that Tiernan delivers to that pub, so it's somewhere else to put on the watchlist, and I know that Tiernan is sizing up that cellar as somewhere to bag up. Jason told me.'

'I'll take her to speak to Webby,' Irene said.

'I'll come with you.' Gary stood up and we trooped to the CID office, where I recited the whole story again.

'The information is useful,' DI Webb said. 'I'll leave it with Eamon and perhaps we can get a name for the other man.'

'Thank you, sir,' I said.

'What are we going to do with her?' DI Webb asked Gary. 'She keeps going off by herself.'

'But I was trapped by accident this time. And I do get some good information,' I argued. 'You just said so.' I was pushing it with my attitude, but I felt aggrieved that I was somehow being held responsible for something that had been unexpected. Okay, I was being nosy, but surely that wasn't a bad trait in a policewoman.

'You do, but I'd rather you kept yourself safe,' DI Webb. 'She's your sprog, Gary, so I'll leave you to deal. A word of warning, Sam. When you come to CID, I won't tolerate you going anywhere without clearing it with someone first.'

I resisted the urge to tell him where he could shove the CID. I just said, 'Yes, sir.'

'Go out on patrol now; we'll talk later,' Gary said.

I trailed out of the CID office. Life was so unfair sometimes.

Chapter Twenty-Five

I lay in bed thinking about Jason Harper, the Jacksons, and Boyle and Barbara.

Jason had suggested—no, not that strong—he had *hinted* at Kevin Lynch's death being not what it seemed, which fitted with what the pathologist had found. I had heard no more from the CID, nor did I expect to, but I would have liked to have known if anyone had investigated. Only a month to go and I would be out of my probation. I still wouldn't be CID though—that would take some time yet—but I might be taken a bit more seriously.

My mind drifted to Hornthorpe Dell. Something still niggled at me since my chat with Minchie and Walter, but I still couldn't pin it down. I floated off into a jumbled dream about flying over the airfield with Pete. Vincent Boyle and Barbara, who was wearing a WAAF uniform, waved at me from outside the clubhouse. She went back into the club, looking briefly over her shoulder before going inside. I put two fingers up at Boyle.

When I woke up, I realised what had been scratching at the back of my mind. Barbara had packed parachutes as a WAAF. Barbara would have become adept at it with practice and wouldn't have forgotten how to do that after she left the WAAF. Barbara hated Summerskill. If the picture Boyle had shown me was indeed Leonard Jackson, he had been outside having a cigarette when he should have been watching the store. It wasn't uncommon for smoking to be banned in places like the parachute stores, even in the 1940s. Assuming that Mr Jackson didn't have Ray's ferocious habit, he'd have been gone perhaps ten minutes: fifteen if he stretched it out. Not long enough to have unpacked and repacked something so large, but how long would it have taken to rearrange a few key pieces, such as the straps, by someone who knew what they were doing. I liked Barbara and I didn't want to be right, but in my heart I knew I was on to something.

I got up and had a cup of tea while I thought about how to bring my theory up with Eamon and Mike, or even if I should bring it up. They had decided that the original findings were correct and Summerskill's death had been a terrible accident, and it would be so easy to leave things as they stood. What would be gained by opening up a new lead? It wouldn't bring Summerskill back, and would ruin Barbara's life. She might have done a terrible thing, but it was in response to a terrible injustice done to her.

I sighed. From what I had learnt in my chats with old colleagues of his, Summerskill had been an unpleasant man: charismatic but arrogant, and mistrusted by most. Did that mean he wasn't entitled to justice? Hadn't I promised to carry out my duties without fear or favour?

I chuckled at myself for sounding so sanctimonious. I could do with some guidance. I would go into work half an hour early and speak to Irene.

*

'Irene, do you know if Eamon and Mike have submitted the file on the alleged historical murder?' I asked when I went into her office.

'I know it's complete, but I don't know if it's been submitted yet. Why?'

'Do you know if they still have the photographs that Boyle gave them?'

'No, sorry. Sam, what's going on?'

'I could do with seeing the pictures. I think Boyle might be right and Summerskill was murdered.'

Irene remained silent for a minute. 'I don't want to disturb them right now. Boyle has died without regaining consciousness. DI Webb is going to arrest Leonard Jackson on suspicion of murdering Vincent Boyle.'

I gasped. That added a whole new layer to things. 'I think Barbara, the manageress of the Hornthorpe airfield club might have been the one who interfered with Summerskill's parachute. My problem is, after all this time, I'm not sure there's anything to be gained by following that line of enquiry. Also, I now feel worse that this has come up on the day her son has died.'

Irene's jaw dropped. 'Whatever gave you that idea?'

'I think I saw a young Barbara on those photos. I could do with seeing those photographs to make sure, first,' I said.

'If it is her, the decision whether to go forward or not is not yours to make. You should put sentimentality aside, report as you find and let the CID decide.' Irene stood up. 'Come with me.' She walked with me to the CID office.

'Sam has a theory about that old accident at the airfield,' Irene called to Eamon. He came over carrying an almost full mug of tea. Irene grabbed it from him. 'Ta very much.'

'I could do with seeing those photographs that Boyle gave you. Do you still have them?' I asked.

'Hang on.' Eamon went to his desk and found the folder. He tipped it out and several photographs landed on his desk.

'I thought that had been submitted,' Mike called from his desk.

'It will be; I hadn't got around to it. Boyle dying has taken precedence for now.' Eamon took the photos over to Mike's desk.

DI Webb came over to see what was going on. 'Oh, not this again. I think we have gone as far as we can. Time to move on.'

I shuffled through them and found what I was looking for. I peered closely at the picture of the WAAF looking over her shoulder and I knew I was right.

I held up the photo. 'On the day Summerskill died, a

photographer was taking publicity shots around the base, including the place where they stored the parachutes. Some of them are on display in the club at Hornthorpe.' I held up the photograph for them to see. 'I believe this is Barbara, the manageress at the club. She had a baby by Summerskill that she gave up for adoption. Summerskill refused to acknowledge that the child was his. Barbara should not have been by the parachute store—in fact, she shouldn't even have been in uniform—she had had to leave the WAAF when she was pregnant, months before Summerskill took his last jump.'

Eamon took the photo from me and scrutinised it. 'There is a resemblance, but this isn't a great image. I'm not sure this would constitute sufficient evidence. I think if she denied it, we'd have nothing.' Eamon turned to Mike. 'What do you want to do, follow this or leave things as they are?'

Mike scrutinised me for a moment. 'This information came from an alcoholic with an axe to grind?'

'Some of it,' I admitted. 'But others have corroborated that she was a WAAF and that she'd had to leave. Nobody has told me that she had been on site that day. I'm the one who realised the photo is probably Barbara.'

'You know what a halfway decent defence would make of that, if you had to stand up in court and say it?' Mike folded his arms.

Mike was right. If I went to court at the present moment, I'd be shredded, the case would be dismissed. I might not have proper evidence, but what I did have was the basis of an investigation that I was sure would garner more acceptable evidence.

'When Eamon and I went to the club at Hornthorpe Dell, I also chatted to the storekeeper that had been on that day. Walter Gower. He told me he had been ill and Leonard Jackson had covered for him until a proper relief was found.' I shuffled through the photographs again until I found the photo that Boyle had alleged was Leonard Jackson. 'This is supposed to be Jackson. Notice that he is by the same building as the WAAF but, judging by the solid door and the bin in the background, I'd say he was out back while Barbara is entering from the front.' I glanced at Eamon. 'Hiding in plain sight.'

'But we don't know that the photos were taken on the same day, or even the same year,' Eamon said.

I tapped the back of the photo which had the date stamp. It matched that on the rear of Barbara's photo.

'Jackson had access to the parachutes,' DI Webb said.

'Walter Gower told me that the jump was already on and the parachutes issued when Leonard Jackson stepped in. Mr Jackson hadn't had to do anything, just be there for enquires until the relief arrived,' I said.

'Eamon said that Summerskill had been late that day, so his parachute would have been there with Jackson,' DI Webb insisted.

'Even if he was, he wouldn't have been alone with it for long, because we know that Summerskill made it in time for the jump. Mr Jackson couldn't have known that he would be asked to stand in for Gower. He wouldn't have had time to damage the parachute in a way that wouldn't be noticed. Packing a parachute is a specialised job.'

Eamon clicked on. 'Barbara was a WAAF trained in packing parachutes. She would have known exactly what to do to cause a malfunction in minimal time.'

'But she was no longer a WAAF at that time,' DI Webb insisted.

'Maybe she kept some of her uniform, or maybe she stole one. Either way, a WAAF on an air force base would not have looked out of place,' I argued.

'Jackson—or this Walter Gower—would have recognised her,' Mike said.

'Yes. So maybe she kept watch and waited for him to leave or go on a cigarette break then sneaked in,' I said.

'It's a thought,' Irene said.

'It's not enough to charge her,' DI Webb said. 'How would

she have known which parachute Summerskill was going to take, any more than Jackson would?'

'I don't know; we'd have to ask her,' I said.

'But would this be enough to bring her in for questioning?' Eamon asked.

'I'll have a think,' Webby said. 'It's very shaky, there's too much that relies on a confession. Nobody would be criticised if the file was put in as it stands today.'

Oh well, it looked like this was going nowhere. Perhaps that was for the best.

'Can you come in on Friday?' DI Webb asked me.

'Yes, but I'd have to clear it with the inspector: I'm supposed to be rest day,' I replied.

'Leave that to me,' Webby said. 'DI Corlett is coming back.' He looked at his watch. 'You'd better get yourself downstairs; parade starts in ten minutes.'

I walked to the stairs and met Gary coming out of the office ready for parade.

'Where've you been?' he asked.

'Speaking with DI Webb. He's going to ask you if I can work my rest day on Friday. That Manx DI, DI Corlett, is coming back. I think it might be that thing they talked about before New Year.'

Gary chewed his thumb as he thought. 'You'll have to take time in lieu, the overtime budget is a bit stretched. Don't worry, I'll talk to Norman. Remember, not a word to anyone else.'

'Well, duh, sir.' I winked at him and continued towards the stairs.

Steve came out of the kitchen as I passed and we went to the parade room together. I wondered if he had heard Gary and I talking, but he asked no questions so I gave no response.

*

Webby had decided that I should parade on at 7am on Friday. I was surprised to see Mike Finlay, Eamon and a few other jacks as well as the dog handler, minus the dog, already in the CID office. A few foot patrols from the morning block were there and, at the back of the room, several unfamiliar, tough-looking officers lined the wall. These were not just patrol officers; I don't think a single one was under six foot, and most were built like Phil.

DI Webb, DI Corlett and the DCI came out of Webby's office. The DCI hardly ever came to Wyre Hall.

'It isn't going to come as a surprise that we have planned a raid,' DI Webb said. 'Is everyone here and have you all been to the toilet?' It wasn't such a daft question. Once he revealed the location, we would have to remain together until it was over, to prevent anyone using the phone to warn the target. Sadly, someone had done just that in the past.

DI Webb continued. 'Right, we might as well begin. A series of raids are taking place across the peninsula. This is a wide-reaching operation and is linked to existing operations: Blue Sky here, and Rainfall in Odinsby. We have named this one Thunderstorm.'

I enjoyed how linked operations were named on a theme. I had had no idea about Operation Rainfall, but it was in a different division. I had often been reminded that policing didn't stop when I was off duty. Things happened that I knew nothing about, even within my own division.

'You will have noticed that this is a bit later than usual; there is a reason for it, but I'm not going to get into that now. I will be remaining here to oversee the operation from this division, and I will be liaising with senior officers in the other divisions,' the DCI said.

DI Webb said, 'Officers from Egilsby and Odinsby will be taking various addresses there and we have a team from the city, who will hit the workshop on Primrose Terrace.' He gestured towards the officers at the back, who stood stony faced as we all turned to them. 'You lot are going to enter a property in

Cornflower Row,' DI Webb continued. 'This is the home of one Fergal Tiernan.' DI Webb held up a large photo. 'Tiernan is a supplier of drugs. He has many underlings and contacts, and runs drug smuggling operations.'

I noticed that he didn't mention the connection to the Hornthorpe club, but now was not the time to question DI Webb.

'It doesn't seem like the home of Mr Big, sir,' one of the tough officers said. 'Look at some of the others that have been caught: they've been in large houses in nice areas. This is a poky terrace on the arse end of a rundown council estate. Sorry, sir.'

'DI Webb commented on the very same thing when we discussed it,' said the DCI. 'However, our intelligence says that he does live there. We have been unable to trace another address connected to him. It could be he isn't as senior as he would like to believe.'

DI Webb gestured to the detectives behind him, 'The dog and you lot, position yourselves in the back ready to catch him if he bales that way.'

'Just a reminder: if I release the dog, you should all remain still while he goes after Tiernan. We wouldn't want him to mistake you for his target.' The handler chortled at the alarmed faces of the jacks. The men at the back of the room glowered, leaving the handler in no doubt that his dog would not fare well if it attempted to do anything other than wag its tail at them.

DI Webb counted the bobbies from the block. 'One, two, three. You uniforms will follow DS Finlay to the door. Four, five. You two will go to assist at the workshop on Primrose Terrace. Does everyone understand?'

'Yes, sir,' we all said.

'Sam, you remain here with the DCI and DI Corlett. They will speak to you about your role,' DI Webb said. 'I will join you later.'

'Yes, sir,' I replied.

'Wagons roll,' DI Webb said and led everyone else out to the yard, where the transport awaited.

I stood awkwardly, waiting for my next instruction.

'So, you're Samantha Barrie,' the DCI said.

It was always a bit worrying when a senior officer knew your name. He didn't look unfriendly though.

'Yes, sir,' I replied.

'DI Corlett has told me how helpful you've been to this investigation.'

I could see DI Corlett grinning behind the DCI. 'Thank you, sir.'

'I expect you're wondering why we're not doing this is the small hours,' the DCI said.

It had crossed my mind, but I remained silent.

'We know that Tiernan is not an early riser on his rest days, and he is not in work today, and we can't risk news of the arrests getting back to the airfield. So we if we go in simultaneously, that negates that risk.'

'I understand, sir, but won't it be difficult with more people being around?' I asked.

'Possibly,' the DCI admitted. 'But we have to work with what we have. Your lesson is scheduled for 9:30 but I think you and DI Corlett can leave soon. It would be best if you were at the airfield while the raids are happening. It makes it less likely a message will get through. DI Webb will be coming to the airfield. We've borrowed some bodies from Tynvoller to wait near the airfield. They won't move in until instructed by DI Webb.

'Yes sir,' I replied. There was not much more to be said.

Chapter Twenty-Six

DI Corlett and I crunched into the car park of Hornthorpe airfield in the hired Aston Martin. At the same time, police officers were positioning themselves out of sight around the outskirts so that, when DIs Webb, Corlett and crew came into the car park, any absconders would be caught as they fled.

Before we got out, DI Corlett said, 'Okay, you just carry on as normal and I'll go back and liaise with Norman and the DCI. If for some reason we're not at the airfield before you're ready to take off, try to stall him somehow. We don't want Pete or Johnny to leave.'

'Got it, sir,' I said. In the distance, a man pushed a wheelbarrow. I saw a small plane, not the Cessna, moving out of the second hangar. 'It looks like they've got a new groundsman. There's at least one other pilot or instructor here, too.'

'They'll all have to come in,' DI Corlett said. 'You never know, we might unearth someone we hadn't expected to be involved.'

That was standard procedure in a situation such as this. Bring everyone in, then sort it all out back at the station. It often left innocent parties feeling peeved, but needs must. It was easier to gather more information and evidence that was needed, than it would be to try to go back because not enough had been collected.

Feeling a lot lighter than I had last time I came here for a lesson, I walked to the club with DI Corlett. It was freezing and I hugged my warm, winter coat around me.

In the club, Pete was nowhere to be seen.

'Hello?' DI Corlett shouted.

Pete's voice came from the club office. 'Hi, with you in a minute.'

We went over to the door and looked in. Pete was finishing a phone call at a desk strewn with papers.

Pete put the phone down and took a deep breath. 'Sorry about this; Barbara's on compassionate leave so I've been organising some cover.'

'Compassionate leave?' I asked. I knew exactly why but I thought it might look odd if I showed no curiosity.

'Her son died,' Pete said.

'Oh dear. She told me he'd been in a crash,' I said.

'Yeah, he never regained consciousness,' Pete said. 'Anyway, you're a bit early, Samantha.'

'Yeah, sorry. Dad's got some things he needs to do so I thought I could just hang around the airfield before our class. That's okay, isn't it?'

'Sure,' Pete agreed.

'Will you be all right to fly after what's happened?' DI Corlett asked, playing the part of concerned father in a most convincing manner. 'I mean, such awful news must be disturbing for you too.'

'I'm fine, Mr Barrie. I barely knew the man. I feel sorry for Barbara though.'

'Right, I'll be back later to collect you, darling. I'll be in the office so ring if you need anything,' DI Corlett said to me. By that I knew he meant ring the station in case of trouble.

'See you then, Daddy,' I replied. I followed Pete to the hangar where Johnny was working on another plane.

I put my thick coat in the locker in the hangar. I was wearing a denim jacket, which would suffice in the cockpit. I wasn't going to fly, but I needed Pete to think everything was as normal.

'Pete, a word,' Johnny called.

'Will it wait?' Pete asked. 'I still have a couple more phone calls to make before taking Samantha up.'

Johnny pointed at me. 'Barbara spotted that Irish bloke she

knocks around with in the hospital. He's a cop; he was asking questions at the nurses station.'

Pete turned to me. 'Samantha?'

I felt my cheeks go hot, but I wasn't the one in the wrong. I would brazen it out.

'Eamon is a policeman, why is this a problem?' I asked.

'He said he was from Downpatrick,'

'He does come from Downpatrick.'

'Why was he asking questions at the hospital?' Pete asked.

Phil, my old tutor constable had instilled in me the importance of being truthful with our customers. But I had also learnt that sometimes, when working undercover, you had to lie to maintain your cover. This was one of those times.

'I don't know. You'd have to ask him. He doesn't talk about his work with me,' I said.

'Are you a copper?'

'No. Look, should I leave? I'll go to the clubhouse and ring my dad to collect me.'

'I don't believe her,' Johnny said. 'We need to move out.'

Pete said nothing. He climbed into his plane and started up the engine. It was too soon. Everything was timed around my 9:30 lesson.

'What the hell, Pete?' Johnny shouted. 'You're just going to leave?'

Pete didn't reply. The plane slowly moved forward. In a second, the plane would be outside, gathering speed, and Pete would escape. Without thinking, I raced to the pilot's door, closely followed by Johnny, threw it open and grabbed at Pete. I had intended to drag him out, but he suddenly had a gun in his hand and pointed it at my head.

Johnny and I both gasped. Where the hell had that been hidden?

'Back off now,' Pete said.

I took one step backwards and Pete relaxed. Just as he turned to the controls, I leapt forward and grabbed the arm with the gun. If I kept it close, Pete would struggle to use it. If I could delay him, he would be caught in Operation Blue Sky.

We struggled for a few seconds until I felt a heavy blow across my back. My knees buckled and Johnny pulled me back. I dropped to the ground and rolled under the plane so Pete couldn't shoot me, and Johnny couldn't hit me again with the wrench he was holding. It felt like he had almost broken my spine.

'Think, Pete. We don't want a dead cop,' Johnny said.

Which explained why he hadn't smashed my head in.

'She's going to tell them about us,' Pete shouted. 'I have to get away.'

'It's over, Pete!' Johnny shouted. 'It'll be a couple of years in prison, that's all. We are just a couple of blokes caught up with Tiernan's plan. We tell them he threatened us if we didn't do as he said. Kill her and it's life.'

They knew Tiernan!

'I'm already facing life!' Pete shouted.

Johnny froze. 'You killed someone?' I could see understanding dawn in his eyes. 'You're Tiernan's enforcer! You killed for him. You're the one who killed Vince.'

I froze, too. Pete had stolen Leonard Jackson's car and killed Boyle. I recalled the description Mrs Yale had given me and it fitted. And what did Johnny mean by "Tiernan's enforcer"? Had Pete killed others?

'Move or I'll move you.' Pete stuck the gun out of the door of the plane and jabbed it towards Johnny.

Johnny moved backwards and Pete lowered the gun. I rolled out of the way of the wheels, too sore to run or fight. A few minutes more and help would arrive. How could I prevent Pete taking off?

'Vince tried to muscle in on the operation. You're the one who told me he would snitch if we didn't give him a cut. You told me that you suspected he had already stolen some of the merchandise. Tiernan said he had to be dealt with. He would have killed us both if I hadn't got rid of him,' Pete shouted.

'You broke Barb's heart, you bastard,' Johnny shouted. He raised the wrench as if to strike Pete.

A crack resounded around the hangar and a small black hole appeared in Johnny's cheek. Johnny dropped where he stood. Blood oozed across the floor.

'Fuck!' Pete stopped the plane again and jumped down. He stared down at Johnny's body. Another pilot appeared close to the door of the hangar and peered in. In a second he had taken in the scene and fled across the field towards the clubhouse. I half-expected Pete to fire the gun at him, but he seemed stunned. I staggered to my feet, surprised that I could stand, and edged towards the door, but Pete came out of his daze and turned the gun on me.

'Get in the plane.'

I backed away.

'I won't tell you again. Another body won't make a difference now,' he said.

He was right; how many life sentences could he serve? Moving awkwardly, I got into the plane, and Pete slammed the door after me. Keeping the gun trained on me, he walked to his side and climbed in.

'Be a good girl and I might let you go when I'm safely away.'

I said nothing, but nodded.

Pete started the engine and we taxied out of the hangar. Through the trees surrounding the airfield I saw police vehicles converging towards us, which gave me a boost. The cavalry was coming. Trainer planes had dual control so the instructor could put right any mistakes before they became dangerous so, as the plane began to taxi to the runway, I tried to apply my brakes, but he had locked me out. Pete saw what I was trying to do and laughed.

At that point, my door flew open, which terrified me and surprised Pete who fired his gun. I felt the air move as the bullet passed my face.

Pete stared at the door for a moment then shrugged. 'It happens sometimes; bloody annoying. Good job we're still on the ground.'

The door sometimes opened for no reason! I had thought the doors were flimsy, but I hadn't expected them to actually open when flying. Another reason to hate flying small planes.

As Pete's attention was taken with the door, we had started to slow. Police cars pulled into the car park. Others were coming from the emergency vehicles entrance. I waved frantically, but I wasn't sure if they would be able to see me.

Pete looked across the field and swore. He picked up the radio and transmitted, 'Code *Awyr Las*, Code *Awyr Las*.'

'Roger,' someone replied. '*Ty Mawr*.'

My nan was Welsh and had tried to teach me the language. I still remembered odd bits, such as *Awyr Las*, or Blue Sky, and *Ty Mawr* or Big House. Despite the circumstances, I appreciated the coincidence of the name.

Steve, in plain clothes and panting for breath, burst through the open door into the cockpit and literally climbed over me to get at Pete. I was too stunned to ask what the hell he was doing there. Pete tried to turn the gun on Steve, but Steve grabbed his hand and forced the gun away from us.

'Stop the damned plane,' he shouted.

Whether at me or Pete, I couldn't be certain, but I shouted back, 'I can't!' Nor could I help subdue Pete, with Steve's weight across me.

Pete managed to get the gun clear and fired off a shot. Steve fell backwards out of the plane, blood staining his chest. He hit the ground in a heap and didn't move. Sore back forgotten, I screeched and grabbed at Pete's eyes and hair, but couldn't get a grip.

Pete pointed the gun at me. 'Sit still.'

'You shot Steve!' I could see cars headed across the airfield towards us. Pete saw it too and I could almost hear the cogs in his mind estimating the chance of success if he fled.

'There's more where they came from. You're going down!' I screamed. I tried to grab the controls, but I heard a click as Pete prepared to fire again.

'I said sit still and you might survive this.'

My survival instinct finally kicked in and I sat still. Pete had shot two people as well as killing Boyle; he wouldn't think twice about shooting me now.

'Shut the door,' Pete ordered.

I shut the door and the plane surged forward; in a few seconds we were climbing towards the clouds, far steeper than I had experienced before. I was momentarily distracted by a wave of nausea as my stomach tried to catch up with us.

I looked down and saw DI Corlett get out of a car and run to Steve, who still hadn't moved. I gulped. My funny, mischievous friend, Steve—who was more caring and braver that anyone gave him credit for—could be gone forever. I gulped. I needed to remain calm now, push my heartache aside and figure out how to help myself.

Chapter Twenty-Seven

After flying in silence for a short while, during which I had thought about how to escape without finding a satisfactory solution, I could see the white-topped Welsh mountains beneath us, but I didn't know exactly where we were.

Pete was muttering to himself.

'How did you know? How did you know about the Jacksons?' I asked.

Pete glanced at me. 'So you are a copper,'

'And you're a killer. How did you know about the Jacksons?'

Pete half-smiled. 'Okay then.'

That was worrying. Pete wouldn't share the story to someone who could take it back to others. Or maybe he had accepted that it was all over for him. I hoped for the latter.

'After Barbara told Vince that his father had died in a parachute accident, he chatted to a couple of the guests about the incident and became obsessed with the idea that his father had been deliberately killed by Jackson. I tried to tell him that it was just Minchie's mouth running away with him, but he took every word that drunk said as gospel.' Pete kept wiping his top lip.

Tom Minchin and his big, flapping mouth again. I stopped feeling the slightest bit of warmth towards him. Did he have any idea how much harm his gossiping had caused? Someone should tell him. Maybe when—if—I got back, I'd tell him.

Pete continued. 'Johnny asked Vince what was to be gained after so long, and he said that he had confronted Jackson and demanded payment in compensation for his father's death.'

'He blackmailed him,' I said.

'He didn't call it that, but he was determined to get some money. When it became evident that Jackson wasn't going to cough up, he had to up the ante. He reported the death to the police.'

'Bet you loved that,' I said. 'Vince attracting all that police attention.'

'Not as much as I loved Johnny telling me that some gear had gone missing, and that Vince was trying to muscle in. I had to tell Fergie and he wasn't best pleased.

'Fergal Tiernan?' I asked. I knew who he meant but I wanted it to be clear.

Pete remained quiet.

'Fergal Tiernan?' I repeated.

Pete gave a little nod. That would have to do.

'Did he supply you at your request or did you take the drugs because he said to? Are you panicking because your source of drugs has dried up, or are you celebrating your freedom?'

'Freedom?' Pete laughed wryly. 'There's always someone else ready to take over.'

That had been my impression. 'By your answer I'd say you worked for him. Did Johnny work for you?'

Pete inhaled sharply at Johnny's name. 'We worked together. Fergie told me that Vince had to go, and that Johnny and I had to pay for the missing drugs, or his boss would be very unhappy.'

'So, you stole Mr Jackson's car and used it to kill Boyle. You thought that because the police knew about tensions between Boyle and the Jacksons, we wouldn't look too closely and just assume it had been Mr Jackson driving.'

Pete remained quiet for a moment. 'If I hadn't, Fergie would have come for Johnny and me.'

I thought for a few seconds. He isn't the first you've killed for Tiernan though, is he? Kevin Lynch?'

Pete looked sideways at me. 'He died of a heroin overdose.'

'Self-administered?' I asked.

Pete shook his head.

'Lee Hatton? A man fitting your description was seen at his address.'

Pete didn't reply, but the tightness around his jaw told me he knew the name.

'How many more, Pete? A handful? Dozens? How could you kill those people just because someone says so?'

'You have no idea what it's like. If I was told to dispose of someone, I had to do it, or Fergie would have killed me.'

'Boo hoo. Fergie threatened you, and he in turn would have been threatened by his boss. Basically, you're the minion of an underling. That can't be good for your ego.' Yes, I was goading him, which perhaps wasn't a good idea at several thousand feet above the ground.

Pete gave me a dirty look. 'You're not exactly top of the heap yourself.'

That was true, but we were the good guys.

'How did you know where Mr Jackson lived?' I asked.

'I followed Vince.'

'Of course you did,' I said. 'You ran Boyle over at the YMCA then wrecked the car at the park gates. You were seen you know; the YMCA has cameras, and someone saw you by the park gates. We got a good description of you.' I wanted him to know he wasn't so clever.

'You didn't get me though, did you.' Pete crowed.

That also was true. The description we had could have fitted anyone and the cameras hadn't got the driver, but Pete didn't know that.

'We were gathering evidence. We've been gathering evidence about your activities for a long time. You're going to prison.'

Pete began to descend. I couldn't see any airstrips around.

'This big house must have a private landing area,' I said. 'There's a register of landing strips, which should narrow it down for the search party; and make no mistake, they will be looking for us.'

'You don't think I actually logged the flight, or flew high enough to come to notice on anyone's radar did you?' Pete laughed.

'I think you'll be surprised how far and how low RAF Valley's radar stretches,' I said. I actually had no idea about their radar, but that was something else Pete didn't know. As a pilot, he would have a good idea of their capability, but perhaps he thought police knew more than the public about things like this.

We came down in the grounds of a grand, old house. Two men ran towards us, each holding a shotgun.

'Are these connected to Fergie too?' I asked.

'Shut up,' Pete snarled. I got the impression he was regretting talking to me.

Pete taxied over to a large metal barn-type outbuilding, steered inside then shut down the engine. The shotgun men took position either side of the plane and pointed their guns at us. Pete jumped down and greeted them.

'What's going on, Pete?' one man asked. A local judging by the accent.

'Her. She's police.' He gestured for me to get out. I complied; you do when there are two shotguns pointed at you and you know there's a handgun somewhere in the mix as well.

The men stared at me.

'I was led to believe that you were making a hasty exit. Why did you bring her with you?' the man demanded.

'I had no choice. Johnny's dead. He might have been working with her.'

'You know he wasn't, you shot him when he tried to make you see sense,' I said, but shut up when the shotgun man gave me a filthy look.

'I repeat: why did you bring her here, Pete? Why isn't she feeding fishes in the Irish Sea?'

I didn't like the way the conversation was going. Instinctively, I edged away.

Pete was looking less confident too. 'We've already had one

death, Morgan.'

'Four. No, five,' I interrupted. 'Apart from Lynch and Hatton, you killed Vince and shot Johnny, and Steve too when he tried to stop you getting away.'

Pete clicked his handgun and pointed it at me with his arm fully outstretched. 'Shut up!'

I shut up.

'Perhaps I should have mentioned I had company, but we're here now so I thought we could put her in the barn and, when things have calmed down, dump her on a mountain somewhere,' Pete said.

Yes, I liked that idea. I could cope with being dumped if it kept me out of the Irish Sea.

Morgan rolled his eyes. '*Twmffat!* We can't let her go; she's seen us and the house, and now you said my name, *pen pidyn*!'

'Hatton and Lynch were for Tiernan…' Pete's voice tailed off.

I didn't understand the Welsh words Morgan had used but I could tell, by his increasing volume and red face, they weren't good. Morgan was evidently the one in charge and judging by Pete's demeanour, I guessed he was something as high, if not higher than Fergie. I wondered if Pete was working for two organisations and had answered to two bosses: Fergie and Morgan. A risky move if he had been.

In a moment of madness I decided that, if I was going down, Pete was coming with me.

'Steve was a policeman,' I said. 'He was my friend. Pete shot him in front of everyone as they came to arrest him.'

'You killed a policeman? You have kidnapped a policewoman? There were other police around to witness it?' Morgan asked but it was not really a question.

Pete blanched. Good.

'I don't want blood everywhere in case the police do come here, nor do I recommend dispatching her in the plane. Forensics can pick up the tiniest splatters these days.'

'Er…' Pete said.

'Oh, come on, Pete, you brought her here. Surely you don't expect me to do it, or are you chicken as well as stupid.'

'What do you suggest?' Pete asked.

Morgan pointed to a wood a short walk away. 'In there. The area next to it is used for clay pigeon shooting, so even if someone hears the shot they won't think it odd. Nothing fancy, just one headshot and a quick burial close by so you don't spread blood around.'

I was shivering and it wasn't just the cold. Morgan hadn't even had to think about where to dispatch me, he'd had experience of this.

Pete nodded and motioned with his gun for me to walk ahead.

'Wait,' Morgan called. 'My friend here will go with you to help dig a hole.' He spoke quickly and quietly in Welsh to the other shotgun man, who nodded, went to fetch a spade from the barn then joined Pete. When—if—I got back, I would have to have a chat with my nan and get her to teach me Welsh. It could come in useful sometime: like now.

I don't know how I managed to walk on my shaking legs, but it seemed no time until we were on the edge of the wood. I had forgotten about my injured back. I thought about how angry Morgan had been with Pete. Now he had sent his mate with us, ostensibly to help bury me, but another reason occurred to me, a reason I could use to spook Pete. If he was distracted I might be able to run for it. But then there was Morgan's friend... I took a deep breath; half a chance was better than no chance.

'You know he's going to shoot you too?' I said to Pete.

'Shut up!' Morgan's friend said.

'You know it's true. My grandmother's Welsh, she taught me the language,' I half-lied. 'He's not here to help you, Pete, he's going to make sure there are no witnesses,' I added.

'Shut up or I'll kill you right here,' shotgun man shouted, confirming to me that my hunch was correct.

'Morgan wouldn't like that, would he,' I said. 'You'd better stick to his instructions if you know what's good for you.'

Pete was looking more and more uncertain, but he waved his gun and urged me forward, deeper into the wood until we came to a small clearing. I was not going to get the chance to run.

'Here,' Pete said. 'We should dig a hole first so she can go straight into it. Keep the blood in one spot and deter animals from moving her body parts around. It would reduce the evidence.'

I shuddered at the image that brought to my mind.

Morgan's friend kept walking. 'Follow me.'

He led the way to a denser part of the wood, half a minute or so from the clearing. Hidden under some undergrowth was a grave-sized hole. I felt perspiration run down my back. I fervently wished I had faith that I was about to go somewhere better instead of becoming nothing but worm food. I considered tackling one of them, maybe trying to get the weapon from them, but the other would simply shoot me. I would have to go for Morgan's friend; he would shoot me without thinking while Pete was already unsettled and might be caught unawares, perhaps giving me the chance to gain the upper hand. Would it be better to accept my fate or to go down fighting?

'It was meant for someone else, but it's big enough for two.' Morgan's friend laughed.

Big enough for two: me and Pete. I glanced around; how many bodies were hidden in this wood?

I made no pretence of bravery. I wept as Pete raised his gun. I'd left it too long to tackle either of them. I closed my eyes and prayed to a deity I wasn't sure existed that my death would be quick. I heard a loud crack followed a few seconds later by another. No pain. I opened my eyes and blinked; the air left my lungs. I sank to the ground and wrapped my arms around me, transfixed by Morgan's friend's body. The top of his head was missing.

'Run,' Pete said.

I turned to him, confused. Did the sadistic bastard want to

make a game of my murder?

'I won't play. If you're going to kill me, you can look me in the eyes as I die,' I declared with more resolve than I felt.

Pete lowered his gun. 'For Christ's sake, run you silly bitch. You're right, I'm a target too. Morgan will miss us soon and come looking.' Pete turned to run.

'Pete,' I said. He turned back to me. 'Tell me about the others you killed for Tiernan.'

Pete pursed his lips as he stared back at me. 'All accidental overdoses. They injected themselves.'

'But it wasn't accidental, was it? You injected them with too much.'

Pete stared at me then turned away and ran without answering.

I stood up on shaking legs and listened for Pete coming back. There was nothing; Pete really had gone and given me the chance of escape. I would get away and tell everyone everything I had learnt. I would tell them about Steve's courage and make sure he got an award.

I ran as fast as my unsteady legs allowed. I had to find a house, a phone box, anything or anyone who could alert the police. I couldn't be sure where I was in relation to the big house, but I couldn't stay where I was.

I spotted telephone wires and made towards them. I stuck to the wood as far as possible and followed them to a stone wall that ran beside a road. In the distance, I saw a phone box half hidden by overgrown bushes. I didn't know where I was, but I wasn't too worried about that; phone boxes usually had little notices with their location in them.

My back was hurting again, and it was very cold. I walked as quickly as I was able towards the phone box until I came to a gate in the wall. If I made a call then came straight back and stayed behind the wall, I could dodge out of sight if Morgan or anyone else came after me. I couldn't see any traffic, I couldn't even hear a car engine, so I half-ran half-walked towards the phone box.

At the phone box, I pulled the heavy door open, which made me wince, and stepped inside. The light didn't come on. I looked up and saw the overhead light was smashed. It wasn't completely dark, I was able to see that the small, square notice that would normally give a location had been defaced. Also, the display at the centre of the dial that normally showed the phone number of the box had been removed, probably by the same person who had smashed the light. Why did people do this? Didn't they realise how important it was? I had always imagined country people were more law abiding. I picked up the handset and dialled 999.

'Which service to you require?' the operator asked.

'Police,' I said.

I listened to the clicking as I was put through to whichever control room covered wherever I was.

'Police, what is your emergency?' She sounded business-like.

'My name is Samantha Barrie. I'm a police officer. I was kidnapped by drug smugglers, but I've escaped.'

'Where are you?'

'I don't know. The location notice has been ruined and there's no phone number. You must have the number, ask the operator to trace the call.' I knew that, if requested, the operator could tell where a call came from, especially from a public call box.

'Can you see any landmarks around? Road names, pubs or something?' the operator asked.

I looked around. 'There's a pub called The White Lion a short walk away.'

'That doesn't really help; there's loads of them. Are you near Bala?'

'I don't know,' I replied. 'Trace my call.' Were things so different in Wales?

The woman sighed. 'Where did you come from?'

'Hornthorpe Dell originally. We went to a house referred to as *Tŷ Mawr*. They were going to kill me, but I got away. I came through a wood and ended up on a road with a wall along it and saw this phone box. Can't you trace my call?' I asked. I was getting as frustrated as her.

'Someone is trying to kill you?' I could almost hear her eyebrows shoot up.

'Yes, but one of them is dead.'

There was a moment's silence. 'Look, this isn't funny. There are people with real emergencies—'

'This is a real damned emergency!' I shouted, cutting off her words. 'My name is Samantha Barrie. I was part of a police operation at Hornthorpe Dell airfield. I was taken at gunpoint in a light aircraft to Tŷ *Mawr*. They were going to kill me. I don't know where I am. I need help.' That little outburst left me panting.

A blue Vauxhall Viva turned off the main road and drove past me and on to the pub. I gasped and turned away when I saw Morgan driving, but I didn't think he'd seen me. I gave thanks to any invisible being that happened to be listening that the light in the phone box was not working.

'One of the men involved has just driven past in a blue Vauxhall Viva.' I told the woman: 'Write down the registration: UFM787K. His name is Morgan. Pass it on, they might be able to narrow down the area. Also, tell them Operation Blue Sky. For God's sake, try to find me soon. I'm going to die of hypothermia, if Morgan doesn't find me first.'

'Is there a house nearby that you could get to?' the operator asked.

'No, there's nothing, just that pub in the distance and I can't go there now I know Morgan's there. Hurry.'

I didn't end the call; I left the handset hanging to make it easier for the operator to trace the phone box and to let the patrol that would attend know that someone had been there.

I hurried back across the road and hid behind the wall. I regretted leaving my warm coat in Hornthorpe Dell. There would be a frost overnight and a denim jacket just wouldn't do. My back was agony. If help didn't come, I would have to take a chance and make my way to the pub or freeze to death. I huddled in close to the wall in the hope of retaining a little more heat than I could out in the open.

Chapter Twenty-Eight

After what seemed hours, I heard a car engine coming closer. I was torn between flagging it down to ask for help or remain in hiding in case it was Morgan. Would he know yet that his friend was dead and that I, and Pete, had escaped? He must have thought it odd when nobody came back after the gunshots, and was bound to have found the body of shotgun man when he went looking. I peered over the wall and along the road towards the pub. How I wished I could have gone there for help. I couldn't see into the car park, so I had to remain hiding in case Morgan came out.

I was about to duck behind the wall again when a police car trundled slowly past the pub from the other side and pulled up beside the phone box I had used. Two policemen dressed for winter in heavy overcoats got out of the Panda and walked over to the phone box. One replaced the handset and looked around. I stood up and shouted and waved my stiff, frozen arms at them like a manic windmill. I tried to climb over the wall again, but my legs wouldn't comply. One spotted me and said something to his oppo. They returned to the Panda and drove over.

'Are you Samantha Barrie?' one asked.

'Yes, yes.' I slid off the wall and collapsed onto the ground.

They came through the gate and one knelt beside me and took my pulse. How had I forgotten there was a gate? Perhaps the cold had affected me more than I'd thought.

'I'm Geraint and that's Neil,' he said. 'Neil, tell control we've found her and to get on to the ambulance.'

'I'm okay, just cold and my back hurts.'

'Best to make sure. You're beyond pale,' Geraint said.

'Ambo making,' Neil said. He didn't say where they were making from. I had heard that sometimes emergency services covered massive areas in Wales.

I shivered and Geraint stood up, took off his overcoat and draped it across my shoulders. It was still warm from his body and I pulled it tight around me.

'Thank you,' I whispered.

'So, what's the story here?' Geraint said. 'Control said someone tried to kill you.'

'That's right,' I said. I was starting to feel sleepy. I once read somewhere once that that was not good in the cold, but maybe it was just the warmth from Geraint's coat that was making me drowsy.

'Well, we've got a bit of time to kill before the ambulance arrives, so tell me. I'll have to do the initial report.'

I took a deep breath to straighten my thoughts. 'We were carrying out a raid on the airfield, Operation Blue Sky. Pete tried to make off.'

'Who's Pete?' asked Geraint.

'One of the flying instructors. He smuggles drugs. I tried to stop him but Johnny, one of the other men involved hit me across the back with a wrench...' My thoughts wandered. I felt so sleepy. Geraint shook me.

'Go on. Johnny hit you with a wrench?'

Oh yes, I was telling them what had happened. I tried to gather my thoughts.

'Johnny realised that Pete had killed his stepson and attacked him.'

'Pete's stepson?' Geraint asked.

'No, Johnny's. I'm not sure if he's married to Barbara or not…' I felt myself drift again.

I heard Geraint say, 'Chivvy up the ambo, she's really not well.'

It was important to tell Geraint what had happened. With a

huge effort I sat straighter.

'Pete shot Johnny. He forced me into the plane and made off. Steve tried to stop him, but Pete shot him too.' I gulped as I remembered Steve falling from the plane.

'Who's Steve? Is he here too?' Geraint asked.

'Steve's my friend. He wasn't supposed to be there. Why was Steve there?'

'I don't know,' Geraint answered.

'They'll have to let the Manx police know,' I murmured. 'Pete killed Boyle; we need forensics. He killed Lynch and Hatton and there's others.'

Geraint looked up at Neil. 'This is hard to follow.'

I forced myself to concentrate. 'Pete shot Johnny and Steve in Hornthorpe Dell. He flew to Tŷ Mawr. I don't know if that's it's proper name. He put the plane in a metal building: a small hangar, or a big barn. Morgan and someone else were there with shotguns. Morgan told Pete to get rid of me. He sent his friend with us but I guessed it was to kill Pete too so there weren't any witnesses. We went into the woods. There's a hidden grave in the undergrowth, it was meant for someone else, but they were going to put me in it.' I had another thought. 'That means they're going to kill someone else.'

Geraint looked at Neil. 'I think we need to let the inspector know what's she's telling us, and CID. Those woods need searching. We'll need lights.'

Neil nodded and wandered off, talking into his radio.

Geraint turned his attention back to me. 'How did you get away?'

'Pete shot the other man, then let me go and he made off.'

'Pete's still in there?' Geraint asked.

I was too sleepy to answer. I closed my eyes.

'Samantha! Wake up!'

I opened my eyes again and scowled at Geraint.

'What happened then?' Geraint asked.

Why wouldn't he let me sleep? I'd answer questions when I

woke up.

'Samantha!' Geraint snapped.

I remembered that I had been telling Geraint about Pete and Morgan. 'I saw Morgan in a blue Viva while I was making the call to 999. He went into the pub. I gave the VRM to the operator. That's why I stayed here, hiding.'

'There was no viva in the car park when we went past,' Geraint said. 'Not to worry. I think we have enough information to work with.'

Suddenly I thought of home. 'Have you let my people know where we are?' I asked.

'Control will see to that. Meantime, I need you to give me a description of this Pete so I can get it circulated.'

I wished for the ambulance to hurry. Maybe then Geraint would let me close my eyes and sleep.

*

A couple of hours later, I woke up in the local hospital. I had slept under several blankets, so I felt warmer. I was still shaking though. A rubber plant leant against the wall in one corner. It looked like how I felt: weak and battered.

Geraint had gone and a nurse told me that Neil was waiting to see what happened. I was glad he wasn't sitting by my bedside, especially when she approached with a bedpan.

'Can you pee?' she asked.

'I could do with one, but not in that,' I said.

'The doctor wants a sample from you before you go to x-ray. You can't walk to the toilet until we're sure what's going on with your spine, so you'll have to go in this.'

'I've been walking all afternoon. My spine's okay, just sore,' I complained.

'Do I have to fetch the doctor?' she threatened.

I groaned but complied.

Needless to say, there was blood in my urine. I was sent for

X-rays and various other tests including one where they injected dye into me to see my kidneys. It was extremely late by the time they were finished with me.

*

My spine was not broken, and my kidneys were declared functioning but bruised. A rib was cracked at the back and so I was admitted for a couple of days' observation.

I thought I had held together quite well until, quite unexpectedly, Gary and my mum walked in. When Mum rushed over and hugged me to her, I dissolved into a flood of tears.

After a minute or so, Mum moved over and Gary embraced me. I clung to him like a shipwreck survivor clings to a rock.

'You're still shivering.' Gary pulled my blanket around me.

'Pete shot Steve,' I wailed.

Gary shushed me. 'He's not dead.'

I gulped. 'Not dead?' I looked into Gary's sombre face. 'But he's seriously hurt, and he might die? Don't lie to me.'

'Last I heard, he was in theatre.'

'Steve's resilient, he'll probably wake up and demand a huge breakfast,' I said without really believing it.

'That sounds like Steve,' Gary agreed.

'Why was he at the airfield?' I asked.

'We haven't established that yet,' Gary replied.

I reached out for the packet of tissues that someone had placed on the tray beside my bed but my hands wouldn't stop shaking. Gary passed them to me, and I blew my nose. Steve might still die. I thought my heart would split open.

'Has anyone told Mrs Patton?' I asked.

'It's in hand,' Gary said.

'That poor woman,' Mum said. That was typical of her; she would have been informed that Pete had abducted me and probably had spent hours reliving the ordeal of my abduction when I was fifteen, but she still had compassion for Steve's mother. I hoped this wouldn't reactivate her hyper-protective instinct, I couldn't live like that again.

'How did you know I was in Wales?' I asked.

'We didn't for certain. DIs Webb and Corlett reported that you had gone towards the Irish Sea. Webby got Ray to ring North Wales Police and Lancashire Constabulary in case you went into their areas, meantime DI Corlett got on to his people in the Isle of Man. When you made your call, the lines between here and North Wales were red hot. Once I found out which hospital you were in, I just went around, picked up Liz and drove straight here.'

'Have they found Pete?' I asked.

'Not yet. The Welsh police are liaising with the Manx police. DI Corlett has hotfooted it to their HQ. They'll find him. There's an APB on him in case he tries to board a ferry or get to an airport.' Gary stroked my hair. 'You must be worried about Steve. I'll make a phone call and check if he's out of theatre.'

'Wait. I have to tell you something. Pete killed Lynch and Hatton, and who knows how many more. All overdoses. He told me he was the one who killed Vincent Boyle. He stole drugs from them, and he was trying to muscle in on the drugs business, so Fergal Tiernan told Pete to deal with Boyle. Pete knew about Boyle harassing the Jacksons, so he stole Leonard Jackson's car and used it to kill Boyle because Pete knew we'd blame Mr Jackson. We need to search Pete's house for forensics to place him with the car.'

Gary chewed the side of his thumb. 'Norman Webb told me that they have the forensic report back from the Allegro, and there are some fibres that don't seem to match anything of Jackson's. Also there is a footprint on the mat that is a couple of sizes larger than Mr Jackson's shoe size.'

'If they go into Pete's address, I bet they find it's his shoe size,' I said.

Gary nodded. 'Tiernan's dead, so's John Poulter. We might struggle to link Tiernan to drugs coming in to Hornthorpe.'

'Tiernan's dead?' I gasped.

'He made off when the raid went down and ran onto the motorway. A lorry hit him.'

I couldn't say I was sorry to hear of Tiernan's death, but it did make it more awkward for the ongoing investigation. I hoped evidence had been found at the other locations.

I thought for a moment. 'Jason Harper. Webby knows all about him. He can link all this together and doesn't have to worry about Tiernan anymore. Oh, Pete admitted to killing Lynch and Boyle.'

'I'll pass it on.' Gary kissed me and left Mum and me to talk.

She sat holding my hand for a couple of minutes. It seemed she was building herself up to say something.

'What is it, Mum? I can feel vibes coming off you,' I said.

'You need to get out of the job. It's too dangerous, you're always getting hurt,' Mum said. 'I think you need to go to Hong Kong with Gary.'

'Won't you miss me?' I asked.

'Of course. I missed you when you went to stay with your aunt and uncle in Canada, and I'll miss you if you go with Gary. At least you'll be safe.'

I closed my eyes. 'Mum, this was a legitimate operation. It's bad luck that it went wrong.'

'Maybe so, but it always seems to be you.' Mum stopped speaking as Gary came back.

'I passed on what you told me. Steve's out of theatre; I can't find out more than that at the moment,' he said.

'That's something.' I felt relieved.

'I met that local lad outside. Neil. Nice bloke. He told me that the car you saw was registered local to where you were found.'

I tried to sit up but yelped as pain knifed through me. A nurse came over.

'I think Samantha needs to rest now.'

'No, I'm okay, I just moved awkwardly. I need to know more about that car,'

The nurse watched me for a moment, then said, 'Five more minutes.'

'Tell me about the car,' I said to Gary.

'There's not much more to tell. The local police will be paying them a visit. They're already checking out the woods by where you were found.'

'From the way Morgan's accomplice was talking, I think there's more than one body there. The grave they were going to put me in was ready for someone else.'

Mum made a little yelp sound and sobbed into her handkerchief. Dammit, I was so busy trying to tell Gary everything, I hadn't considered how it would affect my mother.

'Mum, I'm safe. You and Gary are here with me and I'm safe. Don't get upset but I needed to pass on the information I have.'

'Talk some sense into her, Gary. Make her go with you! I can't cope with this.' Mum ran from the room.

Gary and I stared at each other.

'I have a lot of sympathy for Liz; you do spend more than your fair share of time in hospital. I won't force you into anything, though. As far as I'm concerned, the arrangement we made stands,' Gary said.

'It stands for me too.' I sighed. 'She's going to smother me again. I can't live like that. I'm going to have to find my own place.'

'Why don't you move into the flat?' Gary suggested. 'You already have the key and I'm going to need someone to keep on top of the mail and so on. I was going to ask my mother to pop in from time to time.'

'You wouldn't mind if I moved in while you're away?' I asked.

'I wouldn't mind even if I wasn't moving away.' Gary took my hand.

'We'll have to come to some arrangement, so I pay rent and so on,' I said.

'I own it, so no rent, just service charges, but we'll worry about all the details when you are home.'

I glanced towards the door. 'Have a chat with Mum, would you? Explain to her that I have just been unlucky. Also, warn her that I will be moving out.'

'I think you should tell her that bit,' Gary said.

He was right of course. Mum wouldn't be happy; she couldn't guard me if I lived away, but she'd get used to it and eventually she might even relax a little. Especially if I could keep myself out of trouble for a while. It was going to be an awkward conversation to have with her,

'You'll be off work for a week or two again,' Gary said.

'Dammit, my sickness record is rubbish. They won't hold that against me when I finish my probation, will they?' I asked.

'Normally they would, but you've only been off when you've been injured on duty, so I think you'd have grounds for a grievance if they tried that.' Gary laughed. 'Don't worry about it. Just rest at home and enjoy Liz fussing over you.'

'I just had another thought. Before Operation Blue Sky, Norman Webb was about to arrest Leonard Jackson on suspicion of Boyle's murder. Did that happen?'

'Webby didn't have quite enough evidence to go ahead and charge him.' Gary replied.

I grinned. It wouldn't be any time now before Mr Jackson was in the clear.

Chapter Twenty-Nine

Before I left the hospital, a local detective visited to take a statement from me about what had happened. I was bursting with questions.

'Have you searched the woods yet?' I asked.

'That's still ongoing,' the detective replied.

'How many bodies have you found so far?'

'Like I said, the search is ongoing. I'm not sure I can tell you just yet anyway.'

'Who owns the house?' I asked.

'The National Trust,' he replied.

'Has anyone spoken to the National Trust?' I asked.

'Yes, and no. I don't know what was said.'

'Did Morgan work for them?'

'I'm supposed to be interviewing you,' he complained.

I smiled. 'Yeah, sorry. But I am interested; I almost finished up planted in their land.'

The detective sighed. 'Morgan was taken on as head groundskeeper. As far as we know so far, nobody connected to the house had anything to do with this drugs business. Morgan operated his little kingdom from the grounds. This is a live investigation and no doubt more information will be uncovered before it ends.'

'Have you managed to find Pete Flinders?' I asked him.

'Not yet, but we will,' he said.

'Is that APB still going?' I asked.

'Yes it's still in place and will be until he's caught.'

'Do you know if his house has been searched yet?' I asked.

BLUE SKY

'No, that's a Peninsula job. We're more focused on *Tŷ Mawr.*'

'It's all connected, though. Isle of Man, Hornthorpe and *Tŷ Mawr,*' I insisted.

'Yes. Each force is investigating its own link to it, then it can be married up later on.' The detective chuckled. 'You're not the only police officer, you know. Let us worry about the crime, and you concentrate on getting better. You're going to make a great detective one day. You'll have no trouble getting confessions, you'll just beat them down with words.'

Fine. I'd leave them to it, but Pete would be halfway to Australia by now.

*

Once I was back home, Mum went into full guardian mode. She took leave from work and barely left the house, deigning only to venture to the shop if Gary was with me. I recovered quickly and decided that I didn't need two weeks off as long as I could take it easy at work. Gary promised that I could look after the enquiry office until I was fully recovered, which suited me. I could count my time left as a probationer in days now and I didn't want that important date to pass while I was on the sick again.

I had hoped that Eamon and Mike would go to see Mr Jackson and inform him that he was no longer a suspect in Vincent Boyle's killing, but Gary relayed a message from Eamon that they wanted to interview Pete Flinders before doing that. They had searched Pete's house and some interesting things had been found. The footprint had been the same size that Pete wore; what's more, they found fibres that matched the car mat in the tread of Pete's rubber-soled shoes. As a bonus, tiny glass fragments that matched the glass used in the Austin Allegro were found in a pair of woollen gloves. I was elated; they could forensically place Pete in Leonard Jackson's car at the time of the crash. Leonard Jackson was off the hook. It seemed unnecessary to me to allow Mr Jackson to have this charge hanging over his head in the face of such compelling evidence against Pete. It had to be putting enormous stress on him, but there were procedures to follow. I had no say about that. I was still just the B Block sprog.

*

The day before I returned to work, Gary came to visit, but his solemn expression alarmed me.

'What's happened?' I asked.

'It's Pete Flinders,' he replied. 'They found his body in a ditch close to the woods where you were found.'

I had done the right thing hiding behind that wall and keeping low. 'Was it Morgan who killed him?'

'Probably. North Wales Police are interviewing him,' Gary said.

'I didn't hear a shot after Pete ran off,' I said.

'His throat had been cut. He had been there for a few days and the local wildlife had started on him,' Gary said.

My stomach flipped. 'Morgan must have been looking for me when I saw him. He probably thought I'd go to the pub for help.'

'That would have been the logical thing to do, but you never take the easy option. It was a good thing on this occasion,' Gary said.

'What about informing Mr Jackson that he's in the clear?' I said.

'You made a statement detailing everything, so that and the forensic evidence will suffice,' Gary said.

'I have to say, if it's good enough now, it would have been good enough a few days ago. That poor man has had this hanging over him for far too long,' I said.

'Are you going to tell Webby that?' Gary asked.

'You could tell him,' I suggested.

'Not my place. I wouldn't appreciate him telling me how to

run B Block, so I wouldn't tell him how to run his department,' Gary said.

'Do you think it's been too long for Mr Jackson?' I asked.

Gary took a deep breath. 'Perhaps. But it might have been something cooked up between Pete and Leonard Jackson to get rid of Boyle.' He held his hand up to stop my objection. 'I know, I know, but imagine if Jackson had arranged with Pete to steal his car, kill Boyle and take the blame, then he helped him get away—'

'And then followed him to Wales where he slit his throat in a huge double cross, and the drug running is all a big coincidence,' I interrupted.

'Yes, it's unlikely, but things like that have happened. That is what the prosecutor has to consider, and why Jackson could not be discharged from the enquiry until he's satisfied that Leonard Jackson's involvement with Boyle was a coincidence. Now they no longer have that option, so they can make their move based on the available evidence.'

'He's going to be so relieved,' I said. 'Changing the subject, I thought I'd go and see Steve later on. I'll give his mum a ring and make sure I won't intrude on her time.'

'Will you be okay to drive?' Gary asked.

'Fine. I've stopped taking the painkillers and I've stopped peeing blood,' I said.

'Urgh, too much information. Pass on my regards. Tell him I'll pop in tomorrow.'

'Official visit?' I asked.

'Afraid so. I'm expected to report on his progress,' Gary said.

'Have you reported on mine yet?' I asked.

'Of course,' Gary said. 'Anyway, I'll call in again tomorrow.' He kissed me, shouted his goodbyes to Mum, and left.

Mum came into the room. 'Have you decided to go to Hong Kong?'

I sighed. 'No, Mum.'

Mum plonked herself onto an armchair. 'I deliberately left

you alone hoping that you'd change your mind.'

I had to speak out. 'Mum, listen to me. I joined the police because I wanted to use my bad experience to help others. If I go with Gary, I will be an expat wife, sitting around and serving no purpose at all.'

'You'll be Gary's wife,' Mum said. 'Why can't that be enough for you?'

'I know things were a bit different in the fifties—'

Mum snorted. 'Not that much different. I could recognise a good man then as well as I can now.'

'You'd have followed Dad anywhere, and that's great, but I don't want to throw away everything I have worked so hard for. Gary and I have made our plans, which suit us both.' I took a deep breath. 'I'm moving to Gary's flat.'

Mum blinked. 'What's the point of that? He'll be in Hong Kong.'

'Independence is the point. I love you, but I can't be smothered.'

'I don't smother you; I protect you…' Mum's voice faltered.

'Mum, you are smothering me. I won't be far away, and I'll still see you lots. Gary wanted someone to keep an eye on his place, so this is ideal.' I grinned. 'You know I've been spending most of my time there anyway.'

'Hmm.' Mum stood up. 'Well, if you think that's best, I won't stop you.'

I didn't remind her that I was in my twenties and she couldn't have stopped me. She went into the kitchen, evidently uncomfortable with my plans. I didn't follow her; she would come around.

*

Visitors poured into the long ward. Steve was on the left a couple of beds down, close to the nurses' station, but at least not in a side room. He was chatting to a nurse with auburn hair pinned into a large, loose bun. She was laughing at something he said as I approached. 'Samantha!' Steve reached up and pulled me into a hug.

I caught the beginnings of a scowl on the nurse's face. When I fully looked at her, after Steve released me, that look was replaced by a bland, pleasant look. Was I reading too much into this or did I detect a case of green eye?

'Sam, this is Emma, my favourite nurse. Emma, this is Sam, one of my best friends. The one I told you about.'

Emma's face relaxed and she gave me a genuine smile. 'Steve has told me a lot about you. I'm sure half of it's made up.'

'Probably not,' I admitted. 'How's he doing?'

'He's being so brave,' she replied.

Steve gazed at her as she spoke. Emma looked down at him and smiled. I smiled too; it was about time Steve had a girlfriend, and who better than a nurse? She would understand the rigours of the job and the stresses of shift work. I might suggest that to Steve, if he hadn't already thought of it.

I sat on the bedside seat and plonked a box of Quality Street on his lap. Chocolates were my default hospital gift. I didn't have the imagination to do something like Steve's pirate themed visit to Ken.

'Thanks.' Steve opened the packet and offered Emma one. She selected a strawberry cream.

'Nurse Seton! Stop intruding on that patient's visiting time and stop eating his chocolates,' boomed a navy-blue uniformed sister.

'Yes, Sister,' Emma replied. She turned back to Steve. 'Got to go. I'll speak to you later.' She scurried back to the nurses' station.

'So, am I disinvited to Richard's wedding?' I asked. I wouldn't have minded if that were the case.

'Of course not,' Steve said. 'Mum would kill me.'

'Which of us will you take: Emma or me?'

Steve blushed. 'She's nice, isn't she?'

'Have you asked her out yet?' I asked.

'It wouldn't be allowed while I'm a patient here.' Steve cast a speculative look across to Emma.

'You won't be a patient here forever.' I picked up the clipboard hanging on the end of Steve's bed and flicked through the sheets. 'I see your bowels are opening regularly.'

Steve snatched the clipboard away and tossed it on top of his locker. 'That's private.'

I leant back in my chair. 'I've been getting regular updates about you. You were lucky, you know.'

'So I've been told. I've been kept informed about you too. Hypothermia, damaged kidneys, broken ribs.'

I snorted. 'All exaggeration. I got a bit cold, my back was bruised—still is a bit—and I had a cracked rib. It hurt to breathe for a while. You had a hole blown in your chest. What were you doing at the airfield anyway?'

'It didn't take Einstein to work out where you were. I knew you'd been doing stuff over at Hornthorpe Dell, so when I overheard you and the boss talking, I took a chance and rode over to the service road behind the airfield and parked my bike in the woods. It was really early and the place was deserted. I just hung around and watched until you arrived.'

'So you *had* been eavesdropping from the kitchen,' I said. 'What were you thinking? You could have ruined everything. Didn't you see the patrols around the place?'

'I was keeping an eye on you, for all the good it did.' Steve ran a hand along his chest. 'It all went pear-shaped anyway. I ran behind the hangar you went into, looked in the window and saw the gun. I tried to signal to the patrols that had arrived but I'm not sure they saw me.'

'They'd been told to stay put until DI Corlett or DI Webb ordered them to move,' I said.

'Anyway, when the pilot started the plane up, I ran close to the underside so he couldn't see me and pulled open the door. Then it was just a matter of timing it right to get into the cockpit.'

'When you were shot. I thought you were dead!'

'I don't remember anything after that. I woke up briefly in an ambulance then that was it until I woke up after an operation to repair the damage. Luckily, the bullet missed everything important.'

'You're going to be off for a while though,' I said.

Steve shrugged and winced. 'I must remember not to do that. You'll probably be a jack before I get back.'

I sighed. 'You know, Steve, I might get a nice safe job as a juvenile liaison officer, or in the control room,' I said.

Steve chuckled. 'They have their stresses too. If you check the stats, I think you'll find that the heart attack rate in control room staff is greater than average.' Steve rolled his shoulders and winced again.

'At least nobody will be actively trying to kill me,' I said.

The sister picked up a bell from the desk and it clanged the end of visiting.

'That went fast.' I stood up and pecked Steve's cheek. 'Gary asked me to tell you he's coming on an official visit tomorrow. I'll come again in a few days. Say hi to your mum and dad for me.'

On the way out, I spotted Emma in the sluice room. She waved and came out.

'Can I ask you something?' she asked.

I guessed what it was but said, 'Go ahead.'

'Is there something between you and Steve? Or has there been?'

'No. I have a boyfriend. Steve and I have only ever been friends.'

She grinned. 'Then I won't get you coming after me if I suggest to Steve that we meet up after he's discharged?'

'Absolutely not. I warn you though, he's a complete pain in the posterior and overfond of bad jokes.'

'I don't think I'll ever get tired of listening to him,' she said.

Oh yeah, she had it bad. My good luck, if Steve was busy

with Emma, he'd stop trying to protect me and perhaps his mum would stop trying to get us together.

Chapter Thirty

'Had enough skiving and decided to come back and do a bit, have you,' called Trevor as I walked into the parade room on my first day back. I didn't take it to heart; gallows humour was what kept us going sometimes.

'I heard that you were making a pills of things, so I thought I should come back to show you how it's done,' I replied.

The others laughed in appreciation.

I sat in my place and got out my pocketbook. Ken was beside me, but Steve's place was still empty and would remain so for a few more weeks. At least he was going home soon and would recover.

We all stood as Gary, Alan and Shaun came into the room.

'As you were,' Gary said, and we all sat down.

'We've a few bits of news for you. First of all, welcome back, Sam,' Gary said.

'Thank you, sir,' I replied.

'Secondly, Bert Mason will be coming to replace Alan when he retires.'

I didn't know Bert Mason but judging from the little wave of approval that went around the room, he had to be okay.

'Thirdly, your new Inspector will be George Benjamin. He's newly promoted so be nice to him.'

'What we really need is someone with a bit of experience. How old is he?' Frank demanded. He reminded me of Derek with his tendency to find fault and complain.

'Old enough to be promoted to Inspector. Don't forget, I was newly promoted when I first came here,' Gary reminded him.

'Yeah, but you're good.' Frank grinned and Gary grinned back. It looked like that bridge had been mended.

'I'm sure the new chap will be fine too once he finds his feet. You older blokes can look after him. Finally, we are getting a sprog,' Gary said.

'Yes,' I hissed. About time too.

Alan leant over and whispered something to Gary.

'I've just been informed that we're actually getting two sprogs. That'll ease things,' Gary said.

I wondered who they'd get as tutor constables. Possibly Phil, but he had passed his exams and promotion couldn't be far off. Maybe Mike Four: he hadn't tutored anyone for a long time. Actually none of them had tutored anyone since the little flurry of incoming sprogs that had been Steve, Ken and me.

'Over to you, Alan,' Gary sat back while Alan went through the duties.

'Sam, you can look after the front office.'

'Yes, Sarge,' I replied automatically.

'Go now,' Alan said.

'Yes, Sarge.' I picked up my bag and went to the enquiry office.

'You're back!' Ray exclaimed.

'In the flesh,' I replied. I went into the control room and did a little twirl.

'You're wanted in the CID office,' Derek said. 'Wait for parade to end, they want the boss as well.'

Interesting. I nipped to my locker to put away my hat, then went into the telex room behind the control room and made tea for everyone. The mugs hadn't improved in appearance since I'd been away. I would have to remember to bring in some Brillo pads.

People began to crowd into the office to collect their radios, so I pushed my way through the crowd back into the enquiry office, where it was quieter.

Gary put his head around the door from the sergeant's office.

'Ready?'

Ray spun around in his chair and called, 'Gary, can you have a word with them, please? I don't know what they're planning but we're one man down, we still don't have anyone to cover the front desk and now they want Sam again. It has to stop.'

'You're right. I'll talk to Norman,' Gary said.

I followed him upstairs to the CID office where I was surprised to see DI Corlett sitting at Mike Finlay's desk dressed in his familiar camel coloured coat and maroon scarf. The outfit hadn't been just for show.

'Here she is,' he called. He stood up and held his hand out to Gary, who shook it. 'And the very patient Inspector Tyrrell. Thank you for loaning me your officer. She has been a real asset; resourceful, daring and has a touch of maverick about her. I can imagine that she's a bit of a handful at times.' DI Corlett laughed

'She has her moments,' Gary replied.

I caught Gary's eye and couldn't suppress a giggle.

DI Webb came out of his office.

'Norman, can I have a word when you're free?' Gary asked.

'Sure, just give me five minutes and I'm all yours.' DI Webb turned to DI Corlett and grinned.

'I asked Norman to bring you up here so I could thank you for your hard work before I went home,' said DI Corlett.

'You're welcome, sir,' I said.

'Seriously, we wouldn't have got on as fast as we did without you and I'm certain we wouldn't ever have known about the Welsh connection.'

'I only found it because I managed to get taken hostage,' I replied.

DI Corlett laughed. 'I love your sense of humour.

'Thank you, sir.' I didn't go on to say that I hadn't been joking.

'I've told Norman that he's a fool if he doesn't get you on your CID Aide's course as soon as possible.' DI Corlett grinned at me.

'And I've taken that on board.' DI Webb looked at his watch. 'I don't want to seem rude, but your car is waiting.'

'Righto,' said DI Corlett. He held out his hand to me and we shook. 'If you ever feel like a change of scenery, Samantha, consider the Isle of Man. Contact me and I'll support your application,'

'Thank you, sir,' I said.

'Oi, stop trying to poach our policewoman, you Manx git,' DI Webb said. 'If you want to get to the airport in time, you need to get moving.'

I caught a slight undercurrent to Webby's jokey manner; he wasn't kidding.

DI Corlett made no sign of having picked up anything other than matey banter from DI Webb.

'Okay, Norman. Got to go. Thank you again everybody. Oh, Sam, one more thing. I have put you and Eamon forward for Chief Constable's commendations, supported by DI Webb.'

I glanced across to Eamon who was beaming like the sun.

'Thank you, sir,' we said.

One more wave and DI Corlett was gone, escorted by Eamon.

'Any idea when Steve's back?' DI Webb asked Gary.

'It's going to be a while,' Gary answered.

'He was damned lucky,' DI Webb commented.

'He wasn't the only one.' Gary looked at me. He was right.

'Has Mr Jackson been told he's off the hook?' I asked.

'Sam!' Gary snapped.

I turned to him. 'I was only going to ask if I could go with them to tell him, sir.'

DI Webb looked at Gary. 'I don't mind, but she's on light duties isn't she?'

'She is,' Gary said.

'It's only to deliver a message,' I argued. 'I've had a lot of dealings with them. I would really like to tell them it's all over.'

'Up to you, Gary,' DI Webb said.

'Okay then, but straight back afterwards and into the front office.'

'Thank you sir. Sirs,' I said.

'After scoff. You can go with Eamon,' DI Webb said. 'By the way, what was it you wanted to talk to me about, Gary?'

'Oh, it doesn't matter now,' Gary said. 'Come on, Sam, you need to get back to the front office before I get Ray chewing my ear off again about staff shortages.'

'Yes, sir,' I responded and followed Gary into the corridor. I thought it was clever how he had let Webby know about staffing problems without getting all heavy about it.

I was on my way to the staircase when Gary guided us into his office where he let out a huge laugh. 'I don't think Norman wants to lose you.'

'You picked that up too? Do you think DI Corlett noticed?' I asked.

'Hard to think how he wouldn't have,' Gary said.

'How about you?' I replied.

'Am I in danger of losing you?' Gary asked.

I wrapped my arms around him. 'Never.'

We kissed and hugged for a moment before having to break apart when Norman Webb rattled the door on his way in. I quickly adopted the "at ease" stance.

'Oh, sorry, am I interrupting something?' DI Webb asked.

'*Yes,*' I thought

'Not at all,' Gary said. 'We're finished here. Congratulations again on your commendation, Sam. It will look good on future applications.'

'Thank you, sir,' I replied.

'Dismissed.'

I went to the door.

'Sam,' DI Webb said.

I turned back. 'Yes, sir?'

'You don't want to go to the Isle of Man. I spent a few days there recently and it's shite.'

I was not sure how to respond to that, because I had enjoyed a couple of holidays there as a child. I simply said. 'Yes, sir,' and left.

Chapter Thirty-One

Two milk bottles sat on the doorstep of the Jackson's house in Kensington Road. I had no way of knowing what the Jackson's regular milk order was, but I felt uneasy. It was early evening and, by anyone's standards, it was unusual for milk not to have been taken in.

Eamon knocked at the door, but there was no movement. I stepped backwards and looked up at the bedroom window. The curtains were closed. Eamon knocked again but there was only silence. My feeling of foreboding deepened.

'It's too quiet; I don't like it,' I said.

'I'll check around the back,' Eamon said and clambered over the side gate.

I lifted the letterbox. 'Mr Jackson, Mrs Jackson, it's Sam Barrie, we have some good news,' I called.

Still silence.

Eamon came back and shook his head. 'Nothing. Everything is secure and the curtains are drawn. The good news is, there are no bluebottles at the windows.'

Eamon, like me, had attended many deaths and concern for welfare incidents and one of the first indicators that we were going to find a body was flies at the window. The more flies the older, and smellier, the death.

'We have to break in,' I said.

'We can't break in straight away because we're getting no answer. They might have gone away. Let's check with the neighbours first,' Eamon said. He took the right-hand neighbour while I went to see Lisa, the young mother next door.

'Hello, sorry to bother you but I need to speak to Mr and Mrs Jackson. Do you know if they've gone away or something?'

She peered out. 'Well, Leonard's car is still there, he wouldn't go anywhere without that. He only got it a short while ago after his old one was stolen. I saw Muriel yesterday, it looked like she was having a spring clean. She had all her chair covers on the line and I saw her scrubbing the tops of the cupboards in the kitchen. Our kitchen windows face each other,' she explained.

That was not good. 'Thank you, I'll keep trying.'

I met Eamon back at the house. 'Muriel Jackson was spring cleaning yesterday,' I said.

'It's winter,' he said.

'That's beside the point. We need to get inside. I'll tell Shaun.' I stepped away from the house by habit, sometimes close proximity to buildings, especially in tree-lined roads, interfered with transmissions.

'4912 to control.'

'Go ahead Sam,' Ray replied on the radio.

'Could you let supervision know that we have to force entry to the Jackson's house please? I believe they are inside and unwell or otherwise indisposed.'

I listened as Ray relayed my message to Sergeant Lloyd.

'Right. Eamon, can you get that door open?' I asked.

He looked at the door. 'I'd break my shoulder if I tried to force that.' He picked up a rock and broke the small window to the side. He reached in and furtled around. A minute later he opened the door.

Eamon went upstairs and I went into the living room. It was so clean, it almost sparkled. I moved into the kitchen which was also pristine and smelled of lemons and bleach. Newspapers had been laid out on the floor by the back door and a row of bowls held water and enough dried dog food for about three days. One bowl was empty. In the corner, the Jackson's dog lay curled in its basket. Its tail thumped against the side as I bent to stroke its head. I couldn't remember its name, so I looked at the tag on its collar. Sandy. Sandy licked my hand.

Sandy followed me as I climbed the stairs. I walked past a bathroom bleached to perfection and the tidiest spare room I had seen and joined Eamon in the main bedroom.

Mr and Mrs Jackson were dressed as if going out for the evening, but they lay together on the bed, hand in hand, quite dead. Sandy rested his nose on the side of the bed closest to Mrs Jackson and whined softly. I had heard of people who planned to end their own lives getting everything in order beforehand. All bills paid, house cleaned and so on, so those who had to deal with the aftermath had an easier time but dealing with death was never easy.

A letter lay on the bedside addressed to *"To Whom it May Concern"*. Before I could pick it up, Eamon handed me another letter he had been reading. It was from Leonard to Muriel.

My darling,

I am sorry but there was no other way. This letter is my explanation and my confession that I killed James Summerskill in 1945. I didn't mean to, but it wasn't exactly an accident either.

You know my sister, June, was a WAAF and died of blood poisoning before I met you, but I have never told you the full story. June died following an illegal abortion. My sister was not fast and loose, James Summerskill raped her.

June went to a dance. She was very safety conscious and had taken a torch with her for the walk home. She was not herself after the dance and I became quite concerned about her. She finally admitted to me what Summerskill had done. He asked her to use her torch to help him find his watch, which he claimed he had dropped, but when she went outside to help him search, he pushed her into bushes and forced himself on her.

I persuaded her to report him, which I have regretted all my life. June had had a glass of port and lemon and that was sufficient for him to cast doubt on her testimony. A short time afterwards, she found out that she was pregnant and went to see a woman in Egilsby. Our mother reported her afterwards and I believe she was arrested. It didn't bring back dear June, though.

I confronted Summerskill and we got into a fight, which was broken up by an officer.

A few weeks later, I got my chance for revenge when I was put on cleaning detail. When I got to the stores, the storekeeper was ill and had to rush off. I stayed until someone could take over.

There was a jump on that morning and the parachutes had been issued but Summerskill was late. His parachute had been left to one side for him. On impulse, I opened the rig and pulled about a foot of material out. I wanted him to get a fright and have to use his emergency parachute. I was going to pull more out, but I quickly came to my senses and pushed it all back into the pack. I told myself that such a small amount of material being displaced wouldn't make a difference. However, Summerskill's main parachute didn't open, nor did it cut away. His emergency parachute got tangled and he fell to his death. The enquiry judged it an accident, but they didn't know what I had done. I never had the courage to admit to it.

A few months ago, Vincent Boyle called to the house and told me that he was Summerskill's illegitimate son. Somehow, he had found out that I had killed his father. Boyle tried to blackmail me. He demanded £1,000 but we don't have that sort of money, so he started to hang around the house leading to that unpleasantness where the policeman was hurt. I feel responsible for that poor young man's injury. Boyle learnt my routines and accosted me in the park to demand money. Sometimes I gave him what I had. I suppose you must have wondered why I started to walk Sandy so late at night. Boyle found me then too. That young policewoman almost caught him. I lied to her. I wish I hadn't, Boyle could have been arrested but then my crime would have been revealed.

Eventually Boyle went to the police. He had photographs that he thought proved my involvement. The detectives have been very sympathetic as they carried out their investigation. As you know, they concluded that Summerskill's death was indeed an accident, but I know that I killed him and lied about it.

When my car was stolen, I thought this was Boyle's latest attempt to make me pay more, but we now know that my car was used to run him over. He has died of his injuries and I am under investigation again. It is only a matter of time before the police return and charge me with Vincent Boyle's murder. That would mean life imprisonment, which I suppose is justice even though it's for the wrong man.

I cannot bear to think of people pointing their finger at you because of what I did. It would be better if you were a widow rather than the wife of a convicted killer. Then you would receive sympathy rather than contempt.

I collected my insulin prescription today and I intend to take it all.

I love you my darling and I'm grateful the life we had together.
I'm sorry my love.
Leonard.

I wiped a tear from the corner of my eye with a shaking hand. 'He'll never know he wasn't going to be charged for Boyle's murder.'

Eamon said nothing. I wondered if he was thinking about the investigation he and Mike Finlay had carried out following Boyle's allegation. Eamon and Mike were good at their job and although Mike had not been enthusiastic, they had accepted my input instead of writing off the whole file straight away, which would have been so easy.

Leonard had pulled a little material from the parachute bag. Would that alone have caused Summerskill's death? I knew nothing about parachutes so perhaps.

I picked up the second letter. This was more business-like, intended for us when we found them.

To whomever finds this.
No doubt you will have read Leonard's letter, so I don't need to

explain anything to you.

Had Leonard told me about his past, I would still have married him. We have had almost thirty wonderful years and I don't want to live alone for maybe another thirty years without Leonard.

Leonard didn't use all his insulin, so I am taking what remains of it along with the emergency store of insulin that I keep in the kitchen. I have also taken several aspirins. I am not diabetic so I hope it will work and my passing will be as reasonably peaceful as Leonard's seems to have been.

I know the milkman will call for assistance if the milk hasn't been taken in after a couple days. I tidied up so things shouldn't be too unpleasant for you and left enough dog food for Sandy to get by until someone comes. Please find him a good home.

All our paperwork and copies of our wills are in the black box in the right-hand side of the sideboard. We have no family to contact.

We would prefer a cremation. There should be sufficient money in our account to cover this.

I don't care what happens to our ashes, as long as Leonard and I are together.

Muriel Jackson.

There was no ambiguity here. These had been intentional acts and they were clear about their wishes.

'We should have told him earlier,' I said. 'Someone should have told them what Pete told me. There was no need for this.' I threw the letter down and wrung my hands to stop them shaking.

'We had to be certain Mr Jackson wasn't involved. We had to wait for the forensics to link Pete to the car,' Eamon said.

'We waited too long.' I had liked the Jacksons, and I even had some sympathy with Leonard's attempt at sabotage all those years ago. Their deaths were unnecessary.

I swallowed the lump in my throat. Now was not the time to become emotional; we had a job to do, starting with securing the scene. Then I had to arrange for the RSPCA to come and collect Sandy for rehoming. I could ring the dog pound, but they would only keep him for a week before putting him to sleep and there had been enough death in that house. I was tired of being surrounded by death.

Chapter Thirty-Two

A week later, Gary came into the enquiry office where I was still working, and asked me to come to the CID office with him.

'I don't want to take part in another operation,' I said. 'Can you tell them that you're short staffed or something, or suggest they use Ken.' I had been quite affected by the Jacksons' deaths. Maybe because there had been so much death in Operation Blue Sky, and I had come close to joining their ranks. I really just wanted to spend a few days at home, wrapped in a blanket, but after so much time off, I felt that I should try to compartmentalise it and carry on. As Derek put it, 'Stress is for wimps.' I hadn't even stayed over at Gary's flat, choosing instead to remain at home in my own bedroom, eating lots of chocolate.

'It isn't another operation,' Gary said. 'It's just mopping up from Blue Sky.'

Okay then, that was different. I went upstairs to the CID office with Gary.

DI Webb called us into his office. 'The North Wales police say they have got all the offenders from their end of the investigation.' DI Webb continued. He drew breath. 'They've sent one of their detectives to speak to you, Sam. I'll introduce you shortly. You were right: so far, they've found six bodies in those woods. One dates back at least five years.'

I wrapped my arms around myself and sank onto a chair. 'I was so nearly one of them and you wouldn't have known where I was.' I became aware that I was shaking again. Maybe I should speak to the doctor.

'It's all over now,' DI Webb patted my shoulder. Then he adopted a brisk tone. 'At the time of the raid, Barbara was off work following the death of her son. We visited and told her about Johnny.' He paused, no doubt recalling the visit. How awful it must have been to have told a woman already grieving that she had lost someone else. 'We intend to bring her in for questioning about the parachute incident in a couple of days. I think it would be good—if Inspector Tyrrell agrees—if you could sit in on the interview, Sam, seeing as you were the one to notice the details that everyone else missed.'

'She doesn't know I was undercover,' I said.

'Actually, she does,' DI Webb said. 'She also knows that Pete took you hostage. It doesn't matter any more, though; you don't need to go back to the airfield.'

I need never have a flying lesson again. I felt happier than I had been for days, but my hands still shook.

'Let's take you to meet DC Griffiths,' DI Webb said.

We trooped out of the office to the far side of the main CID office where DS Mike Finlay was talking to the Welsh jack. He stood up as we approached and chuckled.

'I wondered if it might be you,' he said.

I paused for a moment then it clicked. 'You interviewed me at the hospital.'

'I tried to,' DC Griffiths said. 'You hardly let me get a word in edgeways.'

'Sorry, but I had so many questions. I'll let you ask the questions this time,' I said.

'We might as well get started straight away, if your inspector agrees.' DC Griffiths looked at Gary, who nodded his agreement.

'Do you want anyone with you?' DC Griffiths asked.

Instantly my suspicion level rose. 'Do I need to? Will I be under caution for some reason?'

'Good Lord, no. I was just giving you the choice. We can do it right here if you're not bothered,' DC Griffiths said.

So that was what we did. Gary and Mike perched on

neighbouring desks while Webby hovered about, ostensibly supervising the other jacks but listening in to every word I said.

*

When we were finished, DC Griffiths shook my hand. 'It's been great talking to you.'

'And you,' I said.

DC Griffiths left, and DI Webb came over.

'I'd say Blue Sky has been a success. We linked two operations in the Peninsula, as well as connecting them to the Isle of Man and the North Wales police. You were a big help, Sam.'

'I think Steve should be acknowledged too,' I said. 'He's endured the shame of being arrested and remanded into custody when he was innocent. Without that, none of this would have become known. Also, he did try to rescue me.'

Gary and DI Webb looked at each other.

'He shouldn't have been there,' DI Webb said.

'But he was, and he was courageous, even heroic when he tried to stop Pete,' I argued.

'A Chief Superintendent's commendation?' Gary suggested. 'I would endorse that if you wanted to make the recommendation, Norman.'

'You see, the arrest is already having an adverse effect on him. What's wrong with a recommendation for a Chief Constable's commendation like me and Eamon,' I argued.

'A Chief Superintendent's commendation is not to be sneezed at,' Gary said.

'I agree with Sam,' DI Webb said, which surprised me. 'I'm going to recommend Steve for a Chief Constable's commendation for his heroic effort to free Constable Barrie. If they don't like it, they can lump it.'

'I'll endorse that,' Gary said.

*

A few days later, as arranged, I entered the interview room with DI Webb.

Barbara was sitting at the table with a cold cup of tea in front of her. She looked up as we entered and locked eyes with me.

'I told them I didn't know that Pete and Johnny were bringing drugs into the airfield or shipping them out. And as for that little shit, Tiernan…'

DI Webb and I sat down.

'Thank you for coming in, Barbara, but the drugs are not why we need to speak to you today. Constable Barrie will sit in with us, but I will be asking most of the questions. Is that okay?'

'Okay,' Barbara answered.

DI Webb recited the caution to her. 'Right Barbara, you are now under caution. That means that we will make a record of what you say, and we might use it in evidence.'

'Evidence for what?' Barbara asked. 'You said you believed that I wasn't involved in the drugs.'

'We do believe you,' DI Webb said. 'But this is about James Summerskill.'

Barbara's shoulders slumped. 'Right.'

'You had a relationship with James Summerskill in the forties, didn't you?' DI Webb asked.

'Yes, just after the war. I had his baby, but my father made me put him up for adoption.' Her eyes flicked to me. 'Look, let's not mess around. I've lived with this for over thirty years and I'm tired of carrying the guilt. I killed him'.

I gasped and even DI Webb's jaw slackened. I hadn't expected such an easy confession.

'Do you want to tell us about it?' DI Webb asked.

Barbara made herself comfortable. 'On that day, I had an interview to be taken on by the NAAFI. The WAAF wouldn't have me back because I'd had a baby: I'd have sullied their ranks with my loose morals.' She laughed without humour and I guessed that that had been a direct quote by someone.

Blue Sky

'It was pure coincidence there was a training jump scheduled on the day of my interview, but when I heard about it, I got the idea of getting back at James while I was on the camp. I thought I could put the straps across the canopy so it wouldn't fully open, then he'd have to use his emergency parachute. I only ever intended to scare him.' Barbara took a long breath and tugged at one earring.

'The night before, I kept watch outside the camp for James' car. I hid until I saw James and the bint he was with leave the camp. He didn't see me. I was on my bicycle and, although I pedalled like the clappers, they soon were out of sight. But we had gone far enough for me to recognise that he was headed to the small hotel I knew he favoured for his conquests. Me included.

'By the time I got to the hotel, he had parked up and was inside. I sneaked up to his car and let the air out of a tyre with a matchstick in the valve. I guessed he wouldn't find it until next day and that would make him late. I should have stopped with that, but I was angry and hurt and wanted revenge for losing my baby boy.' She stopped speaking and a teardrop ran down her face. 'My baby boy,' she murmured. She tugged at her earring again.

I swallowed the lump in my throat. It's hard to sit in a room so filled with grief. I felt nothing for Boyle, but Barbara was a mother who had been delighted to be reunited with her son. Now she had lost him again, forever. And she had lost Johnny.

'Do you want to take a break?' DI Webb asked.

She shook her head. 'Let's get this out of the way. My interview was early next day. The supervisor wanted to see me before they were busy with breakfast. I had my old uniform hidden in a bag. When I was finished, I went to the ladies and changed into it. I went to the stores and waited for Walter, the storekeeper, to go out for a smoke. I had a spoonful of floor cleaner in a little bottle. When Walter went out, I sneaked in and put it in his mug of tea then scarpered. I didn't put enough in to harm him, just to make him sick to get him out of the way. I knew he wouldn't taste it because he took his tea so strong with loads of sugar.

'I hung around outside, waiting for him to come out again, but after a while I saw Leonard Jackson come over. I hadn't planned on that. I hid and then I saw Walter racing off like the hare on a dog track. I waited until Leonard came out for a cigarette and nipped in.'

'What did you do?' DI Webb asked.

'I saw one rig put to one side and guessed it was for James. I rearranged the straps. When he jumped, he should have cut away the canopy, but he didn't and when he deployed his emergency 'chute, it got tangled. I didn't mean for him to die.'

Neither Leonard Jackson nor Barbara had meant for Summerskill to die, but dead he was.

'May I ask a question?' I asked DI Webb. He held his hand out to Barbara, inviting me to go ahead. 'Was the parachute out when you went in and put floor cleaner in Walter's mug, or had it been put out later?' I asked.

Barbara looked towards the ceiling as she thought. 'I think it was already out.'

'So we can assume that it was not Leonard who took it off the shelf?' DI Webb said.

'Yes. If James had rung to say he was late but on his way, Walter would have done that to save time when he arrived. It wasn't just a matter of hauling a parachute off a shelf and tossing it to the man, it was properly controlled. That's why I had to make sure James would be late by letting the air out of his tyre.'

'Do you have any other questions?' DI Webb asked me.

'If the rig hadn't been out, how would you have known which rig to target?' I asked.

'I wouldn't have known,' Barbara said.

'Would you have taken a guess?' DI Webb asked.

'No, no, it would have jeopardised an innocent man. I knew James was going to be late, I also knew that the stores would be informed of a latecomer. In those cases, it was normal to prepare the rig to save time.'

DI Webb put his hands over his face and exhaled heavily 'You took steps to make sure Summerskill was delayed, you poisoned Walter Gower to get him out of the way, you tampered with Summerskill's parachute, directly causing his death. You weren't reckless, you were methodical.'

'Yeah, I know. I didn't intend to kill him, but he died anyway. I don't really care anymore. Johnny is dead, my son is dead.' Her voice broke. 'My life is over.' Barbara exhaled. 'Charge me. I'll plead guilty. I won't be in prison for long.'

DI Webb glanced at me then said, 'Barbara, you understand that murder and even manslaughter carries a life sentence?'

'Oh, I'll serve life.' Barbara patted her left breast. 'Cancer. Now Johnny's gone, I've told the hospital I don't want any more treatment, so I've got maybe a year. Like I said, I won't be in prison for long.'

'But that's suicide!' I exclaimed. I realised I had spoken out of turn. 'I'm so sorry.'

'Don't be,' Barbara said. 'To be honest, the treatment wasn't working as well as they hoped anyway.'

'But it could have given you more time,' I said.

'What for?' Barbara responded. 'I might have had another five or six years, but I've got nothing left to live for. I've had enough. They can keep me comfortable but let me go.'

More death, so much death. I tucked my shaking hands under my thighs.

DI Webb stood up and I followed suit. 'Barbara, come with me to the charge office and we'll get you charged.' Turning to me he said, 'Make sure she has a warm blanket, not one of those old, ratty ones. Get her two if she wants and get her a fresh cuppa.'

I went to the female cell area and set one up for Barbara, then returned to the charge office to escort her. She walked with me back to the cell and I made sure she was comfortable.

'Do you have medication with you? Will you need painkillers? I can arrange the police doctor to come out to see you,' I said.

'I've got painkillers. They're with my property the sergeant took. You don't have to be so nice to me, it's what I deserve,' she said.

'Nobody deserves what you've been through,' I said quietly.

Barbara watched me for a moment. 'You're a nice woman and a good copper. I didn't have a clue about your true identity until after Johnny died. Never lose your caring side.'

I didn't know how to respond so I simply said, 'If you need anything, just press the bell and someone will come.'

Back in the charge office, DI Webb was organising Barbara's appearance in court and eventual transfer to a remand centre. It would be rare for someone to be given bail after being charged with such a serious offence.

'Make sure it's noted that this lady has terminal breast cancer,' he said down the phone. 'I'm not mollycoddling her; it's plain human decency,' he said in response to something the other caller said. He ended the call and banged the phone down. 'Wazzer.' He looked at me silently for a moment. 'So that's that.'

'We have two confessions,' I commented.

'Yeah, but only one person we can charge,' DI Webb said.

'I hate the way this has panned out. I wish I had left things alone,' I said.

'Once you made the connection, it was out of your hands,' DI Webb said.

'But what good has it done?' I asked. 'It sounds like he was a complete bastard.'

'It doesn't sound like he was a nice person,' Webby agreed. 'Look, Sam, we can't choose what law to enforce. If we know, or even suspect a crime, especially one as serious as a killing, we have a duty to follow it to its conclusion, even if we don't like where it goes.'

'If I had kept quiet, you would never have known, and Barbara would have been able to live what's left of her life at home.'

'You would have known,' DI Webb said. 'And I think you

have too much professional pride to have let it go.' He slapped me on the shoulder. 'You know what you need?'

Chocolate, a warm blanket and an hour alone with Gary, I thought.

'You need to come out with us for an after-work drink. It's great for decompressing and bouncing ideas.'

'I'll mention it to the inspector,' I said.

'No, I'll mention it. He should come too.'

'Okay, sir,' I said. Webby might be right; it was one thing to decompress with my block, but they hadn't been part of Blue Sky and wouldn't fully understand. And if that didn't work, I'd try the chocolate, blanket and alone time with Gary option.

Chapter Thirty-Three

I enjoyed my evening out with the CID, even though it got a bit rowdy. I had taken the second option as well. All in all, since then, I was feeling a lot better than I had felt recently.

I had come to terms with the whole Barbara thing. I still wasn't sure that I had made the right decision, but I couldn't undo it and I was not going to beat myself up over it.

I might be called to give evidence at court over Operation Blue Sky, but that was nothing too terrible. Life was returning to normal, except Gary was leaving in just a few days. I refused to dwell on it. We had made our plans and we were happy with that. I wouldn't half miss him though.

I walked past the sergeants' office on my way to the parade room, for what was probably my last parade as a probationer. My confirmation hadn't come through, which made me a bit anxious. I didn't recall Ken or Steve not having their confirmation so close to the end date. I hoped I wasn't going to have my probation extended.

'Sam.'

I turned to see Shaun Lloyd coming out of the office with a policewoman. Mid-twenties, five-foot-eight at least, with long, slim legs and blonde hair swept back into a French pleat. Her makeup made my lick of mascara and lip gloss look inadequate. I wondered if the superintendent had met her; he didn't like his policewomen to look like "painted ladies"—his words, not mine. Her jacket nipped in at the waist, accentuating the curve of her hips. She had to have had that altered to fit; my jacket hung like a sack.

'Sam, this is Charlotte, she's our new recruit,' Shaun said.

Charlotte's eyes travelled over me and, in less than five seconds, I felt that I had been assessed and found wanting.

She put her hand out. 'Charlotte Leader, graduate entrant.'

I took her hand and shook it. 'Samantha Barrie, traditional entrant.' Neither of us really needed to know the other's entrant status but I had the feeling that Charlotte had decided she was somehow a princess amongst peasants and wanted to establish her credentials early on. I turned to Shaun who practically had his tongue hanging out as he watched Charlotte.

'Do you want me to take Charlotte to the parade room?'

He turned to me as if waking from a spell. 'What? Oh, no. I'll introduce her to Ray and Derek then bring her down with Alan and the boss.'

'Okay. Nice to meet you, Charlotte.' I continued to the parade room.

Outside the room, facing the door was an unfamiliar police officer. He seemed nervous and I could almost hear him counting before opening the door.

'Hello,' I said.

He jumped and spun around. 'Oh, hi. I'm Andy. I start with B Block today.'

I smiled. 'I'm Sam Barrie. I'm on B Block.' We regarded each other for a few seconds. He was a nice-looking lad, a little younger than me, with clear skin the colour of caramel and hazel eyes, not unlike my own eye colour.

'Did you know that you're supposed to report to the sergeants' office before your first parade?'

His eyes widened. 'No. I'm sorry, nobody told me.'

Nobody had told me either. 'Come on, I'll show you the way. Sergeant Lloyd is our patrol sergeant. He's okay. Charlotte is already there.'

Andy rolled his eyes. 'Of course she is. Has she told you she's a graduate entrant yet?'

'Funny you should say that.' I laughed.

'The next thing she'll probably say is something like "Leader by name and leader by nature". She's convinced she'll be a Chief Constable one day.'

Well, that was interesting. I couldn't see such an attitude going down well with the others on the block. She'd soon be taken back down to earth. Andy would fit right in.

At the sergeants' office Charlotte smirked at Andy. 'So you made it?'

'I didn't know we had to report to the sergeant before our first parade. You might have said something, Charlie,' Andy complained.

'You know I prefer to be called Charlotte. It's more professional,' Charlotte said.

'I'll leave you to it.' I returned to the parade room grinning. Charlotte was in for a rude awakening.

Ten minutes later, just before parade started, Andy and Charlotte came in with Shaun, Alan and Gary, who made brief introductions.

'Finally, you're no longer the sprog,' Alan said to me.

'About time, Sarge,' I replied.

Alan told Charlotte and Andy to sit down. Charlotte went to a vacant chair on the other side of the room, and Andy came and sat by me, in Steve's seat. I would gently advise him to move along one when Steve returned. I introduced him to Ken. Once they were settled, parade resumed, and our sprogs were allocated tutors. Phil got Andy, which I thought was good. Phil was a phenomenal tutor-constable. Charlotte got Frank on Mike One, who covered the south end of town. I had no idea how that would turn out.

'Sam, Not only are you no longer the sprog, when we get back from rest days, you will no longer be a probationer.' Gary said.

'I'm being confirmed?' I asked, a big grin across my face.

'You are indeed, unless you do something really stupid. Congratulations. The Chief will speak to you later. Next you need to start thinking seriously about your career path. I suggest a driving course first.'

'Yes, sir,' I responded.

That was a relief. Gary had told me that it would have been unreasonable for the brass to have held my sickness record against me given the circumstances, but it had been at the back of my mind as I approached the end of my probation. Now, no more class days to brush up on theory, no more tick boxes so Alan could see what type of jobs I did, and only annual assessments from now on. Instead, I had to think about my future in the police. Driving, departments, promotion, or jack the whole lot in and follow Gary to Hong Kong next year. I pushed it from my mind. I had plenty of time to think about that.

*

Eamon came down as we were getting our radios and doing our test calls.

'Sam, have you heard about Jason Harper?' he shouted above the din.

I pushed my way to the corridor. I still didn't like being crowded, but I was tolerating it better.

'No. Has he been in court already?'

'He has. He got three months in custody.'

'I suppose it was only to be expected, given that he was arrested for burglary whilst on bail for the drugs arrest.' I still felt sorry for him and Joan.

Eamon grinned. 'Suspended for twelve months.'

'So he's out?'

'He is. It'll still show as a custodial sentence on his record, but he'll be able to get on with life now, as long as he stays out of trouble.'

'I think that's disgusting,' Charlotte said from behind me. 'Someone commits burglary while on bail for a drugs offence. I'd have him banged up for a long time.'

I turned around. 'You know nothing about this case, Charlotte.'

She pulled herself to her full height, so she was looking down on me. 'But I could hear everything you said. A criminal who belongs in prison is walking the streets.'

I refused to be riled by her. I lifted my chin and met her gaze. 'You were not part of the incident, nor were you part of the conversation.'

'Well, pardon me.' Charlotte stalked off.

'Who was that?' Eamon asked.

'Charlotte Leader, graduate entrant.' I chanted. I leant closer and lowered my voice. 'I've been told that her mantra is "Leader by name and leader by nature".'

Eamon chuckled. 'Be careful, she might be your boss one day.'

'Our other sprog tells me that is her intention. Going back to Jason, do you think that they somehow knew how he'd helped us?' I asked.

Eamon shrugged. 'I couldn't say, but I know the defence really laid it on about his injured grandmother, and how he'd wanted to go straight but had been threatened by a known criminal.'

Despite what I'd told Jason about deals, I had the distinct feeling that something had happened in the background. Perhaps Webby, or maybe someone higher, had had a word with the prosecutor and he had come to an arrangement with the defence where he wouldn't object to a request for a suspension. Justice had to be done, or more to the point, it had to be seen to be done, and a suspension of sentence fulfilled that requirement, whilst allowing Jason to work on getting back on track. I was satisfied with that.

*

Once our test calls were done, Ken and I walked to our beats together.

BLUE SKY

'Two of the musketeers are together again. How long do you think it'll be before the third will rejoin us?' Ken asked.

'A few weeks yet. Between Steve's arrest, your eye, my kidnap, and Steve's chest, it seems like months since we were all together discussing Steve joining the air force,' I said.

Ken chuckled. 'It'll make a nice change not to have to go to the hospital. I spent so much time there visiting you two, I thought they were going to start charging me rent.'

'I know the feeling,' I said. 'I'm so tired of hospitals. I worried that it would affect me completing my probation. I half expected it to be extended.'

Ken thought for a moment. 'We should have a party. Steve didn't do anything when he was confirmed, I didn't get a chance to, and now you're coming out of your probation.'

I hesitated. 'To be honest, Ken, I'm not in a party mood. Gary is flying out in a few days.'

'Well, Steve isn't going to be able to party yet. I suggest that we leave it until he's back and you're feeling more with it, then hire a function room and have a do,' Ken said.

'Perhaps the police club can do something for us. We can make it a three musketeers themed party.' I recognised Steve's influence rubbing off on me.

'That's sorted then. I suggest June sometime.' Ken stopped walking. 'This is where I leave you. Have a good day and see you at scoff.'

'See you.' I continued on towards my beat.

I hadn't gone very far when I spotted Joan Fletcher headed towards the supermarket. I could still see some bruising, but it was nowhere as bad as it had been.

She waved when she saw me and trotted over. 'I thought it was you, Constable Barrie.'

'Hello, Joan. Your face looks so much better, how are you feeling?'

'Oh, I'm fine. Did you hear about Jason?' she asked.

'I heard he got a suspended sentence,' I replied.

'Yes, but apart from that,' Joan said.

'I don't think so then.'

'He's been taken on as an apprentice with the council. He's going to train as a gardener. He'll be going to college part time and be looking after those fancy roundabouts and so on the rest of the time.' Joan looked ready to burst with pride.

'Are they aware of what's happened?' I didn't want to spoil her excitement, but I wasn't sure that would still happen given his recent convictions.

'That nice Mr Webb sorted it for him,' Joan said.

'Detective Inspector Webb?'

'He came to our house and had a long chat with us. He thanked Jason and asked what his plans were. Jason told him how he wanted to earn a living by gardening—properly, not just labouring—but he knew that any decent company wouldn't take him on because of his convictions. Mr Webb told him that the council were advertising and to go ahead and apply. He wrote a letter for Jason to show them.'

I couldn't believe what I was hearing. Webby hadn't said a word.

'What type of letter?' I asked.

'Not a reference exactly, Mr Webb explained that police weren't supposed to give references, but he told them that Jason had been really helpful to an investigation. In fact, he said they would not have been able to solve it without his help. There was a lot more, but I can't remember it all now. It did the trick.'

That was really good news. As long as Jason stayed out of trouble, he had a bright future.

'I'm really happy for him; for you both. It's a new start.'

'It really is. Also, my niece is expecting a baby and she asked Jason to be godfather. I said I'd get the gown for the baptism. I'm looking for something special, but I haven't seen anything I really like so far.

I had a lightbulb moment. 'Actually, I know someone in the market who might be able to help you. She made me a fabulous silk scarf for my mum. Karen Fitzroy, she's in the annex hall near the rear exit. She's reasonably priced and does a first-rate job.'

Chapter Thirty-Four

The day was clear, the sky a diamond blue with strands of white cloud. Gary had said his goodbyes to his family the previous night, so we were alone. I wouldn't have minded his mother coming to the airport with us, but I appreciated her thoughtfulness.

We drove to the airport in silence. I had so much in my heart, but I couldn't express any of it. Each time I glanced at Gary he was staring ahead. Thinking of his new life in the East or thinking about us? Maybe a bit of both.

I parked up and walked with Gary to the departure hall.

'Have you remembered your passport and so on?' I asked, simply for something to say.

Gary patted his pockets. 'All here.' He went to check in and then we walked towards passport control, until I couldn't go any further. We faced each other. Was this the moment we parted forever?

'Remember, I will come back on leave and you can come out to visit,' he said.

I opened my mouth but instead of the bland agreement I had intended, I blurted, 'If you meet someone else while you're out there, just tell me, don't pretend…' My voice trailed off.

'I love you, Sam, and I wish you were flying out with me, but I don't expect you to be a hermit either. You must still go out, meet friends, go dancing, see films. A year from now we will talk about the future,' Gary said. 'I will accept your decision, whatever it is.' He kissed me and I held onto him, breathing in his scent.

Blue Sky

'Thank you,' I said. 'Thank you for giving me time, thank you for guiding me through hard times and thank you for showing me that my life didn't end when I was fifteen.'

We kissed once more, and he went through the gates, turning briefly to wave to me. I stood staring after him for a moment, holding back the heartache that had threatened to consume me, then I walked to the viewing terrace and sat by a small tea stand and sipped tasteless brown liquid as I watched planes leave and land. I was shaking again.

When it was time for Gary's plane to take off, I walked to the edge of the viewing platform and looked out for a large British Airways plane. I spotted one backing out from its place at the terminal. It made its way to the runway in the distance and joined a queue of three. No other British Airways planes were moving, so that had to be the one carrying Gary.

I watched the plane take its place at the head of the runway, then move faster and faster until it lifted into the air. I waved, even though I knew Gary could not see me, and I kept on waving until the plane was invisible in the blue sky.

THE END

Did You Enjoy This Book?

If so, you can make a HUGE difference.
For any author, the single most important way we have of getting our books noticed is a really simple one—and one which you can help with.

Yes, you.

Us indie authors and publishers don't have the financial muscle of the big guys to take out full-page ads in the newspaper or put posters on the subway.

But we do have something much more powerful and effective than that, and it's something that those big publishers would kill to get their hands on.

A committed and loyal bunch of readers.

Honest reviews of our books help bring them to the attention of other readers.

If you've enjoyed this book I would be really grateful if you could spend just a couple of minutes leaving a review (it can be as short as you like) on this book's page on your favourite store and website.

Acknowledgements

I have a few people I want to thank.

First, thanks to Pete and Simon for agreeing to take on this unknown writer and being willing to take my ideas and whip them into shape. Thanks also to the beta readers for their time and enthusiasm. Thank you to my old friend, Christine Winton, who walked the same streets as me, and who, four decades later, pointed me in the direction of Burning Chair.

A big shout out to the Crime and Publishment gang. Your passion for writing and your encouragement is priceless. Thanks to Graham Smith who organises the C & P weekends. I have learnt so much since I started attending. Thanks to John Coughlan for sharing his knowledge of parachutes.

Thanks to Andrew Wille, for his advice and counsel.

Thanks to my family for putting up with me talking about the characters as if they really exist (they do in my head). Thanks to my husband, who is willing to discuss the plausibility of scenarios with me and will point out likely locations for foul deeds.

Finally, to police officers everywhere who do a thankless, daunting and often dangerous job. Few could do what you do. I thank you.

About The Author

Trish Finnegan has spent her whole life living on the Wirral, a small peninsula that sticks out into the Irish Sea between North Wales and Liverpool. She has always had an overactive imagination and enjoyed writing and reading, sometimes to the detriment of her schoolwork.

She first met her husband, Paul, in the charge office of a police station: where they both were serving as police officers. She has three grown up children and currently spends her time wrangling grandchildren and writing.